GLOVE SAVE

TEAGAN HUNTER

Editing by Editing by C. Marie

Proofreading by Judy's Proofreading & Julia Griffis

Cover Design by Emily Wittig

For anyone who needs to hear it…

You're strong.

You're worthy.

You're enough.

CHAPTER 1

"I'm telling you, asswipe, that's what I did. I tried to deke him, but he's too good."

"Well, then you didn't deke him right. If you make it convincing enough, he'll bite. Ask the goalie—he'll tell you."

Moe and Larry—no, scratch that. That would make me Curly, and the Three Stooges we are not.

Tweedledee and Tweedledum—*much better*—going quiet has me glancing up from my beer, the same one I've been nursing for the last hour. The cloudy amber beverage is warm, and my stomach is turning at the thought of trying to finish it.

Well, it's either that or the pit that started forming the minute I hung up the phone with my mother.

My stomach turns yet again just thinking about the call.

Yep. That's it.

"Well, Mr. Hotshot Goalie? Any input?" Fitz, the forward for the Carolina Comets, asks impatiently.

"Fitz is right, Hayes. You have to sell it harder. I've given up a few soft goals on good dekes."

Fitz throws his fist into the air and lets out a loud whoop. It's obnoxious enough to draw eyes, something I really don't want to do tonight, so I tug my hat down lower.

"Shut up," I hiss with a scowl.

"What?" He shrugs, glancing around. "Nobody is paying us any attention. Besides, it's Slapshots—they know better than to mess with us in here."

That's usually true. This place is a haven for those on the Comets, but sometimes there are nights when people don't care that it's our off night and want to hound us.

I don't typically drink during the season, but I couldn't say no when Fitz and Hayes invited me out. We've just come off an eight-game winning streak where I recorded not one but *two* shutouts.

It's February, and we're on a roll. I feel fucking unstoppable right now, and I don't want to let that feeling go just yet, especially not right now when we're walking into a six-game homestand. We kill it on home ice.

"Come on, man. Lighten up." Hayes claps me on the shoulder. "We're hot as hell right now, so have fun and stop scowling at everyone."

I glance down at Hayes' hand, which is still resting on me, and that scowl deepens. I look back at him with one brow raised in an *Are you seriously touching me right now?* kind of way.

He lifts both hands in the air in surrender. "S-Sorry," he mutters.

I nod once, letting it go. I'm not big on touchy-feely shit, but he's the rookie, so I don't expect him to know that.

I can't seem to let go of the call I had with my mother just before we stepped into the bar, the one that's put a damper on my whole evening.

She's getting married.

Again.

Or should I say again again *again*. It's her fourth marriage, and I don't even know how many "serious relationships."

I want to be happy for her. I really do, but it's difficult when I know this one will end in the same heartbreak as all the others.

"What's up with you, Greer? You seem grumpier than normal, *and* you just chased the rookie off."

I glance up to see that his seat is, in fact, now empty.

Oops.

"Just tired," I tell him.

Fitz's eyes narrow, and I'm annoyed by how hard he's staring at me. He knows I'm lying.

"Does this extra scowly-ness have anything to do with that mysterious phone call you took before we came in?"

I sigh, then toss back the rest of my beer because why not? I'm already miserable as fuck. May as well go for broke at this point.

I cringe as the warm liquid slides down my throat. I

know some people love their warm beers, but I am not that type of person. I want it ice cold, like so fucking cold you feel like you need to wear gloves to tip the bottle back. The coldness matches my dead, black heart, and I relish it.

"I'll take that as a yes," Fitz says.

I nod. "It was my mom."

"Oh? I fucking love talking to my mom." He glances around, then points at me. "Don't tell anyone I said that or sounded so damn excited." He clears his throat and pushes his shoulders back.

I try to hide my smirk at how tough he's trying to look.

"I love talking to my mom too," I tell him, and he relaxes at my words. "She's getting married."

"Married? That's awesome! Congratulations to her."

I scoff, and Fitz doesn't miss it.

"Uh-oh. Do you not like the guy or something?"

"No clue. I haven't met him."

David seems like a nice guy from the few times I've said hello on FaceTime, but so did Archie, Harry, and Kenneth, and not one of those relationships endured. Besides, I learned a long time ago not to get attached to anyone my mother is dating because the likelihood of it lasting is slim.

"Does *she* seem happy about it?"

"She's fucking ecstatic." And that's the truth. The problem is, she's *always* happy about the wedding. It's the whole making-a-relationship-work part she's not so keen on.

"Then what's the issue?"

"It's not her first wedding." Far from it. "The last one…I wasn't on my best behavior."

"You slept with a bridesmaid, didn't you?"

I wince. "Three."

"Huh?"

"I slept with three of them."

Fitz's eyes widen. "At the same time?"

"No! Well, kind of. Two of them, yes. The third, no. I slept with her at my mom's second wedding. She was not happy when she walked in on the threesome and caused a scene."

Fitz's mouth is hanging open at this point, and I can't say I blame him. I was shocked, too, when the door to the coat closet flew open and I had two sets of lips wrapped around my cock. I was just about to come when Maggie—or was it Mary? I can't remember—started screeching and chased away my orgasm.

"So, is this your mom's third wedding? Maybe the third time is the charm for all of you?"

"Fourth," I correct him.

"Fourth…" Fitz swallows once, twice. "Well, that's okay. Sometimes things don't work out."

My lips twitch at how diplomatic he's being right now, choosing his words carefully so he doesn't offend my mother or me.

"Also, maybe don't sleep with bridesmaids and ruin your mom's big day this time?"

"Therein lies my problem—she wants me to bring a date to the wedding. Guess she thinks it'll prevent me from sleeping with anyone from her salon, which I assume is who will be in her wedding party."

"A date? Yikes."

It's a well-known fact to everyone on the team that I don't do relationships. Period. *Ever.*

It's why, as much as I like my teammates, I don't hang out with them often anymore. Wright and Rhodes are both hitched, Lowell has a damn kid—hard pass on that shit—and now even Miller found someone to love his dumb ass. Having to see them all wrapped up in their lovey-dovey shit? Yeah, no-fucking-thank-you.

It's why I'm hanging out with Fitz so much lately. He's single, therefore he's not shoving all that happy, hearts-in-the-eyes bullshit down my throat. I swear I can feel my esophagus swelling at the thought of having to watch all the puppy-dog looks those guys seem to have. It's annoying. What the fuck is so great about love anyway? All it does is beat you down and break you and lead to misery. I'll pass on that.

"It's just a date, though, right? Not like you're the one getting married."

I gag, and Fitz laughs, slapping me on the back.

"Don't be so dramatic. I'm sure it's not that bad."

"You think *marriage* isn't that bad?" Is he drunk? Am *I* drunk?

Fitz shrugs. "Yeah. I mean, hell, look at the other guys. They seem happy enough."

"So did my mom during her first marriage. Oh, and her second and third. My dad has fathered children with multiple women he's had long-term relationships with. He just called me last week to inform me that he and his latest baby momma are 'taking some time apart.' Is that the kind of happiness you want?"

Fitz grimaces. "Maybe not."

"That's what I thought." I raise my glass to my lips, but I'm disappointed to see that it's empty. Fitz talking about marriage left such a gross taste in my mouth that I somehow forgot all about my awful warm beer.

I slide the empty glass across the counter. From the other end of the bar, the bartender tips his head in a silent question: *Another?*

I signal that I'm done, figuring I'd better quit while I'm ahead. This night is clearly a wash.

"Okay, so you're not rushing down the aisle. I get it, but one date won't kill you, especially if it's for your mom. Do you know the number of horrible dates I've been on for my mother? You'll be fine for one night."

"Then you're a better son than me. I'm not bringing a date."

"Scared you won't be able to find one?"

I narrow my eyes, not liking the cocky smile that's taken over his face. He's trying to bait me, and fuck me, it's working.

I hate that it's working.

"I can find a date just fine."

"Damn straight you can," Hayes says, slipping back onto his empty stool. "You were the NHL's first star of the week last week—you could have your pick of women. Hell, I bet there are at least ten ladies here tonight just waiting for you to ask them to go home with you." He inclines his head toward the other side of the bar. "Including those babes over there."

"Don't call them babes. You sound like Miller," Fitz says to him before I can.

"Babes, women—whatever. When I was getting my drink, I heard them talking about us. They're definitely interested. Could make for a fun night." Hayes bounces his brows up and down.

I slide my eyes toward the group he's referring to. A few hours of rolling around in the sheets doesn't sound too bad. It may be just what I need to turn this now-soured evening around.

There are four women sitting at a round table. One is a blonde looking this way, her lashes fluttering as she takes a sip of her drink, which looks like it's more sugar than alcohol.

When I make eye contact with her, another throws her head back. She slaps the shoulder of the other woman next to her, who is also laughing. It comes off as forced and fake, especially with the way they both keep looking over here as if they're waiting for us to pay attention to them.

Finally, there's the woman with dark hair who is

partially hidden from view and isn't looking over her shoulder to get a glimpse. In fact, she has an elbow resting on the table, and she's twirling her straw in her drink. She seems bored, like she wants to be somewhere else right now.

I want to go over and ask her where that place is.

"Should I go talk to them? I should go talk to them, right?" Hayes asks, already pushing himself off the stool.

I'm quick to reach out and grab the back of his shirt, dragging him back down.

"Leave them alone, Hayes." I shove his shoulder down hard, letting him know I'm not kidding.

"Why do you ruin all the fun?"

"Because two of the women have wedding rings on their fingers. If you want to make headlines, do it on the ice, not off it."

"Oh shit." Hayes gulps. "I missed that."

"I didn't."

"Yeah, that's because you're allergic to commitment, so you pay extra attention to that shit," Fitz comments.

I don't argue because he's right.

"We should get going anyway." The forward rises from his stool. "Coach Heller said the practice isn't mandatory, but he did that eyebrow thing he does that means he'd like to see us there anyway."

Hayes groans. "But…but…babes!"

"Don't call them babes, Miller Jr." Fitz shakes his head, tugging the young player up by his arm. "Coming, Greer?"

"Yeah. I'm going to take a leak. Meet you out front."

"Sounds good." He steers Hayes away from the poor, unsuspecting women and toward the door.

I chuckle to myself when I see his bottom lip come out. *Fuckin' rookies, man.*

As I cross the bar toward the restroom, I can't help but let my eyes wander to the table of women Hayes pointed out. They are hot; I'll give him that, and burying myself between a set of legs does sound better than drowning in alcohol.

But…I should go. It's the responsible thing to do. We're on a heater right now, and I don't want to risk that by staying out too late or drinking too much or for some random pussy.

This season is all about no distractions.

We have a Cup on the line, and I intend to make it mine.

CHAPTER 2

The minute the strip turned pink, telling me I was pregnant at nineteen during my freshman year of college, I settled into the fact that the fun, partying part of my life was over. Going to clubs, going to bars, and dating around weren't in the cards for me anymore. I had a kid to raise, and Macie was going to come first no matter what.

I guess what I didn't plan on was that kid growing up so damn fast or her wanting to spend time with her aunt and not her mother. Since when did she become so independent at ten?

So, when Bianca Macbeth, a mom from my daughter's school, called to invite me out for a girls' night, I didn't have any reason to say no. In fact, it sounded like fun. A night out with fellow moms having a few drinks? Hell yes! It was just what I needed.

Now that I'm here, though, sitting at a bar surrounded by women I *should* want to hang out with, I'm miserable and would much rather be sitting at home on my couch with my kid and a Disney movie pulled up. Well, it would probably be a hockey game instead of a movie since she's obsessed with the sport.

I hate saying this, but…I'm *bored.*

I'm not interested in the same drink I've been sipping for the last thirty minutes or the music that's thumping through the speakers. Hell, the only thing that really has my interest right now is the TV sitting above Bianca's head that's playing a recap of the Carolina Comets game from last night. I blame Macie for that one, seeing as I was never interested in hockey until she became obsessed. Now, though, I can't seem to escape it. Even my younger sister, Scout, is involved in hockey since she's dating a player on our local team. My life is now more entwined with the sport than I ever thought possible.

It's probably why I have zero interest in the conversation between Bianca and the other moms right now. They've been going on for ten minutes about the three Comets players sitting on the other side of the bar, but I'm just not as starstruck as they are.

I won't even get into the fact that they shouldn't be batting their lashes and pushing their tits up like they are, considering two of them are married and one is in a long-term relationship. That's their business, not mine.

Besides, I don't want to rock the boat with the only moms nice enough to invite me out. It would be an understatement to say it's been a struggle to make mom friends. The groups are already formed, and the rumors about my failed marriage have already been spread. It's hard to fix the image everyone seems to have of me.

"Seriously, he's *so* hot. I want to lick his jawline so badly. I—oh god! He's looking over here!" Bianca hisses, running her fingers through the ends of her hair.

"Never in my life would I think a guy missing a front tooth would be so cute, but *oh my god*, Fitzgerald makes me swoon."

I can't help but grin at that comment from Denise, another mom, because Fitzgerald *is* cute, especially when he has his tooth out. He also happens to be the sweetest guy ever. Quiet and polite, I love it when he stops by my sister's donut truck.

But I don't tell them that. I have no interest in advertising that I'm familiar with the players they're fawning over. There's no attention on me right now, and I'd like to keep it that way.

The girls keep giggling and staring at the hockey players. One must get up because Bianca's eyes track him across the bar, and I swear she licks her lips. I want to laugh, but I don't.

If only they saw the side of the players I see. They're just like everyone else and not worth getting all flustered over. Some are sweet—like Smith, Miller, and Fitzgerald—and some are downright assholes, like Greer, the grumpy goalie who is never, ever nice, not even to Macie.

"So, Stevie, I heard a rumor…" I inwardly groan as Bianca turns her ultra-white smile on me. "Is your sister really dating a Comets player?"

Crap. So much for keeping that part of my life quiet.

"She is. Grady Miller."

"Miller?!" Denise fans her face. "God, that man is *so* hot. He makes me tingle in all the right places."

Hearing her talk about my sister's boyfriend like that makes me uncomfortable. I don't know how Scout handles this stuff every day, and I know she deals with it because I see her social media accounts. So many people accusing her of only having a publishing deal because of her "famous hockey boyfriend" is bullshit. If only they could have seen what I did over the years. She's been through some rough stuff. I know how hard she worked for what she has, so the comments annoy me, just like Denise's do.

"How'd she meet him again?"

"Well, she owns Scout's Sweets. It's—"

"That's the cute little donut truck, right?" Bianca interrupts.

I force a smile. "Yes, that's the one. Several of the players on the team stop by often."

Sometimes too often if you ask me. *Especially* Greer. I could go the rest of my life without ever seeing him again, and it would still be too soon.

Is he possibly the most gorgeous man I've ever laid eyes on? Yes.

Does it erase what a giant dick he is? Not even a little.

"What about Fitzgerald?"

"Hmm?" I ask.

"Does Fitzgerald ever stop by? Because if so, I might need to make a trip there."

"Kerry! Don't ask that. It's none of our business," Bianca scolds, but her eyes drift my way anyway like she's waiting for me to say it's okay and spill all the secrets of the players.

I'm not going to do that.

"Actually, I—"

"Hello, ladies," a deep voice says, quieting me and the rest of the group.

I turn to find a stranger standing at the end of the table, a tumbler of something brown in his hand. He's tall with deep blond hair and ruddy cheeks. The scent of alcohol wafts off him, and I'm certain it's not coming from his glass. It's him.

I glance at the other women, and none seem bothered by him interrupting our evening. In fact, Denise sits up higher, and Bianca grins his way like she can't wait to sink her claws into him. Kerry seems interested as well.

"Hi," Bianca says breathily.

"You ladies want some company?"

Before any of us can even respond—because I damn sure would say *no*—he sits down.

Right next to me.

I slide away from him as subtly as I can.

He grins over at me, and I muster up the tiniest of smiles back. There's something about him I don't like, something that puts me on edge that I can't quite place my finger on. The other girls don't seem to mind him, smiling and flirting. Maybe it's all in my head.

A hand appears in my field of vision, and I jump in surprise.

"Hey, easy there, sugar. Just wanted to say hi."

I glance up to find the guy smirking at me. I assume it's supposed to be cute, flirty, or something of that nature. It's not. It's making me extremely uncomfortable.

I scoot away from him farther. He doesn't miss it.

In fact, he laughs and leans into me. "Playing hard to get, huh? That's all right. I like a good chase." He winks, and I want to vomit. "I'm Kyle."

It hits me.

Michael.

He reminds me of my ex-husband. His perfectly coiffed hair, his stupid collared shirt, those hideous khakis —even the red that's staining his cheeks is reminiscent of my ex, who loved a bottle of whiskey more than he ever loved Macie or me.

Michael was a drunk and an asshole. This guy is giving me those exact vibes, and I really, really want to be anywhere else. My hands are clammy, and the pace of my heartbeat quickens.

I wish I were at home. I wish I were at home. I wish I were at home.

Shit. I didn't tap my heels together.

"I'm going to use the restroom. Excuse me."

I shove out of my chair and away from the table faster than I ever have in my life. I barrel through the bar and down the hall. I never thought I'd see a bar bathroom as a sanctuary, but the air that whooshes back into my lungs the moment I swing the door open makes it feel like one.

Pressing my back against it once it's closed, I suck in breath after breath.

I'm not sure how long passes until my breathing finally evens out some, but when my racing heart finally settles down, the shame washes over me. I haven't felt like this since the night I finally walked away from my ex. I hated it then, and I hate it even more now. I hate that he has a lasting effect on me.

I don't want him to. I'm stronger than this—stronger than *him*.

Pushing off the door, I give myself a shake as I head for the stall. I didn't really have to pee, but now that I'm here, I might as well.

I take my time, folding the toilet paper with precision instead of wadding it up. I wash my hands three times, doing everything I can to extend my time in here so I don't have to spend another second at the table with the intrusive stranger who reminds me so much of my ex it makes my skin crawl. When I've exhausted all options, I take a steadying breath and pull the door open.

I'm two steps into the hallway when I regret my decision.

A dark shadow falls over me, and I don't even need to look up to know who it is. I can smell him.

"There you are, sugar. Thought you ran out on me."

In an instant, he's in my space, crowding me against the wall and trying to get his hands on my waist.

"Don't touch me."

I hate how breathless I sound, hate the fear that's racing up my spine. The same fear has me frozen in place instead of running.

"Oh, come on. You don't mean that." I'm sure he thinks he's being charming, but he's not. "I'd love to take you home tonight."

"No."

He laughs, reaching for me again, and I do everything I can to block his touch. How is nobody seeing this? Why is nobody helping?

"Stop, please."

Another laugh that has my stomach revolting.

"I said *no*."

I squeeze my eyes shut when he leans in, turning my head so if he does kiss me, at least it won't be on my mouth. I want to puke. I want to scream. I want to run.

But none of those things happen. Instead, a rush of cold air hits me, and the breath returns to my lungs in a *whoosh*. There's some grunting and someone talking, a few cuss words thrown around.

I swear I don't care who my savior is; I'm going to give them a big ol' kiss.

When I finally peel my eyes open, I hate myself for making that promise, because I know exactly who I'm staring at, and kissing him is the last thing I want to do.

Greer.

CHAPTER 3

"Don't touch me."

The voice carries through the door of the restroom. They must be speaking pretty loudly because Slapshots isn't a quiet place.

"No."

What the hell…

"Stop, please."

I tug the door open. There's a man standing in the darkened hallway, and it looks like he has someone crowded up against the wall.

"I said *no*."

It's a small voice—a *scared* voice, and there isn't a single atom in my body that hesitates to jump into action. I grab the asshole by the back of his shirt, yanking him away from the woman who clearly doesn't want him in her space and shoving him against the wall, my forearm on his throat.

"Hey! What the fuck?!"

I shove into him just a little harder. "She said no, you dick."

"Mind your own business." The asshole tries to push me off him, but it's no use. I'm bigger and stronger, and it looks like I've had about eight drinks less than him.

"Douchebags taking advantage of women *is* my business."

"F-Fuck off." He tries to fight me again, and I strengthen my hold until he chokes out a cough.

I get a sick satisfaction from it, but I don't give a shit. I'm glad he can't breathe. I'm sure the woman he was bothering felt the same way with him all up in her face.

"F-F-Fuck y-you." He barely gets the words out.

"You're hurting him," a soft voice says beside me.

"Good."

Watching the red deepen on his cheeks and the fear grow in his eyes makes me happy. Fuck this guy. Fuck him for hitting on a woman who clearly isn't interested, and fuck him for trying to touch her when he wasn't invited to. He deserves to feel the same fear she did.

I barely register someone touching me. It's a soft touch, light and feathery.

"Greer."

The single word pulls me from my stupor, and I glance at the woman I just rescued from this asshole. She's standing next to me now, and it takes me all of two seconds to realize who she is.

"Greer," she says again softly. "Let him go."

The soft plea in her voice has me releasing my hold on the asshole. He shoves at me again, but I don't budge.

"When a woman says no, she means no. You got it?" He doesn't answer, and I shake him. "Do you fucking got it, prick?"

He sputters out another cough, his air supply dwindling slowly. "I—I got it."

"Good. Now, you're going to walk out of this bar and not even look at another woman. Clear?"

He nods several times, his face contorting with pain from the pressure against his throat. I give him one last shove, just for good measure, then let him go. His knees buckle, and he nearly falls to the floor before catching himself on the wall, then stumbling down the hall and back into the light of the bar.

I stare after him, making sure he leaves as instructed. With the number of people and chairs he bumps into, I wonder if he even has his eyes open.

My fists, which have been clenched at my sides since I let him go, relax slightly.

"You could have seriously hurt him."

I whirl around to the woman standing in the hallway. Her arms are crossed, and her lips are twisted into a disappointed frown.

"That was kind of the plan, something I planned to enjoy, yet you stopped me."

"Because you could have seriously hurt him."

"Your point?"

"Your career. Or did you forget about the eight-game heater you're currently on?"

A grin pulls at my lips, and I cross my arms to match her stance. "You've been watching me, huh?"

She rolls her eyes, the ones I know are deep blue. "Not even kind of."

"Then how do you know we're on a heater?"

"Um, because I live here, and people talk? For some reason, you have fans."

"I have fans because I'm a damn good goalie."

"You're cocky."

"I'm good."

She looks like she wants to argue that one, but she doesn't. Instead, she drops her arms and turns on her heel, marching back through the bar.

I follow.

She leads me—and I say that in the loosest of terms—to the exact table Hayes was pointing at earlier. So this is the mystery dark-haired woman.

"Stevie!" the blonde says when we stop. "We were just about to come look for you."

She's lying, and it's painful how obvious it is. I bet they didn't even realize Stevie was missing, which means they had no clue she was about two seconds away from being assaulted.

The woman's eyes land on me, and they widen. "Oh. I didn't realize you were…busy." She grins, then bats her lashes. "Hi, I'm Bianca. It's nice to meet you."

I don't respond because it's not nice to meet her.

Maybe if she gave a shit about her friend and didn't blatantly lie to her, I'd play nice, but not right now. Not after Stevie just went through what she did.

Stevie doesn't miss my lack of manners, glaring at me before turning a sweet smile her friends' way. "I'm sorry. I got…held up." Her smile falters, and if her friends notice, they don't indicate it. "It was my daughter, so I need to get going."

"Aw, so soon?" Bianca pushes her lip out. "Bummer."

"Such a bummer," another woman echoes, though she's not looking at Stevie. Her eyes are on me as she twirls a strand of hair around her fingers…one of which bears a wedding ring.

See? Marriage doesn't mean shit.

"I'll walk you out," I say to Stevie.

Her eyes narrow, telling me she wants to argue with me yet again, but the way her eyes flit toward her friends says she doesn't want to cause a scene.

"Thank you."

The words come out forced, and I can't help but smile.

Stevie slides her coat over her arms, pulling her hair from under the jacket. An aroma of something fruity hits my nose. I can't quite place my finger on the scent, but whatever it is, I don't hate it.

"Thanks again for inviting me out," Stevie says to the blonde.

"Of course. You'll have to come out with us again

sometime." Her eyes slide to mine, then back to Stevie. "*Soon.*"

Lady translation: I want all the details.

Too bad for them there won't be any juicy details. Stevie hates me, and I'm not interested anyway.

"Oh, you dirty, dirty dog, you." Hayes rests his hand on my shoulder, whispering so only I can hear. "And you said we should stay away." He grins. "Ladies, lovely to meet you."

I glance over at Fitz, who shrugs. "We were wondering where you were. He barreled over here, so I figured I'd follow."

"Remind me to tell Lowell you're a horrible babysitter."

"Pfft. My nieces love me."

"Yeah, that's clearly because you don't watch them and let them do whatever they want."

"So, ladies, how's your evening going?" Hayes asks, laying the charm on thickly.

"It's much better now," the blonde answers, tossing her hair behind her shoulder. "I'm Bianca," she tells him in that same sultry voice she tried to use on me. This time, it works. Hayes takes the bait like he hasn't eaten in days.

Jesus. They're so obvious it's painful.

I turn my attention back to Stevie, but she's not there. I look left, I look right.

She's gone.

"The brunette?" Fitz asks.

"Did you see her?"

He hitches his thumb toward the door. "She left."

"Fuck," I mutter. "I gotta—"

"Go," Fitz finishes for me. "I'll take care of Hayes."

I want to tell him given the fact that he let him just waltz back in here, I doubt that, but I don't. I head for the door, bursting through it in about two seconds. I scan the street to my left, then look right and spot her just a few feet up the sidewalk.

She stands just outside the light of the streetlamp, her own phone illuminating her face as she scrolls through whatever's on the screen. Her long dark lashes cast a shadow against her cheek. Her jacket may be puffy and bulky and not do any favors for her figure, but her jeans sure as hell do, fitting her like a second skin.

Her dark hair is covering part of her face, but even from here, I can see the lone tear running down her cheek, can hear her sniffle.

I take a step toward her, and her head whips my way at the sound of my shoes against the concrete. She immediately takes a step back into the light, but I notice the way she relaxes when she sees it's just me.

"What do you want."

It doesn't really come out as a question. It's more like she's annoyed that I've followed her.

"I…" But nothing comes out.

What *do* I want? Why did I follow her out here?

She lifts her brows in impatience. "Well?"

"I wanted to see that you were okay."

Her head jerks back in surprise, and I can attest that the feeling is mutual.

My statement is honest, though. I *do* want to see that she's okay.

"Oh." The word is quiet, but I hear it all the same. "I'm fine."

Her chin wobbles, and another tear slips down her cheek.

I take another step toward her. "Are you sure?"

"I'm fine." She swipes at her face, rolls her shoulders back, and gives herself a shake, tips her chin up. "I'm fine."

This time, the words come out stronger. It's almost like she believes the harder or more she says them, the truer they'll become.

"Okay."

"Okay," she echoes. Another sniffle.

"Do you need a ride home?"

"I got an Uber. It'll be here in ten minutes."

"I'll stay with you, then."

"You really don't need to."

"I'm waiting for my Uber too."

That's a lie. I haven't called for a car, though I do need to. I'm not drunk and didn't have much, but I don't want to risk anything.

"So, did you know that guy?"

She shakes her head. "No."

"Good." And it is good. I don't like the idea of her associating with someone like that.

"He was drunk."

Now it's me who is surprised. "Your point?"

"I'm just saying…he was drunk."

"That's not an excuse to assault someone."

"I know that."

"Do you? Because it doesn't sound like it."

She glowers at me. "I *do* know that. I'm just saying maybe he wouldn't have been so…forward if he wasn't drunk."

I snort. "Right. I fucking doubt that. Guy gave *me* the heebies."

I shake my head, annoyed she's defending him but also not trying to blame her. She's probably in shock, probably trying to rationalize what just happened. I don't need to pile on her right now.

"I don't watch you, you know."

"Hmm?"

"Before, you said I must be watching you. I'm just telling you I don't."

"You already said that."

"And I'm reiterating it. *I* don't watch you. My daughter does."

"Scrawny little shit with braces, right?"

Another glare. "Her name is Macie. She's obsessed with the Comets."

"She has good taste, then."

"She doesn't like you."

Now it's my turn to glare. "That so?"

"She calls you The Jackass."

I tuck my lips together so she can't see my smile because, honestly, it's a good name for me. I *am* a jackass sometimes. Everyone says so.

"She seems…"

"Careful, Greer. She's ten, and I will scratch your eyes out."

I rock back on my heels, impressed by her tenacity. "I was going to say she seems like she's got some fire in her."

Stevie lets out a light laugh, a smile curving her lips. "You could say that."

"Who is her favorite player?"

"I think this week it's Miller."

"Miller? Seriously?"

She lifts a shoulder. "He makes her aunt happy."

I roll my eyes because *of course* it has to do with love and all that sappy relationship shit. "Miller is an idiot."

"He truly is sometimes. He asked me yesterday if goose and geese were two different animals."

"He did not."

"Oh, he did. I've never had secondhand embarrassment so hard in my life." She shakes her head with a smile. "But he's sweet too, and he loves my sister so damn much."

An involuntary groan leaves me, and Stevie doesn't miss it.

"What was that for?"

"Love."

"Excuse me?"

"Love." I lift my hat, running a hand through my hair before putting the cap back on backward. "It's a crock of shit. The idea of waiting around to find the right person is sickening."

"Ah." She nods. "That makes sense now."

"What makes sense?"

"Well..." She waves her hand in my direction. "You."

"Meaning?"

"Meaning *everything*. The scowl that never leaves your face and the way you treat people, like you're uninterested and holding them at arm's length—the lack of love in your life explains that well."

"I have love in my life."

"Who? Because last I checked, you're single and have never been married."

"You know, that sounds an awful lot like you've looked me up."

Stevie huffs. "I have not."

It's a lie. We both know it.

I just want to know why: why she looked me up, and why she's lying.

Scratch that—I probably know why she's lying. She knows I'll never let her forget it.

"I have love in my life," I insist again, though I don't know why. Stevie is nobody to me. I don't need to convince her I'm not missing something by not being in a relationship.

I already have to convince my mother of that; I don't

need to add someone else to the list. She's enough to deal with, thank you.

"I'm sure you do." Her words are the exact opposite of the look on her face. She doesn't believe me at all.

That's fine because I don't believe me either.

Do I have love in my life? If you count the fact that my parents both love me, sure. Other than that…well, no, not really. I like my teammates and would consider them friends, but do I love them? I don't think so.

So, fine, maybe I *don't* have real love in my life. But I'm fine.

I am *fine*…right?

A car pulls up to the curb, and Stevie steps toward it.

"Wait!" I call out, startling us both.

"What?" she asks, staring up at me with her brows drawn tight together.

"You don't even know if that's your Uber."

She lifts her eyes skyward. "It's mine."

"But I ordered one too." *That's a lie.* "It could be mine."

"It's not. It's mine."

"Says?"

"Um, the app?" The sarcasm drips from her words as she holds her phone my way, and I take a quick look at the information, then check the car in front of us.

It's her ride.

With a groan, she shakes her head. "I don't even know why I'm showing you this. I'm leaving now."

"Can you wait a second?"

A loud sigh falls from her lips. "What."

She's clearly annoyed by me. I would be too. Honestly, I don't even know why I want her to wait; I just do.

"Are you sure you're okay?"

She stares up at me for a moment with her head tipped to the side like she's studying me. I don't like being under scrutiny.

"That's the second time you've asked me that. Why do you care so much?"

"Because I'm not a heartless monster."

She snorts out a laugh. "Sure you're not." Her hand lands on the rear door handle. "Can I go now?"

"Yeah, go." I wave my hand toward the car. "You're welcome, by the way."

A pause.

A slow turn my way.

A heated stare.

"Excuse me?"

"I said, *you're welcome*. For rescuing you."

Stevie scoffs, then pulls the door open before leveling me with one last glare I'm sure I'll bear the burn marks from tomorrow. "Good night, *jackass*."

Before I can register what she's just said, she climbs into the back of the car, which promptly pulls away from the curb, and she disappears down the road. I stand there like an idiot, staring after her for far too many minutes, trying to figure out why I don't exactly feel great right now.

"Wow."

I spin on my heel to find Fitzgerald shaking his head at me.

"What?"

"She's right—you really are a jackass."

This time…I think I may agree.

CHAPTER 4

"Wait, wait, wait. He said *what*?"

"*You're welcome for rescuing you.*" I shake my head. "Who the hell does he think he is?"

I toss the dough I've been working for the last forty minutes onto the counter, annoyed it's not doing what I want it to. I'm sure most of that is my fault. I'm distracted. I can't stop thinking about last night or Greer's parting words. They've been grating on me since I got into the Uber, and my poor driver had to listen to me complain the entire ride. I'm sure I'll be seeing the karmic response to that at some point and get stuck with a driver who doesn't stop talking.

But I was pissed.

I *am* pissed. Greer's comment was just so…*him*.

"A jackass," says Rosie, the head baker at my sister's donut truck, Scout's Sweets. "A complete and total moron, too. Why the hell would he say that?"

"Because he's the worst. I hate him."

"I hate him too."

"You do?"

"Of course I do. Solidarity!" Rosie says, lifting a fist in the air. "I'm here for you."

I chuckle. "Thank you. I appreciate that." I peek over at my sister, who is standing at the back of the truck, a donut in hand. "Any solidarity from you?"

She takes another bite of her donut—a Strawyummy Cake, my favorite—then chews and swallows. "Sort of."

I take a step back because I am genuinely surprised by Scout's comment. "Sort of?"

"Greer is definitely a jackass…but he *did* step in when you needed help. I can't fault him for that. You're my sister, and I'll love anyone who keeps you safe."

She's right. I know she is.

And while I'm super grateful for Greer pulling that douchebag off me, and I know I owe him for it, it doesn't change the fact that he was just so…*Greer* about the whole thing. Cockiness radiated off him, and I wanted to wipe the smug smile right off his face with my palm.

I'm sure somewhere deep down, Greer is a nice guy —he did help me, after all—but sometimes, no matter how many good deeds someone does, it doesn't erase their douchebaggery.

"I still don't like him," I mutter.

"I'm surprised. You're normally Miss Sunshine who loves and gives everyone a chance. Why not Greer?"

"Have you met him?" I counter.

She has a point, though. Even with my checkered past with my ex, I still love and trust people. I'm friendly.

I like to talk. But there's just something about Greer… He does something to me that I can't describe, probably because it's nothing I've ever experienced before.

"He's hot," Rosie comments, working her hands through the dough in front of her like she didn't just drop a bomb.

"What?!"

Rosie shrugs at my outburst. "He is. That jawline of his is…*wow*. It's too bad it's always covered by his goalie mask."

Her words remind me of Bianca last night and how badly she wanted to lick Greer's jaw. That's two women obsessing over him. Is it even that good? I've never noticed before.

"Oh please. Yes you have."

Crap. Did I say that out loud?

"There's no way you could have missed it." Scout backs Rosie up. "Pretty sure it's sharper than his skates."

"Don't you already have a hot hockey player to drool over?"

A dreamy look crosses her face, and Scout sighs. "I do. My hot hockey player agrees with me, though."

"That Greer is hot?"

"Yep." She nods. "I had him rank all his teammates one night when we were bored."

"And?" Rosie asks, setting her dough aside, fully invested in the conversation now.

"Greer was at the top. Then Rhodes because his scar makes him hotter. Fitz because of his missing tooth,

Lowell because he's a daddy—though now that I'm thinking about it, I'm not sure if he meant daddy or *Daddy*. Wright was at the bottom of the top five." She shakes her head. "Wait, that's not right. If I went with his *real* top five, he himself would come after Fitz. We argued for thirty minutes about whether or not he could be on his list. I won."

She grins, clearly proud of herself.

"He put *Greer* before Fitz?" Rosie looks stunned. "Is he nuts?"

"I don't think so. I'm also very honored. I'll have to thank him for that."

A chill runs up my spine.

I know that voice.

I turn on my heel with reluctance. I don't want to see him. Not right now, or ever again.

"Oh god. He's going to kill me for telling you that." Scout gulps audibly.

"Please, Miller worships the ground you walk on," Rosie tells her. "He's so completely obsessed it almost makes *me* want to gag, and that's saying something because I adore a good romance."

Scout sighs, then says something to Rosie, but I don't catch it. I'm too engrossed in the staring contest I've been roped into with Greer. He's looking at me with green eyes that remind me of a summer day. He's not smiling, nor is he frowning. He's…watching.

I hate it.

Almost like he can read my thoughts, a small smile

pulls at the corners of his lips, lifting them into a smug grin.

I hate that even more.

"Stevie." His voice is deep, a low timbre that has no business sounding as good as it does.

"Greer."

His stupid lips pull up higher, somehow making his already smug smirk even smugger.

"What are you doing here?"

"I'm getting a donut."

I lift an eyebrow. "Since when?"

"Since I always do. It's Saturday."

"Your point?"

"I come here every Saturday I can."

Now both of my brows go up. *Does he?*

"You're usually not here."

That's true, but how does he know that?

Saturday mornings are typically reserved for Macie, but since she stayed with Scout and Miller last night, I figured I'd help Rosie for a few hours. Scout's donut truck business has picked up since word of her dating Miller got out. Customers are flocking here faster than ever before in hopes of getting a glimpse of one of the Comets players. I'm sure if Greer had arrived just an hour earlier when the line was to the parking lot, he would have been hounded incessantly for autographs like Miller was. He took Macie, and they're hiding at McDonald's across the street.

"I'm helping out."

I don't tell him I'll probably be here more often from now on. The law firm I work at is merging with another firm, and they don't need two receptionists. I'm aware it's likely my head on the chopping block.

"So, are you going to help me out, then?"

"Excuse me?"

He points to the rack of donuts behind me. "Donuts. I want to order."

"We're closed."

He barks out a laugh just as Scout lets out a squeal.

"Stevie!" she admonishes.

"What? I'm on the clock today, not you. We're closed."

"Stevie!" my sister says again, shoving me out of the way and pasting on her best customer service smile. "Ignore her, Greer. What can I get for you?"

"I got it," Rosie says, already boxing something up.

"How do you know his order?"

She shrugs, setting the box on the counter, then moves toward the iced coffee. "He comes here a lot."

"He does not!"

"I do too," says the man in question.

"Well, you can't. Not anymore."

He lifts a perfectly arched brow, and I momentarily wonder if he gets them waxed and shaped to look like that.

"I don't."

"What?"

"My brows. I don't get them waxed or shaped, whatever the hell that means."

Shit. I have to stop saying what I'm thinking out loud, especially with Greer here. The last thing I need is to think something positive about him and accidentally say it. I don't want him to get any ideas about me liking him.

I shudder at the thought. Liking Greer? Please. That will *never* happen.

"Here you go." Rosie slides an iced coffee his way. The cup's contents are pale, like it's loaded down with milk and sweetener.

He sticks a straw in the drink and takes a healthy swig almost instantly. He exhales loudly, smacking his lips together in the most annoying manner. "It's perfect, Rosie. Thank you."

The way he says it…it's so…*nice*. So unlike Greer.

"It's on the house, too," Scout tells him, hitching her thumb my way. "Because of her."

Another smirk. "Well, *thank you*, Stevie. Wasn't so hard to say, was it?"

I narrow my eyes. "You can leave now."

My sister yells my name for the third time. "Stevie! You can't work here if you're going to be mean to customers."

"I'm not. Just to Greer."

Scout drops her head into her hands. "Good lord."

"It's okay, Scout," he says magnanimously. "I don't mind. I can take it."

"Well, *I* mind. You were so nice to her last night, helping her out. She should maybe be a bit nicer," Scout says through clenched teeth, eyes narrowed at me in warning.

"Talking about me, huh?"

God, I want to jump over this counter and wipe the arrogant look off his face.

"Go away, Greer."

"Not until you say it."

"Say what?"

"*Thank you, Greer.*"

I snort. "Not a chance."

"Come on. Don't be that way. I thought we had a connection last night."

"The only connecting we'll ever do is my palm with your face."

"That's okay. I like it rough." He bounces his brows up and down, and I hate it so much.

The only thing I hate more is the pull I feel between my legs at the thought of anything rough and sexual with him.

"Is that something you like too?" he asks, leaning closer. I want to get away, want to do anything to put space between us, especially when his green eyes are boring into me the way they are—like he's entirely too invested in my answer—but I can't. That would give him the idea that he's affecting me, and I'd rather him not know that.

So, I don't move. I don't answer him. The only thing I do is swallow the lump that's suddenly formed in my throat.

"Interesting," he murmurs, not missing it.

"Leave."

He lets out a low, sinister laugh. "Say it."

"Not going to happen, Greer."

"Why not? Scared you'll have to acknowledge I helped you and you owe me?"

I curl my lips in disgust at the word. "I don't owe you anything."

"Sure you do, and I intend to collect on it."

"For the tenth time this morning, leave."

"I'll go, but only because I have somewhere to be." He lifts his drink Rosie's way. "*Thank you*," he says, giving me a pointed look. "I'll see you ladies later. Steve."

"Jackass."

He chuckles, then spins on his heel and treks back through the parking lot with entirely too much swagger in his walk. It's obnoxious how confident it is. It's almost as annoying as how well his long-sleeved shirt clings to his back, showing off the build he hides under his pads.

But I don't care about that because I don't care about Greer. I dip my hands back into the dough, kneading away, trying to channel all my frustration into shaping donuts. I beat the pile of dough over and over, shaping, then reshaping the same donut. I'm so annoyed I can't even make a damn Long John.

"Ugh," I groan, tossing the dough aside. "He is so…so…"

"Insanely hot?"

"Rosie!" I glare at her. "I thought you were on my team. What happened to solidarity?"

"Oh, right." She straightens her back. "Ugh. He's *so* gross. The worst."

It's the worst acting job I've ever witnessed. Not a single word that tumbles from her lips is believable.

"I can practically hear all the dirty thoughts running through your head right now."

"Nah." She waves her hand. "The only one I'm fantasizing about is Fitz." She lets out a dreamy sigh, and it's kind of funny how head over heels she is for him and how oblivious he is to it.

Scout points to her head baker. "I'm with her. Well, not the whole fantasizing-about-Fitz thing, but the Greer-being-hot part. Because he is."

"He's…fine looking."

My little sister gives me a look that says I'm full of shit.

I ignore it.

Is Greer good-looking? Yeah, of course he is, but do I care? Not even a little bit. He's an ass on a good day. He's grumpy, and he thinks he's better than everyone else. I don't think that's hot at all.

"Mom!"

Now *that* I do care about.

I turn toward the parking lot just in time to see an excited Macie running my way.

"Mom!" she calls again once she's closer. "You won't believe what happened!"

"What's up?" I lean against the counter, watching as she skids to a stop before the truck, just barely tall enough to reach the counter.

"Uncle Grady"—my heart melts a little when she says that—"paid for everyone's lunch, then we took some food to Eddie. After that, he took me to the store and let me pick out *thirteen* things. Anything I wanted."

My brows go up at the last thing. "Thirteen?"

I slide my eyes Miller's way, unsurprised to find him smiling unapologetically.

"What?" He lifts his broad shoulders. "It's my lucky number."

"Uh-huh," I say, turning back to my daughter, who is practically bouncing on her heels with excitement. "What'd he let you get?"

"Well, I got candy. Like, *a lot* of candy, because he said if I got some of the same kind of stuff, it didn't count as more than one thing."

Of course he said that. "How much is a lot?"

"Less than Halloween."

"That's a terrible unit of measure," Rosie mutters, and I agree.

"Plus, I got a Spiderman pajama set, two new books, a DVD about when the Comets won the Cup, a new goalie stick, and *so much* more."

"That sounds like—"

"The best thing ever? I know!" She claps her hands together. "I'm so happy! He said it was a late Christmas gift."

I want to point out that Miller already got her an incredible Christmas gift—tickets to several Comets games, including the one tomorrow—but I don't, not when she's as excited as she is. I should also tell Macie to maybe not get used to being spoiled like that, but I can't bring myself to ruin her high right now.

"That was really nice of him. Did you tell him thank you?"

"Her mom can't say it, so why should she?"

I glare at Rosie, who quickly turns her attention back to the dough she abandoned, whistling like she didn't just say what she did.

"Duh, Mom. I even told him *thirteen* times." She rolls her eyes, and before I can yell at her for it, she runs off, sprinting toward the picnic table where Miller set her bag of goodies.

Scout laughs, and I turn my glare her way.

She lifts her hands in the air. "Hey, I didn't say anything."

"Yeah, but you're thinking it."

"I'm just saying…you owe him."

"I don't owe him anything."

That's not true. I *know* it's not true. I should thank him. What kind of example am I setting for my daughter if I can't even tell someone thanks for doing something so huge for me? It's just…it's *Greer*. I don't want to give him the satisfaction.

Not to mention I'm embarrassed there's even anything I have to thank him for. What happened last night…I thought I was done feeling that helpless, thought I was finished feeling like that. I don't want Greer, of all people, to know I need to be rescued.

Scout's hand lands on my shoulder. "It doesn't make you weak to need help," she says softly, like she knows exactly where my mind has gone.

With a sigh, I say, "Fine. I'll do it."

"Good." Scout smiles proudly.

"Why do I feel like I missed something?" Miller asks, his eyes bouncing between his girlfriend and me.

Scout waves her hand. "It's nothing."

It's not nothing, though. I know that, and Scout knows it too. I promised myself eight years ago I'd never indebt myself to someone again.

It looks like it might be time to break that promise.

CHAPTER 5

Game days are my favorite days ever. The excitement that hums through me from the moment I open my eyes is unlike any other high. I mean, I've never actually been high, but I assume it's better. It has to be. I'm getting paid to play hockey—how fucking incredible is that? How could anything get better?

It can't. It's impossible.

"You really shouldn't frown like that. Your face is going to get stuck."

I glance over at the idiot who has just flopped down on the bench next to me. "Go away, Hayes."

"What? I'm just saying, keep scowling, and you're screwed. You're going to be as wrinkly as Coach before you're even thirty."

"Wrinkly or not, I'll still be a better hockey player than you."

He scoffs. "Please. You wish."

"Why are you here?"

"Uh, because we have a game?"

"I mean *here*, talking to me. You know—"

"You hate being talked to before a game." He rolls his eyes. "I know. I just thought…"

"Ah, see, there's your first mistake, rookie—thinking."

He glares at me. "The guys are right. You are a dick."

I grin, wearing that badge with pride. "Thank you." I let my smile fade. "Now fuck off. I need to get ready."

The kid saunters away, leaving me on my own, just how I like it.

Every guy has their own pregame routine, and shutting out the world is mine. I don't like talking to people, not even my teammates. I don't want music or television or any sort of distraction. The only thing I want to do is sit here and just *be*.

It helps me get into the right headspace. It's what's helped me win eight games in a row, and it's what's going to help us lift that Cup this season. I can feel it in my bones. I'm definitely not going to let the fucking rookie trip me up.

Not tonight.

I let my eyes fall closed as I rest my back against my cubby. The all-too-familiar sounds in the room wash over me, and I take slow, deep breaths. It's kind of like meditation, only there are about ten other dudes in here, it smells like a disgusting locker room, and they have no fucking idea how to shut up.

But…I love it. It's all part of playing the greatest game ever to exist.

Someone plops down next to me, and I know in an instant who it is.

"You have to stop being mean to the rookie. He's going to think you don't like him."

"I don't like him. Or you, for that matter."

"That's a lie."

"It's truly not, Miller. Please fuck off."

He laughs, then slaps my thigh. "And miss an opportunity to annoy you? Not a chance."

I peel my eyes open, turning a heated glare his way. "Why are you bothering me?"

"Because I like doing it."

"How does Scout not smother you with a pillow?"

"Because it turns out I'm really good with my tongue." He sticks said tongue out, licking the air.

It's annoying…just like he is. I want him to go away, and I think I know just how to make that happen.

"I heard a rumor…"

His brows rise. "About me?" He rubs his hands together. "I hope it's an exciting one."

"I think it is." I cup my hands around my mouth. "Hey, Wright!"

The defenseman lifts his head across the room. "What's up?"

There's hesitation in his voice, and I get it. When I say I don't usually talk to anyone before a game, that's not an exaggeration. I like the quiet, the solitude, because I want to win, and that's why getting Miller far, far away from me is so important.

"Did you know Miller made a list ranking all the guys on the team by who's hottest, and you're number five?"

"Five?!"

"Oh crap," Miller mutters, shrinking as Wright rises from his cubby, stalking toward us.

"What the hell do you mean *five*, Miller? I am way hotter than the other guys!"

"Hey! I take great offense to that," Lowell chimes in.

I point to the captain. "He said you're hot because you're a daddy."

"Like a daddy or a *Daddy*?" He bounces his brows up and down.

We all look to Miller for the answer. He doesn't respond. He can't. He's too busy holding his breath and squeezing his eyes shut, pretending he doesn't exist right now.

"He definitely meant *Daddy*. It's Miller. For the record, I'd like to be left out of this list."

"Too bad. You're number two."

"Two?" Rhodes growls, sounding very much like he doesn't want to be left out at all. "Then who is number one?"

"That would be me." I smile proudly. "I'm number one, then Rhodes, Fitz, Lowell, Wright."

"Fitz is before me?" Lowell's mouth opens in shock. "What the hell for?"

"Because of his missing tooth." Miller shrugs. "It's cute."

Fitz grins, poking his tongue through the hole. "I knew this would win me some points."

"Miller is right," says Surkov, another forward. "My husband and I made a list too. Just swap out Lowell for Wright and it's spot-on."

"What!" Lowell explodes at the same time Wright yells out, "Ha! Suck it!"

"I'm still hotter than both of you." Rhodes grins, awfully proud of himself.

"What are you smiling about?" I say to him. "I'm number one."

"Yeah, number one pain in my ass."

"He took *my* spot?" Miller presses a hand to his chest and juts his bottom lip out. "I'm hurt. Truly."

"You're an idiot. Truly," Rhodes mocks.

"Nah. You love me."

"I really, really don't."

"Lies!" Miller says, rising from the bench to follow the defenseman, who is now retreating from the room. He glances back at me, then peeks around before holding his hand to the side of his mouth. "Also, your vibrator is on," he whispers.

What the…

"Did you just say what I think you did?"

"Hey, no judgment!" He holds his hands up. "But maybe turn it off so you don't burn out the battery?"

"What the fuck are you on about? I—"

"There it is again."

I'm about to tell him he's a complete idiot, but this time, I hear it.

"That's not my vibrator—which I don't even have—it's my *phone*."

"Sure. Right."

"Miller…" I growl, and that's all it takes for him to scramble away, off to annoy someone else.

I pluck my phone from my bag, surprised I completely forgot to shut it off. I'm two seconds from doing so, but it buzzes again.

It's my mother.

I should ignore it. I know I should. I have a game to focus on. I'm ready to take our win streak to nine.

But if she's called me this many times, something has to be wrong, right?

I slide my finger across the green button.

"Mom?"

"Oh, thank gosh! You finally answered!"

The way she rushes out the words in complete panic has me sitting forward, now on high alert.

"What's wrong? Is everything okay?"

"No! Nothing is okay. The cake company I wanted to use says they're booked for that weekend, and I had my heart set on their vanilla and raspberry three-tier cake. It's the one I had when I married Archie, and I want it again, not to mention my seamstress is a complete pain to nail down. We're down to just one month. I need things done, Jacob."

My jaw drops. "You called me about the wedding?"

"Of course I did." She huffs. "I need to know your date's name for the place cards."

"Why?"

"Because I need to know who is sitting next to you! I'm trying to do this one right."

She wanted to do her other wedding "right," too. And the one before that. It's obvious how well those events turned out.

"Well?" my mother prompts when I don't answer.

"I don't have a date yet, Loretta."

She sighs. "You're not distracting me with that."

I chuckle because she knows me so well. If I ever want to change the subject, I call her by her first name. She hates it when I do it and always goes off on a tangent about how I shouldn't call her anything but Mom.

Guess I've used that strategy too many times, and she's onto me.

"And what do you mean you don't have a date yet? We have one month until the wedding. One month!"

"Oh, really? I hadn't heard." I roll my eyes even though she can't see me, and it's a good thing, too, because that would definitely earn me a smack to the back of my head.

"Don't roll your eyes at me, Jacob Greer."

How the hell did she…

"Mom sense," she answers, like that explains everything. "Please let me know your date's name by Friday, or you're off the guest list."

"Excuse me?"

"You heard me, son."

"And do you mean it?"

She hesitates for a moment. "I mean it."

"But I'm your dude of honor."

It feels like tradition at this point. While my mother has plenty of friends—being a hairdresser means she's a people person—I've still always been the one to stand beside her. I refuse to let this wedding be any different.

"I'll have a date by Friday."

"You promise?"

"I promise, Loretta."

"Jacob." She sighs. "You're lucky you're my favorite kid. You know that, right?"

"I'm your only kid, Mom."

"That you know of. Your father, on the other hand, is obsessed with procreating, so who knows if you're his favorite or not."

I laugh because she's not wrong. My parents never married—a shocker for them both—but they still went on to have several other long-term relationships. While my mother prefers to marry her partners, my dad likes to have kids with his. My mom may be going into her fourth marriage, but my dad has her beat—he's on kid number six.

"Lucas is killing it on points this season. He's probably the favorite."

My half brother plays hockey too. He's a forward for

St. Louis, and I love playing him because as hard as he tries, he can't crack me.

"Don't be like that, Jacob. Your father loves all his kids equally."

I have to hand it to my mother. No matter how often my father has moved on with a different woman or a different family, she has never said a bad word about him. In fact, it's the opposite—she praises him for being such a good father, and she's not wrong. He's attentive to us and always wants to make sure none of us feel left out, which I don't. I know my dad is proud of me. I also know he's a *huge* fan of competition, and even though the Comets are on a hot streak right now, my brother had a four-point night two games ago. He's definitely Dad's favorite at the moment.

"Oh!" my mother exclaims. "Your game! You're playing tonight. Why am I bothering you? Oh gosh, I'm the worst mother ever."

"You're not. You're just excited about the wedding."

She sighs wistfully. "I really am. Is that silly? I've done this so many times. I should be over it by now."

"Nah, Mom. It's not silly."

"I just…I love him *so* much. He makes me happy. I really feel like this could be the one, you know?"

This is the same speech she's given me multiple times over the years, so it's a little hard to muster up the same enthusiasm she has. I'm glad my mother is happy, but I'm not really excited about the inevitable heartbreak that's going to follow when this marriage fails just like the others. It's hard to watch over and over again.

Do I hope this one *actually* is the one? Sure, but do I have much hope that it is? Well, no. I'm sure that makes me an awful son to some, but to me, it's just being realistic. When you've grown up seeing it constantly happen, hope is something that goes out the window rather quickly.

"I'm glad, Mom."

Another soft sigh. "I'm sorry I haven't been able to make it stick for you. It wasn't fair to ask you to grow up with so many men in and out of your life."

I don't say anything because I'm not sure what to say. It's no big deal? I learned to keep myself distant from everyone? I don't believe in love at all?

I can't break her heart like that.

"Oh my gosh! I'm a terrible mother. Here I am bothering you about all this stuff when you have a game tonight."

That's right, bring it back around to hockey. Keep feelings and shit out of it.

"It's fine, but I really should be going. We have to hit warmups soon."

"Of course, of course. Thanks for making time for your old mom. Go kick some ass, son."

"I'll try. Love you."

"But never as much as I love you."

I grin. It's the same thing she's always said to me, and

it always brings me that same warmness no matter how many times I hear it.

"Friday," she says once again as a reminder.

"Friday," I echo.

I hit the red button, then relax against my cubby.

So much for no distractions before the game.

"I have no damn clue how we pulled that out of our asses, but we'll take the two points. Eight AM ice time tomorrow."

It's all Coach Heller says before he walks out of the room. He's disappointed, and I don't blame him.

I'm disappointed, too, especially in myself. I played like shit out there. My focus was completely gone, which resulted in me giving up sloppy goals. Sure, we got two points, and yeah, it might have been fun for fans to watch the back and forth, but it was a terrible performance by our entire club.

"Fuck, that sucked." Our team captain sinks down next to me. "Like really, really sucked."

"It was my fault."

"Not true," Rhodes says to me. "That was on me."

"I let so many pucks skip over my blade." Wright shakes his head. "Played like complete shit."

"I was amazing. I got two goals and an assist," Miller says, clearly proud of himself. He should be; he did play well.

"Quit with the fucking pity party," a loud voice booms through the room.

Every head in the room snaps toward Smith, who is standing with his hands on his hips, looking like a dad ready to tell his kids he's not mad, just disappointed.

"You all could have been better."

"I—"

"Missed two practically empty nets." Smith interrupts Miller, who was just about to pat himself on the back again. "Every single one of you skated slow. You didn't finish your checks, and you battled the boards like it was your first damn game. You sucked, plain and simple, but it's not the first time and won't be the last. Take the two points and get the fuck over it. Get your shit ready because we have another game on Tuesday against the top defense in the league. We need the points more than they do, so whatever made you all play like shit tonight, figure it out and leave it in the damn locker room next time."

He spins on his heel and disappears out the door.

"Damn, I miss playing with that old grump," Miller comments.

The rest of us are quiet because we know he's right. It was a team effort—or lack thereof—tonight. We just have to figure it out.

Me especially.

. . .

Mom: Sorry about the game. I can't help but think it might have been my phone call that threw you off.

I scoff. I can't say it's definitely my mom's fault, but she didn't help.

Mom: But please remember…Friday.

Mom: Love you!

With a groan, I toss my phone back into the cubby, the same feeling of dread that filled my stomach before the game hitting me again. I have to get this date thing figured out.

Tomorrow. I'll fix it tomorrow.

CHAPTER 6

"Ughhh."

I try my hardest not to roll my eyes at my ten-year-old daughter. She has been sighing nonstop since the end of the shootout last night.

The Comets, who have been doing incredible, struggled against the team that's currently ranked last in the league and came entirely too close to losing. She's convinced they will tank their entire season and miss the playoffs now. I've been trying to tell her it's just one game, one bad performance, but she's not buying it.

Hence the eighth sigh of the morning—and it's only seven AM.

"Macie, you're killing me."

"Well, we're even, then, because the Comets are killing me, *Mom*." Another sigh, another dramatic toss of her head.

When did she get so theatrical?

"They won, though, didn't they?"

She gives me an incredulous look. "Yes, but they

should have played…well, better!" She raises her hands in the air. It's cute and a little funny but also slightly annoying.

"Okay, well, they will next game. It'll be fine."

"Fine? *Fine?* It needs to be better than fine! I want to see them win the Cup again!"

She drops herself back onto the bench, her head resting on her backpack. I have to leave to take her to school in about ten minutes, and I'm betting I'll get at least three more sighs before then.

I attempt to placate her. "Everyone wants to see them win again, and they will."

She huffs, and I chuckle, turning my attention back to the coffee pot I'm working on refilling. I want to make sure the truck is prepped for Rosie while I'm fighting the school drop-off line.

"Everyone, huh? Does that mean you?"

Macie springs off the bench at the same minute I nearly drop the coffee pot.

Where the hell did he come from?

I peek up to find Greer strutting toward the truck. He's close, giving me zero time to hide or pretend I don't see him, and I *really* don't want to see him. The last two times I ran across him, it wasn't pleasant, and with my daughter being her sassy little self, I'm not sure I'm up to dealing with it today.

"You!"

Speaking of my kid…

Macie jumps off the picnic table, her finger pointed directly at Greer, who stops in his tracks.

"This is all *your* fault!"

His brows go up. "What exactly is my fault?"

"That game!"

I can see Greer's shoulders deflate from here. Ah, so he's upset about them barely coming out with two points too.

"You guys *barely* showed up for twenty minutes. It was pitiful."

"Macie!"

Greer holds his hand up toward me, his attention still on my kid, who is now standing just a foot away from him, her little finger still pointed at him and a scowl that could rival his on her face.

"What could we have done better?"

"Everything!" She throws her hands into the air. "Literally everything. The passing, the skating, the *goaltending*." That last word is punctuated with a glare that would probably have any other grown man trembling.

Not Greer, though. He just stares back at her, eyes sharp and serious as she continues going over what they could work on. He's listening to her.

Like *actually* listening to her.

It's weird. I'm not sure I've ever seen Greer so serious about something, and that's saying something because he is *always* serious.

She lets the pro-hockey player know if the team passed

just a few beats faster, they'd hit the tape every time. If they didn't get stuck in their own zone for so long, they could take shorter shifts, allowing them to skate harder and faster and beat the other team to the puck or at board battles. If they hadn't kept feeding the puck to the goalie's right and instead went to the left, they could have capitalized on it being his weak side and scored top shelf without breaking a sweat.

I admittedly have no clue what she's talking about, but Greer clearly does because he nods when she's done telling him all that.

Then finally, he says, "So you think his left is his weak side?"

"Yes! And it's yours too, especially if they're shooting just above the pads. You leave too much space open. A puck can squeak in there like *that*." She snaps on the last word for emphasis.

Greer nods again. "I think you're right."

Macie's eyes light up. "I am?" She clears her throat, pushing out her chest. "I mean, I am. I'm right. So tighten it up out there."

There's the slightest twitch to Greer's lips, but it's gone as quickly as it appeared.

"Duly noted."

Her brows squeeze together, clearly not understanding what he's said, but he's already walking away from her and toward the truck before she can ask him. He approaches the window, the annoying cocky smirk that I hate lining his lips.

"Steve."

I level him with a blank stare. "Greer."

"Nice kid you have there."

I raise a brow, daring him to say anything even remotely awful about my daughter.

He doesn't.

"What do you want."

"Some hospitality would be good."

"Damn, we're all out of that."

"I guess I'll have to settle for an iced coffee, then."

I turn to make his drink, annoyed with myself for remembering his order from the other day.

"You know, your daughter sure does have a lot to say about my performance."

"She's a big hockey nut," I tell him as I pour the coffee into the to-go cup.

"I can tell. She come to the games ever?"

"Sometimes, whenever I get time off. Miller hooked her up with some tickets."

"You'll have to tell me when. Maybe we can get the backup goalie in the net for her critiquing and get him on a hot streak too."

"Didn't look like you were on too much of a streak last night," I comment, sliding his finished drink in front of him.

His perpetual scowl deepens. "Coach Heller Jr. over there is right. I played like shit."

"Why?"

The word tumbles out of my mouth before I can stop it. I don't really care why Greer had an off night…do I?

He lets out a long sigh, long enough to rival the ones Macie's been letting out all morning. "Phone call gone wrong."

"You took a phone call before the game?"

He tips his head like he's wondering why I'm questioning him on that.

I shrug. "Miller has pregame routines he's gone through with Macie before. I know some players are stringent about not having their phones on before games."

He nods once. "I usually don't, but I guess I didn't turn the volumc all the way off. It buzzed, so I answered."

"Someone important?"

"My mother."

"Momma's boy?" I can't help the grin that slips across my face.

He narrows his eyes. "No."

"Sure."

"I'm not," he insists, and I love how it's clearly riling him up. "She's getting married."

"Oh. Well, congratulations to her. Hope it lasts longer than my marriage did."

He snorts. "Doubt it. She's determined to Elizabeth-Taylor life."

I tip my head, unsure of what he means.

"It's her fourth."

"Oh." I was only married once and it was brief, but

that experience was so awful that I'm not sure I could do it again, let alone four times.

"Yeah." He drags a hand through his dark hair, the slight wave to it flattening for only a moment before it goes back to its normal disarray. "I'm sort of in a jam with it."

"With the wedding? Is it during the season or something?"

"Yeah, but that's not the problem. She lives here, and she planned so I'd be home for it. It's something else, something…"

He trails off, a dark look crossing his face.

"That bad?"

"A date."

"Huh?"

He looks up at me. "She wants me to bring a date to the wedding."

"Is that all?"

He gives me a disbelieving look. "What do you mean, *is that all*? I don't date."

"Ever?"

He shakes his head. "Ever."

"That's…surprising."

"How so?"

"I don't know." I shrug. "You're a hockey player—aren't you all supposed to be slinging your man bits around and hooking up with women hanging around the rink?"

"Man bits?"

I flick my eyes toward my daughter, who is sitting far enough away that she *shouldn't* hear this conversation, but I don't trust it all the same. There have been many times I thought I was being sneaky with a conversation, only for her to have heard every word, including when I spilled the beans that Santa wasn't real. It was a mess, and I don't want to risk that again.

"No, I am not slinging my *man bits* all over or screwing around with anyone. I've learned my lesson there, thank you very much."

Interesting…

"So, no dating?" I ask.

"No dating. Except for this, apparently." He groans, dropping his head to his hands.

I roll my eyes. He's as bad as Macie with the dramatics. "It's not that bad. It's just a date."

"A date is always more than just a date. It's an expectation."

"Of?"

"Everything!" His voice comes out loud and high-pitched, something I've never heard from him. "They'll want flowers and doors opened for them, an expensive dinner. Then they'll want me to walk them to their door at the end of the night. They'll want a kiss and a phone call. It's everything I don't want to deal with—everything I don't have *time* to deal with."

"Oh nooo, you'll need to be a gentleman. How *awful* for you."

"It truly is. You wouldn't want any of that because

you're *you*."

I want to take offense to that, but he's right. I wouldn't want any of that, especially not with him.

Greer shoves a hand through his hair, turning it into more of a mess than it already is. He looks around the empty lot. If he had come just ten minutes earlier, this place would have been packed, but everyone's already on their way to the office, leaving just Macie and us.

He takes a few sips of his coffee, then faces me again. "You're being nice to me today. Haven't told me to leave once. Why?"

"Am I?" I need something to busy my hands with, anything at all, so I grab the nearest rag and begin wiping down the countertop that's completely spotless. "I hadn't noticed."

That's a lie. I definitely noticed. Greer and I have never spoken this much before, at least not without an insult being thrown.

"Hang on…is this your way of thanking me? By being nice to me?"

Okay, so maybe subconsciously, that's what I'm doing.

But also, Greer intrigues me. He's just always so… unpleasant to be around. I want to know why. Plus, he damn near broke my kid's heart last night, and I'm eager to figure out what's bothering him so maybe it won't affect his game any longer.

"I guess so."

"I can think of a better way for you to thank me."

I rear back, curling my lips up. "*That* is *never* going to happen."

"What? You think I mean…" He leans in closer. "Sex?" He throws his head back, laughing and making me want to reach over the counter and slap him. "No. Definitely no. But I'm flattered that's where your mind went."

No? What the hell does he mean *definitely no*? I don't want to sleep with him either, but *definitely no*? And said so sternly?

Screw him.

I glower at him and his stupid smiling face. "You can leave now, Greer."

"But you haven't heard my proposal."

"And I really don't want to."

"Oh, but I think you do." He points toward my daughter, who is back to lying on the bench of the picnic table, her face stuck in some hockey book. "It will benefit her."

"How?"

"Free tickets to games."

"Miller already beat you to that. Besides, we're perfectly capable of buying our own, but thanks for insinuating I can't afford that."

"I wasn't…" He shakes his head. "Never mind. But if free tickets are off the table, how about jerseys?"

"Yours?" Now it's my turn to laugh. "She wouldn't want that. Trust me."

"She hates me that much?"

I lift my shoulders. "Guess she has good taste."

"Okay, fine, not mine. Other jerseys."

"I can buy her jerseys."

He groans. "You're really killing me here."

"Am I? Because you're offering up a lot of stuff but not telling me what you'd want in exchange."

"A date."

I stop scrubbing at the already clean counter and lift my eyes to him. "Excuse me?"

"Be my date for the wedding."

"Don't make me gag."

"Be my date for the wedding," he repeats.

Holy shit. He's serious. He's like *really* serious.

"No. Absolutely not."

"Why not?" If I didn't know any better, I'd say he's offended by me not falling at his feet.

"Well, for starters, I don't even like you."

"That's unfair."

"Is it, though? You're not exactly the nicest guy ever."

"I saved you."

That's the reminder I didn't want.

"You know, it doesn't really count as a nice gesture if all you're going to do is throw it in my face."

"That's fair," he says, his concession surprising me. "But you do owe me."

"I do not. I already said thank you."

"Except you didn't. You were just nice to me, which isn't the same thing."

Crap. He has me there.

"How about this: if you'll be my date, I won't make you say thank you."

"How about this: I'm not saying thank you because I didn't ask for your help. I don't need you or anyone else to step in and rescue me like some helpless princess."

He holds his hands up, the ice in his now half-empty cup jiggling around. "All right. Calm down, Kelly Clarkson."

I lift my brows, unimpressed by his reference. "Again, go away, Greer."

"I'll coach her."

"Huh?"

He nods toward Macie, who is still completely wrapped up in her book. "I'll coach her. She's a hockey fiend, right? I'm assuming you have her signed up for the youth league. I'll coach her."

"Do you have time for that?"

"No."

"Then I—"

"I'll make time."

"Greer…"

"Steve…" he says in the same tone, and I want to yell at him for calling me Steve. Only Scout can do that, and she's not supposed to do it either. That nickname was reserved for my father, who passed away a few years ago. She's just lucky I like her.

Macie shuffles around on the table, and I drag my gaze back to my daughter, who doesn't know I'm having a conversation that could change her entire life.

I didn't sign her up for the youth league. She mentioned she wanted to play, but I know hockey isn't cheap. I'm also not sure I'd have the time to take her to and from games. I'm only one person.

But if Greer is offering, it means she'd be getting training from a professional, something she probably needs since she's ten and already behind the other kids who have been playing for years. She'd have an honest-to-God expert teaching her, something I'd never be able to afford. She would love it, even if it is Greer.

I'd be a fool to pass up this opportunity for my daughter, especially when it's going to cost me just one night of my life. What's the worst that could happen? I get free drinks and dance by myself? I can deal with that.

"Come on," Greer says. "I'm desperate here."

"Wow. Way to make a girl feel special."

"If I were you, I'd take it as a compliment that I'd rather spend my night with you than some woman I'd definitely be falling into bed with afterward."

Images of Greer and me wrapped up in silk sheets—he's rich, so I assume they're silk—assault my mind. Worse, between my legs…

I give myself a shake, refusing to let it continue any longer. It's Greer, for shit's sake. I'm not interested in him at all. It's just because I haven't been with anyone in a long time. That's all.

"Okay, if this is happening—and I haven't said yes yet—we need rules, and that's number one. I am *not* sleeping with you."

"Why do you have to say it like that?" he asks.

"Like it's the most disgusting thing I could ever think of?" He nods. "Because it is."

He grabs his chest, taking a stumbling step backward. His feet dragging across the gravel has Macie lifting her head, her eyes narrowing on us like she's trying to figure out what's going on. It only lasts a second before her nose is buried back in her book.

"That's the meanest thing you've ever said to me, and that's saying something."

"Trust me, Greer, I've bitten my tongue around you a lot. I have a lot of meaner things I could say."

"Please." He steps back up to the counter. "Tell me what I did to make you hate me so much."

"For starters, you're mean to my daughter."

"She's mean to me."

"You're upset a ten-year-old chirped you?"

"I'm just happy you know what chirping is. You're going to make a great hockey mom."

"A hockey mom? Why are you a hockey mom?"

Greer and I both jump at the sudden intrusion that is Macie. I didn't even see her get up.

"Mom?" she asks impatiently when neither of us answers. "Why are you a hockey mom?"

She looks between me and the NHL goalie, her eyes brighter than I've ever seen them before, and that includes this last Christmas when Miller surprised her with all those tickets.

"She's signing you up for hockey."

"You are?!" Macie's little voice rises about two octaves, and her feet come off the ground as she bounces up and down several times.

"And I'm going to coach you."

The bouncing comes to an immediate halt as she stares up at Greer, her brows pinched tightly together. "You are?"

"Well, shit, don't sound so excited about it."

"You can't say shit. You can say *ass* if you put *jack* in front of it, but you can't say shit."

"You just said shit twice," Greer points out.

Her eyes widen as she looks up at me, terrified she's about to get in trouble.

"Leave her alone, Greer."

"Yeah, leave me alone, Greer," Macie tells him, crossing her arms, looking mighty proud of herself.

"That's about to be Coach Greer to you."

Then, because he's a grown-ass adult, he sticks his tongue out at her.

I shake my head at their antics. "Glad to see this relationship is off to a great start."

"Does that mean yes?" Greer gazes up at me with hopeful eyes. I've never seen him look this desperate before. I want to say no to spite him.

"Yeah, does that mean you're really signing me up for hockey, Mom?"

Crap. I can't say no to Macie when she looks even more desperate for a yes than Greer does.

Do I have the time for hockey? Well, with my other

job probably laying me off soon, yes…at least until I find something else.

Maybe we scrimp for a few months. Maybe we cut back on other activities, eat out less—not that we do that often now, but still. Hockey is important to Macie, and Macie is important to me. I want her to be happy. I want her to get everything she wants in life.

I can do this for her.

It's just one date with Greer. I can survive that…right?

With a sigh, I say, "Yes. The answer is yes."

"Yes!" Macie throws her hands in the air, jumping up and down over and over. "I'm going to play hockey!"

Greer watches her, and if I'm not mistaken, his lips twitch, clearly amused by her happiness. He nods toward her as she jumps away—literally—and says, "Her enthusiasm? That's what's happening on the inside for me."

"You're the grumpiest person I've ever met, so I highly doubt you've ever been that excited in your entire life."

"One, you've met Smith, and he's far grumpier than me. Two, I have too been that excited."

"Name a time."

"I got tickets to see *The Lord of the Rings* at midnight once. Best night of my life."

"Including when you lost your virginity last month?"

"Hey, I'm not Miller."

"You're right. He's prettier."

His eyes narrow, but it's not his usual pouty look. Instead, it's something…else.

Before I can speculate any more, he changes the subject. "So, date—us."

I sigh at the reminder. For a brief second, I forgot about my end of the bargain. "Unfortunately."

A smirk pulls at his lips like he's enjoying my pain. "You're going to have fun."

"I doubt that."

He taps the counter twice. "I'll be in touch, Steve."

"Oh joy."

Another smirk.

He turns and heads for the parking lot, but not before throwing a wave at Macie, who is still doing a little dance.

"Get some gear. You'll need it."

"Okay."

"And nice braces," he calls to her over his shoulder as he heads toward the parking lot.

Macie, used to assholes picking on her, flashes him a big smile. "They're Comets colors, but another game like last night and I'm getting them changed!"

I swear I hear Greer laugh.

What the hell did I get myself into?

CHAPTER 7

Greer: When are you available?

Stevie: Who is this?

Greer: Your favorite person on the entire planet.

Stevie: Greer?

Greer: I knew you liked me.

Stevie: I really, really don't.

Greer: Keep telling yourself that, Steve.

. . .

Stevie: Stevie. S-T-E-V-I-E! It's not that hard.

Stevie: Again, what do you want?

Greer: To set a date.

Stevie: We already did.

Greer: Not OUR date. I mean a date for the first training session.

Greer: I am flattered that you're so excited about our date. Can't stop thinking about it, huh?

Stevie: Can't stop thinking about what I'm sure is going to be the most embarrassing moment of my life? Yes.

Greer: You think telling people you're dating me is embarrassing?

. . .

Stevie: Yes.

Stevie: Now stop being annoying and just get to the point of the conversation.

Greer: Ooooh. Someone's testy.

Greer: I kind of like seeing you get all worked up, especially over me.

Stevie: Greer…

Greer: Fine.

Greer: We have practice tomorrow morning. If you two want to come and check things out, we can do a trial run after.

Stevie: A trial run? I thought this was part of the agreement. You teach Macie, and I'll be your date.

. . .

Stevie: No trial runs.

Greer: What if we aren't compatible? What if she bites me?

Stevie: She's ten. She's not going to bite you.

Greer: I was a ten-year-old biter.

Stevie: Why does that not surprise me?

Stevie: She won't bite you. I promise.

Greer: I'm not so sure I believe you. You don't even like me. You probably want me to be bitten.

Stevie: I never said I didn't like you.

Greer: Yes, you did. Multiple times even.

. . .

Stevie: Fine, I don't like you.

Stevie: But I'm not lying. She won't bite you. She hasn't bitten anyone in like six months or something.

Greer: Wow. I am SO glad I get to test out her biting sobriety like this.

Stevie: To be fair, that kid bit her first.

Greer: Your daughter sounds scary.

Stevie: She can be.

Stevie: But she won't bite you.

Greer: Promises, promises.

Stevie: How much time do I need to block out?

. . .

Greer: At least two hours.

Stevie: Wait—are we watching you practice too?

Greer: Yes.

Stevie: Why?

Greer: It might be good for her to see a professional practice before getting on the ice.

Stevie: Oh. That makes sense.

Greer: We good, then?

Stevie: Just one more thing…

Stevie: How'd you get this number?

Greer: I have my ways.

. . .

Stevie: Miller?

Greer: Maybe.

Greer: Why?

Stevie: Just needed to know how big I should dig the grave.

Greer: Your daughter scares me, but you scare me more.

Stevie: Good.

Stevie: What kind of equipment should I bring?

Greer: Well, skates are a must.

. . .

Stevie: Anything else?

Greer: No. We'll start with just skates. We have some sticks and pucks she can play around with at the practice rink.

Greer: I really just want to get a feel for where she's at.

Stevie: She's at zero.

Greer: Meaning?

Stevie: She's, uh, never played before.

Greer: At all?

Stevie: No.

Stevie: Well, she's played on rollerblades, but not on the ice.

. . .

Greer: Oh god.

Stevie: Surprise?

Greer: Yeah, big surprise.

Greer: This is going to be a lot of work.

Stevie: She's willing to learn.

Stevie: She's been practicing since yesterday.

Stevie: I also got called into the principal's office yesterday because she got into a shoving match with some boy who didn't believe she's going to be training with you.

Stevie: "Great, Mom! My first trip to the sin bin! Goalies don't go to the sin bin!"

Stevie: That's what she told me yesterday.

. . .

Greer: She's right. Someone else takes the brunt of the punishment for us.

Greer: Trust me, though, it feels just as bad as sitting in there yourself.

Stevie: Goalies don't get in trouble?

Greer: Oh, we do.

Greer: There are some meathead goalies out there. They do some stupid shit.

Greer: We take penalties but don't have to serve them. Someone who was on the ice when we took the penalty does, so not only is your coach pissed at you, your teammates are too. It sucks.

Stevie: Have you ever been in trouble?

. . .

Greer: Plenty of times.

Stevie: What for?

Greer: Tripping. Slashing. Roughing on that fucker Colter. Even got me a game misconduct once when I first started in the league.

Greer: Not yet been in a goalie fight, though it's on my bucket list.

Stevie: Hockey players are so weird.

Greer: And goalies are even weirder. We're a different breed.

Stevie: And to think my kid wants to be one.

Greer: She's got the fire, that's for sure.

Greer: Just bring the skates. I'll take care of the rest.

. . .

Stevie: Aye, aye, captain.

Greer: I CAN'T HEAR YOU!

Stevie: What?

Greer: Oh. I thought we were doing a SpongeBob thing. Never mind.

Stevie: Oooooooh.

Greer: WHO LIVES IN A PINEAPPLE UNDER THE SEA?

Stevie: We're still not doing it.

Greer: Right.

Greer: See you tomorrow.

. . .

Stevie: Unfortunately.

Stevie: What time should we be there?

Greer: You have got to be kidding me.

Stevie: What?

Greer: It's 5 fucking AM.

Stevie: It's 5:15, thank you.

Stevie: And good morning.

Stevie: What time should we be there?

Greer: Are you always up this early?

. . .

Stevie: Pretty much. Sometimes when I'm feeling feisty, I sleep in until 5:30, but that's a rarity.

Greer: I hate you.

Stevie: Hey, that's my line!

Stevie: So…time?

Greer: 9 AM.

Greer: I'll need a little bit afterward, but I'll meet you on the ice within fifteen minutes.

Stevie: Gotta see your groupies first?

Greer: Puck bunnies.

Stevie: What about bunnies?

. . .

Greer: That's what hockey groupies are called. Puck bunnies.

Stevie: Oh. They sound so cute.

Greer: They really aren't.

Stevie: Uh-oh. Bad experience?

Greer: Hell no. I'm not stupid enough to get swept up in that shitstorm. I've had some clingers though, and that was terrible enough.

Stevie: Ah, that's right. You're anti-love.

Greer: Who said I was anti-love?

Stevie: You did. And I quote, "It's a crock of shit." I don't even know what a crock means, but that's what you said.

. . .

Greer: It's really too early for this.

Stevie: Go back to sleep, your highness.

Greer: Highness? What am I, a king?

Stevie: Just of hell.

Greer: Now, Steve, don't go getting all sweet on me. I'll start thinking you like me or something.

Stevie: That'll never happen.

Stevie: And for the millionth time, it's STEVIE.

Greer: Until you start being nicer to me, it's Steve.

Stevie: That's mean.

Greer: And so are you, so I guess we're even.

. . .

Stevie: I'm rolling my eyes really hard at the grown man I've seen be a dick numerous times calling me mean.

Greer: You started it.

Stevie: Are you five?

Greer: No. You just bring out the worst in me.

Stevie: Lovely.

Stevie: Go back to sleep, Greer. I need you rested so you can teach my kid.

Greer: I'm already awake now. Might as well start my day.

Stevie: You're welcome. And who knows, maybe you'll like getting up early. It's refreshing to start your day early.

. . .

Greer: Not when it's still dark outside, it's not.

Stevie: You're awfully dramatic.

Greer: You'll get used to it.

Stevie: Oh, I have. Hello, ten-year-old daughter, remember?

Greer: She's not going to be dramatic on the ice, is she?

Stevie: Not sure. But if she is, it's your problem.

Greer: Don't smile at that!

Stevie: Sorry. Can't talk. Things to do.

Greer: Evil woman.

Stevie: *smiles*

CHAPTER 8

"All right. I noticed during the last game that you were struggling with your blocker side, so I want to focus on that today." Bill, my goalie coach, bangs his stick on the ice a few times before skating backward and firing a shot at me without warning.

I miss it.

I really shouldn't miss it. I should be alert. I should see it, should know it's coming, but it still goes flying past me and into the net.

I can hear the goal horn ringing in my head. See the red light lit up, showing that the other team scored. Envision all our hopes and dreams for making a Cup run going right out the window.

"Don't do that, Greer. Don't beat yourself up for missing one puck."

"But one puck is all it takes," I argue back, annoyed with myself, annoyed that he can tell I'm already thinking negatively.

"Yeah, that can definitely be true, but it's not the end of the world."

"Could be the end of my career," I mumble, grateful for my mask that luckily blocks my words. Bill would have my ass if he heard that, and I don't blame him.

I shouldn't let it bother me. I'm not going to block and save everything. There are just some days it bothers me more than others.

I can't help but wonder if today it's because there are two sets of eyes in the stands watching me. I don't even have to look up to know she's watching because I can feel it—that's how hard Stevie is staring at me right now. Macie too.

I'm used to spectators coming and watching during practice. It happens all the time, but this time…it feels different with them here. I'm sure it's just because I'm coaching Macie after this and want to make a good impression—so she doesn't bite me, obviously.

Yeah, that has to be it. That's why I'm so worked up. I just need to get them out of my head is all.

I take a deep breath, then another. I nod to tell Bill I'm ready, then get set as he skates farther away. He pulls the stick back and shoots.

He turns his hands at the last split second, and the puck goes where I'm not expecting.

I make the block.

"Good!" he calls out. "Again!"

He winds up and fires.

I block.

Again.

I block.

Again.

I miss.

"Fuck!" I skate out of my goal crease and wander the ice a bit, murmuring to myself. "Come on, man. Don't get mad at missing one. It's fine. You're fine. Don't let this shit get in your head. You've seen it happen too many times to too many good goalies. They let in a few soft goals, and suddenly they're on a bad streak. You fucking got this."

I beat my chest with my glove a few times and take some deep breaths. I skate back to the net, plant my skates where I want them, and hunker down, ready to defend.

Bill fires ten shots my way.

I block them all.

We keep going, this time with my teammates jumping into the mix, firing puck after puck my way. They get up in the crease, smothering me and battling for the puck. I let a few more goals in, but they don't bother me like earlier. I'm calmer and more collected. I feel confident and ready.

I'm not saying maybe Stevie was right about getting up early, but there's no way being up and having over half of my to-do list knocked out before hitting the ice is just a coincidence. I don't feel like there's anything niggling at the back of my mind, and it's allowing me to get recentered quickly.

Maybe the evil woman was right.

A whistle sounds, pulling me out of my head and back into practice.

"Boys!"

The whole team skates to the middle of the ice where Coach Heller is. A few of us take a knee while some of us stand, but we all have our eyes trained on our coach. He's not the biggest of guys, but he sure as hell knows how to command a room. When I learned I was signing with the Comets, the first thing I did was hit YouTube and look up my new coach.

He's a fucking beast. Probably one of the best goons the league has ever seen. More penalty minutes than I could ever dream of. When he was actually on the ice, he assisted on quite a few plays too. All around a solid player.

Now, he's a damn good coach.

"We're looking good in the standings, and we're on a homestand, where we know we play well—but all of that is no reason to take our foot off the gas. We may have walked away with two points, but our last game was sloppy. We looked better today, but there's always room for improvement, and that's what we need to do—keep improving. We want to pad the points. We *need* to pad our points. Then we want to head into the playoffs feeling good, feeling ready. So give it your all out there, boys. Nothing in this league comes easy, and no lead is safe, not even ours."

He looks us each in the eye, nods once, then skates off. Practice is over for the day.

"I have a few quick things to go over, then you're free," the assistant coach says. "Practice tomorrow morning is optional. I need you to…"

He goes on for a few minutes about what we need to work on, who needs to see the team docs, who needs to hit the weights. After he's done with his spiel, we're cut loose.

"Hey, we're thinking of hitting up The Madhouse for grub. You in?" Miller asks. "Scout's writing today, so I want to stay out of her hair."

"Go out in public with you? I'm good."

"Hey, we've been in public together before."

"Your girlfriend's donut truck doesn't count."

"Does too," he mutters.

"Besides, I'm busy."

"Doing what? Being grumpy at the wall?"

"Hey, if the wall has it coming, it has it coming."

He looks genuinely confused, so I roll my eyes.

"I have plans."

I look toward the area that's slowly emptying out. There are a few stragglers—there always are—who are trying to get pictures, pucks, and sticks. Then sitting up at the back of the bleachers are Stevie and Macie. The kid looks like she's about to fly out of her seat, her little legs bouncing up and down with excitement.

I swear I see Stevie say to her, "Not yet."

"Wait…are they not here for me?"

"Nope."

"What the hell, ladies?" Miller yells, throwing his hands up in the air, apparently not caring that he looks like a complete idiot.

Stevie exaggerates a shoulder shrug, and then Miller shakes his fist at her. She laughs, and it's a genuine laugh.

I'm not sure I've ever seen a genuine laugh from her, but I am really sure I don't like that it's Miller making her do it.

"Don't you have somewhere to be?" I say to him, but even I hear it come out as more of a growl.

If he does, he doesn't show it. He just grins at me with that obnoxious, toothy, golden-retriever-energy grin he's always sporting and chuckles.

"Aw, don't sound so sad I'm leaving you."

"Trust me, I'm not."

"What are you doing with them anyway?"

"Coaching."

His eyes widen. "*You're* coaching a kid? But you hate kids."

"I don't *hate* kids," I mutter. "I just don't particularly like them."

"That's hating them."

"Not entirely."

"Macie's a good kid, though. No need to hate her."

"I'll have to remember that."

He takes a step toward me, his eyes never leaving mine. "Be sure you do, because they're good people,

Macie and Stevie. Some of my favorites, actually. I like them a lot more than I like other people."

It's a threat. It's a little veiled, but the message is there all the same: if I hurt Stevie or Macie, Miller is going to hurt me.

"You hear me?" he asks.

I nod. "I hear you."

"Good." And just like that, his perfect grin slips back into place as he puts distance between us once more. His hand lands on my shoulder. "See you tomorrow, man."

Then he skates off, catching up with Hayes. The two laugh all the way off the ice.

I don't usually see that side of Miller—in fact, I don't think I ever have—and it kind of makes me respect the guy more. It's what I would do if I had someone I cared about.

I glance back up the bleachers at where Stevie and Macie are sitting, but they're not there anymore. Instead, they're making their way down toward the ice.

I give them a wave to get their attention. Stevie tips her head at me, and I point toward the locker room and hold up my hand.

Five minutes, I mouth.

She nods, then lifts the skates in her hand. They're not the greatest quality, but they'll do for now. Maybe if today goes well and I don't get bitten, I'll buy Macie a better pair.

I head for the locker room, stripping off some of my gear on the way there. A few people try to stop me along the way—mostly Hayes and Fitz—but I ignore them, trying to get my shit together so I can get this training session over with as fast as possible.

After I get changed, I spritz myself with some cologne, covering up the stench and feeling like I'm in high school all over again.

At least it's not Axe, I tell myself.

I make sure to let George, the rink manager, know I'm going to be using the ice for a bit. He's perfectly fine with it, not that I thought he wouldn't be.

Macie and Stevie are sitting right beside the tunnel when I come out.

"Oh my gosh," Macie rushes out. "I am like *sooooooo* excited." She claps her hands together and attempts to jump up and down, but she wobbles. Stevie reaches out for her at the same time she catches herself on the boards.

It'd be almost comical if it wasn't worrisome.

"You've never been on skates, huh?"

Macie is instantly defensive, crossing her arms over her chest and tipping her chin up. "I have too."

"Yeah? Because your mom says you haven't."

"Mom!" Macie yells, her jaw dropping. "I've gone rollerblading!"

"Trust me, kid, it's similar, but it's not the same thing. The ice is slippery."

"Well, duh." Macie's eyes roll right into the back of her head. "I know that."

"Hey, I've been around this game my entire life, and

sometimes players still seem to forget it's a game played on ice while wearing really, really sharp shoes."

"I won't forget, gosh."

"Hmm. I'm sure you won't."

I cross my arms over my chest, then look over her outfit. It's a little much with the huge puffer jacket, but I'll let her be the judge of if she should wear it or not.

I take a closer look at her skates, then drop to one knee.

"What are you doing?"

"Fixing your skates." I pat my leg. "Up here."

"But…they're sharp. You just said so."

"Just trust me, will ya, kid?"

She huffs but does what I ask and gingerly places her foot on my thigh. I grab it, tugging her closer to me.

"I'm wearing protective gear under my pants. It helps to protect against blades," I explain as I adjust her skates. "It's something every hockey player wears. It's a little weird at first, but you'll get used to it fast."

I look up to make sure she's listening, and she nods several times. Her eyes are wide, and she looks scared. Probably just nerves, I'm sure.

I glance at her mother, who is hovering over us, watching every little interaction. She shoots me a small, equally shaky smile, and there's a punch to my gut I'm not expecting when I see that. It almost feels like I don't like that they're scared or nervous. I…I want to shield them from those feelings, protect them. I want to—

Whoa. What the fuck?

I have no idea where that came from, but it's not me.

I give my head a small shake, then continue tightening the skates on Macie's feet. When I'm finished, I set her back on her feet and rise. "How do those feel?"

"Good. Better." She looks at her mom, a small frown pulling at her lips. "Sorry."

Stevie smiles, her eyes crinkling in the corners as she gazes down at her daughter. "Don't be sorry, silly. This is a learning experience for us both." She looks at me, her smile slipping the second our eyes meet. "For all three of us."

Make that my second not-so-veiled threat of the morning, and it's not even ten.

"Right, Greer?"

"Does anyone call you your real name?" Macie asks before I can answer her mother with something smartassy.

"My real name? Greer is my real name."

"It's not your first name. Your first name is Jacob, full name Jacob Lee Greer. You were born in Saskatoon, Canada. You started playing hockey when you were five. You used to be a forward, but you ditched that when you were my age. You—"

I hold my hand up, stopping her. "I'm pretty sure I know my own life story from Wikipedia, but thank you."

She rolls her lips together, a red hue creeping into her cheeks.

"Are you ready to get on the ice?"

Her eyes slide toward the rink, and there's a hitch to her breath as she stares out at it. She's nervous.

I don't want her to be nervous. I need her to be the opposite of that if this is going to be a successful day.

"Or you can sit on the bench like a big wimp instead."

"Greer!" Stevie yells, stepping forward in front of her daughter, almost like she's shielding the kid from me.

Macie, much to my delight, pushes past her mom and shoves her chin up once again. "I'm ready to whoop your *jack*ass."

Stevie doesn't admonish her daughter for cursing. She's too busy looking proud.

Frankly, I am too.

"Let's go."

I take off, not waiting for Macie to keep up. It takes a few steps before she finds her balance—each almost fall punctuated by Stevie's gasps—but eventually she makes it to the edge.

"You ready?" I ask her once more.

She nods. "Let's do this."

I hold my hand out, tugging her onto the ice without another word.

"Whoa! Ohmygodohmygodohmygod!" she yells as I tow her backward, but her cries of fright quickly turn sweet as she yelps with laughter and her face freezes into a smile.

I don't remember the last time I had to pull someone around the ice. Maybe when I was sixteen with one of my pseudo-siblings? It's long enough to have forgotten how fun it is to watch someone fall in love with the same thing I love.

And that's exactly what I just witnessed. She loves it out here. This ice…it's her home. She belongs on it.

"It's cold!" she calls out to me as I pull her along. "It feels good."

"Yeah? You want to try it on your own?"

Her head bobs up and down frantically. "Please!"

"All right," I say, slowing us down and skating closer to the wall. "I'm going to let go slowly. If you get scared, I'm here. The wall is here too. Right now, we'll just stand here so you can get your balance."

"Okay," she says, staring down at her feet.

"Don't look at your feet. Look at me. Looking at your feet is going to make you even more nervous."

"I'm not nervous."

Those might be the words that leave her mouth, but the hitch in her breath and her hands shaking in mine say the exact opposite.

"You know," I tell her, "the first time I got on the ice, I was terrified. It's slippery as hell, so who wouldn't be scared? But I rode along the wall, and it took me a full thirty minutes to get around the rink. And it was a kiddy rink, nothing big like this one."

"How'd you get over it?" she asks, not even noticing that in the time I've been talking, I've been slowly letting her hands go.

"Practice. I rode the wall for two whole days before I

finally convinced myself to just let go and try it on my own." I step back, folding my arms across my chest. "I guess you're already doing better than I did in that aspect."

It takes her almost ten seconds to realize I've let her go and she's standing all on her own.

The second it hits her, she begins to wobble, and I ready myself to catch her.

But the fall doesn't come. She's doing it.

"I'm doing it!" she shouts, echoing my thought. "Holy crap!" She clamps her hand over her mouth, eyes wide. "Don't tell my mom I said crap. She doesn't like that word."

"But she lets you say ass?"

"No, she lets me say jackass. Totally different."

I chuckle. "Right. My bad." I glance down at her feet, trying not to laugh at how she's standing, her toes tucked in and pointed toward one another. "How are you feeling?"

"A little wobbly."

"That's expected. But this"—I kick her feet out just slightly—"will help with that."

"Ohmygod stop! I'm going to—" Her words are cut off when she realizes I'm right. She's much more stable now. "Wow. That is a lot better."

"Yeah?" She nods. "Good. Now, let's try to move."

"Move?!"

"Well, yeah. You have to move to play hockey."

"Right, right. Let's move."

I instruct her on how to move her feet for optimal skating; for the most part, she does really well. There are a few moments where she's unsure and scared, but she gets over them quickly. I teach her the proper way to fall, then help her when she needs to get back up.

It takes about fifteen minutes before she's able to skate more than twenty feet on her own, but she's doing it, and I was right—she was made for the ice. This is exactly where she belongs.

"Do you love it?" I ask, skating slowly—at least it's slow for me—beside her.

"So much. I want to do this forever."

I can't help but smile at that. "I know the feeling."

"Can we go faster?"

"Are you ready for that?"

She nods. "Yes."

"Okay, but remember, I'm here if you start to feel like you're going down. Brace yourself in the right way, and you'll be okay."

"Got it."

She picks up speed, striding faster and faster as the seconds go by.

I see it the moment it happens. She starts going too fast with too little control.

Then, it happens.

And I hear the scream.

CHAPTER 9

I've had some scary moments in my life, like when I got pregnant by a guy I wasn't in love with and realized he would have to be in my life forever now. Getting married to the same guy because it was "the right thing." The first time my ex had too much to drink. The other night in the bar when that asshole cornered me.

But this moment right here? It's the worst of them all.

Macie's a crumpled pile of skin and bones, and I'm sitting on the bleachers dumbfounded and unable to move.

The sound of Greer's skates against the ice is what snaps me out of my haze and has me sprinting down the steps and onto the slippery surface. I don't have the right footwear on, so I'm unsurprised when I land right on my ass. Pain shoots through my backside, but I don't care. I need to get to my daughter. It's the only thing that matters right now.

I crawl my way across the ice, my hands frozen and

my knees likely bruised. Greer has her cradled in his arms. He's speaking to her, but I can't make it out.

All I see is a nod. She's moving.

Thank god she's moving.

"Macie! Macie! Macie!" I chant, reaching for her.

Her arms fly up, circling around my neck and hugging me tightly.

I grip her, holding her closer than I ever have before, rocking her back and forth. "You're okay. You're fine."

"Mom…" she says weakly, and for the first time since I saw her go down, tears begin leaking from my eyes.

I try my hardest not to let out the sob that seems to be caught in my tight chest. I don't want to scare her. I don't want her to know I've never been more terrified in my entire life.

"Are you okay? Is anything broken?"

She shakes her head. "It hurts, but—"

"Where?" I pull her away, running my hands over her face and her head. "Where does it hurt?"

I keep pressing all over her body, feeling for anything that could even possibly be out of place.

"Just…sore. Everywhere," she says, but I keep checking.

She's missing something. I'm missing something.

"I need to get to a doctor."

"Stevie." A heavy hand lands on my shoulder, and it takes me a second to remember we're not alone.

Greer.

"Doctor," I say to him.

"I can have the team doctor look at her, but she's okay."

"I want to be sure."

He tucks his lips together, likely stifling his need to tell me she's fine, then nods. "Okay." He shoves up from the ice, bends down, and picks Macie up with zero strain.

"Hey!" she complains as he scoops her up in his arms.

"Quiet," he argues back. "Your mom said so, and since you didn't bite me today, I'm definitely more scared of her."

"Why would I bite you?"

He doesn't answer her. Instead, he puts his hand out to me. "Come on."

I slide my palm against his, letting him pull me up, which he does effortlessly. *Geez, how much does this guy work out?*

No. Don't think about that now. Think about your daughter.

He takes short strides as we make our way across the rink.

"I can skate," Macie protests.

"I'm sure you can," Greer says.

"I want to have you checked out first," I tell her.

She rolls her eyes.

Any other time, I'd chastise her, but not right now. Not when she looks so small and frail in Greer's arms.

When we finally step off the ice, we head down a carpeted tunnel and make a right. There are all kinds of equipment strewn about: helmets, sticks, stacks of pucks.

Photos and plaques line the walls as we make our way down the hall, shouts coming from all directions and loud music playing as we pass what looks like a gym. It definitely *feels* like a sports atmosphere.

We turn into an office, and I'm surprised to see someone up on the table in the middle of the room.

"Collin!"

He looks up from whatever the doctor is doing to his leg and grins. "Oh, hey. What's going on?" He looks down at Macie in Greer's arms. "Everything okay?"

He's asking Greer, not me.

"She's fine, but mom's worried."

"I'm worried because she's my kid."

"Oh, I'm aware. You are two peas in a damn pod," Greer mutters, shuffling said kid around.

"Learning to skate?" Collin asks Macie.

"Yes, and I'm *fine*." She stretches the word out, completely annoyed with me.

I get it. She *could* be okay…but she could also *not* be okay and just not want to say anything. It's my duty as her mother to have her checked out, even if it's against her will.

"Where can I set her, Doc?"

The doctor tucks his lips together, raises his brows, and nods toward the other unoccupied table. "Over there is fine." He looks at Collin. "I'll just be a moment."

Collin, who also looks like he's about two seconds away from laughing, says, "It's fine. Take your time. I'm avoiding Harper right now anyway."

"What for?" Greer asks as he sets Macie down. "I thought you two were all stupid in love."

"Oh, we are. Like stupid, stupid in love, but she wants me to model this new design she's working on, and it's painful. How actors do it, getting all covered in makeup, prosthetics, and whatever else for hours and hours…I don't get it. I'd rather get slammed into the boards by Milan Lucic every single day than sit through that shit."

"Dude, Lucic is a beast."

"Exactly my point," Collin says.

The doctor stops in front of Macie, looking down at her. "Does it hurt anywhere?"

"Just my ego."

"Oh, you're definitely hockey player material with that one." He laughs, then points to her legs. "May I?"

She nods, and the doctor spends the next five minutes going over every part of her body, checking for bumps, bruises, and anything else I can think of.

"You didn't hit your head, right?"

"No."

"You're lucky." The doctor frowns over at Greer. "Though next time, maybe wear a helmet?"

Greer pales, his hand going to his stomach like he's about to puke. It's the same way I feel seeing my kid lying on the cold, sterile bed.

"Yeah. Next time," he mutters.

"Next time?" It comes out a squeak, and even I hear the panic in my own voice. All the eyes in the room are on me, including Macie's, whose baby blues look about twice their normal size.

"Well." The doctor claps his hands together. "Everything looks good to me. You may be a little sore tomorrow—especially that ego—but everything looks fine. Perfectly healthy."

"Really?" I ask.

The doctor nods. "Really."

I take my first real breath in minutes and let out a slow, steady exhale of relief.

She's okay. She's going to be okay.

I look down at Macie, who is staring up at me with worried eyes.

"I told you so," she says defiantly, though the bite her words usually carry is missing.

"Yeah, you did," I say quietly. I grab a strand of her hair, the same color as mine, running it through my fingers while I let my heart calm down. "You're okay."

I'm not saying it to her; I'm saying it for me.

She's okay. She's going to be okay.

If I keep repeating it, then it's true.

"Can I go back out there now?"

My heart begins to hammer in my chest again, and I see her crumpled on the ice all over. The panic that races through me is unlike anything else. I hate it. I hate it so much I want to scream.

But before I can, Greer steps up.

"I think we should call it a day."

"But—"

"Hey, life ain't all about you, kid. I have my own shit to take care of."

I want to yell at him for cursing in front of my kid, but I don't have it in me. I'm just too glad she's okay.

"Fine," Macie mutters. Then she looks up at me. "Can we go, then?"

"Yes. And we're getting ice cream on the way home."

"Okay." I've never heard her be less enthused about ice cream before. "I'm going to go put my shoes back on."

I nod as she hops off the table. "I'll be right behind you."

She walks out of the room and down the hall. I watch her until she disappears around the corner toward the ice.

She won't go on it. I know her well enough to know she won't risk getting in trouble like that.

"You good?"

I whirl back around to find Greer staring at me. Collin too. The doctor isn't paying any attention.

"I'm fine," I tell Greer.

He tips his head to the side, his lips twisted as he studies me. After what feels like hours under his hot stare, he rights his head and nods.

"Okay."

Then he brushes past me and out the door without another word.

"I think what he meant to say was he's sorry Macie got hurt," Collin says.

I let out a half-huff, half-laugh. "I'm sure that's not what he meant at all."

"For what it's worth, I'll talk to him."

"Thank you, Collin. Really." I shoot him a smile, then give the doctor a wave.

I knew this whole thing with Greer was a mistake, and today really proved me right.

Now I just have to figure out what I'm going to do next.

"So she's done?" Scout asks quietly.

I look out at my daughter, who is sitting at her favorite picnic table after a long, grueling day at school. She has her nose back in that same hockey book as before, only this time, she looks a lot less excited to be reading it.

"She's done."

This morning as she sat on her favorite barstool eating her favorite breakfast—waffles with peanut butter—she announced that she no longer wants to play hockey.

It broke my heart all over again to see her shoulders drop and her chin wobble when she said it. I asked her if she was sure, and she nodded. I wasn't going to push the subject anymore, so I did what I do every morning: I drove her to school with SportsCenter playing on the radio, kissed her goodbye, and went to work.

She hasn't said a word since I picked her up.

"That's just…sad. She loves the game so much."

"She's still going to watch," I tell Scout. "But not play."

Scout frowns. "It's not the same, I'm sure."

"Probably not, but it's what she said she wants."

"I still can't believe she fell."

"Oh man, Scout. It was awful. I've never been so scared. I don't know how you watch Miller play knowing it's your heart out there on the ice like that."

She shrugs, her favorite well-worn overalls slipping off her shoulders a bit. She tugs them back up. "It's not always easy, but you have to remember that they love the game. It's what makes them happy. It's what drives them. They need it."

"Yeah…" I cast one last look at Macie just as my phone buzzes in my pocket.

I pull it out, and my lips shift into a frown when I see what's on the screen.

King of Hell: Are you avoiding me?

"You okay?" Scout asks.

"It's Greer. He's worried I'm avoiding him because I haven't answered him about Macie's next training session."

"You haven't told him yet?"

I shake my head. "No. She just told me this morning that she doesn't want to play again. I haven't had a chance to get in touch with him."

"Still so weird to see you two getting along."

"I wouldn't go that far," I say.

"No? I mean, he's training your kid. That's getting along."

"Was—he was training my kid. So now we have no reason to play nice."

Me: She doesn't want to play anymore.

King of Hell: Seriously?

Me: Yeah. Sorry to have wasted your time.

King of Hell: SERIOUSLY?!

Me: I'll still be your date if that's what you're worried about.

"I don't give a shit about the date."

I jump, and my phone goes sailing out of my hand,

landing on the floor of the donut truck with a loud clamor.

"Well, I do, but I have other worries too."

I pick up my phone, immediately annoyed that my worst fear has come true—it's cracked.

"Great," I mutter, pushing up to my feet, only to be met with Greer standing just on the other side of the counter. "Were you texting me from the parking lot?"

"Yes."

"Why? That's creepy."

"I wanted to know why you were avoiding me."

"I'm not."

He lifts his dark, heavy brows as if to say, *Really? I call bullshit.*

Yeah, I call bullshit too. I was totally avoiding him.

"Hey, Greer," Scout says.

"Lady Miller," he answers, and my sister giggles like a little schoolgirl.

It's annoying, but mostly because Greer is annoying.

"What do you want?" I ask the goalie, hoping whatever it is, I can get it for him and make him leave faster.

"I'm not here for the food. I have a game tonight."

"Then why are you here?"

"Because…" He looks over his shoulder at Macie, who is trying very hard to pretend she's actually reading the book in her hands and not listening to our conversation.

Note to self: My kid would make a terrible actress.

Greer leans in closer to the truck and quietly asks, "Why doesn't she want to play again? Because of the fall?"

I nod. "I think so."

"That's bullshit."

"Greer!" I hiss at him. "She's ten. Leave her alone."

"Well, I'm just saying. That's bullshit. I know she wants to play."

"She's scared."

He narrows his eyes, giving me that same annoying hard stare he gave me yesterday, the one that made me squirm and want to be anywhere but under his gaze.

"Can I talk to her?"

"Why?"

"Because."

I sigh, not in the mood to deal with his crap. "Be my guest, but she's not very talkative today."

"Hmm." It's all he says before he stalks away, going straight for the table Macie's sitting at.

Watching him try to tuck his long legs in is almost comical, but the look on his face is anything but. He seems serious, even more serious than Greer usually is, and that's saying something.

"What's going on?" Scout asks, nodding toward them.

"He wanted to talk to her."

"What for?"

I shrug. "Your guess is as good as mine."

"They're both wearing the same frown. It's adorable," Scout says.

She's right. They are both frowning, and they're taking turns shooting quick glances this way. It's clear they're talking about me. Or us.

Whatever it is, it's quiet, and neither of them is giving away much of anything. It's taking everything I have in me to stay rooted in the cute baby blue truck and not march out there and demand to be part of the conversation.

After what seems like hours, Greer finally pushes away from the table and comes back up to the truck.

"It's you," he says quietly.

"Excuse me?"

"The reason she doesn't want to play anymore—it's you."

"What!"

"Shh!" Greer says. "Lower your voice." He peeks back over his shoulder to see if Macie is watching. Naturally, she is. He sends her a wave, then glowers back at me. "Way to keep that casual and not suspicious at all."

"Hey, you were talking about *me* first."

"Yeah, because your kid is afraid to confide in you because she doesn't want you going all mom on her."

"Going all mom?"

He shrugs. "That's what she called it."

"That's…"

"Probably accurate," Scout says, joining in on the conversation.

I whip my head her way. "What the hell does that mean?"

"Sorry." My younger sister winces. "But it's true. I'm betting your reaction to the fall was worse than Macie actually hitting the ice. She probably doesn't want to scare you again. So even though she loves the game, she's saying she doesn't want to play so she doesn't upset you."

Greer points his finger at her. "Bingo."

"What? That's just…"

My words trail off as I look out at my daughter. She's watching us, her bottom lip tucked between her teeth, a look of worry etched across her face. It's that same look she gave me in the doctor's office yesterday when he got done checking her out. She wasn't scared because she fell. She was scared because she thought she wasn't going to be able to play again.

"True," I finish. "That's just true."

Greer sighs. "You need to tell her it's okay to play."

"But…how?"

"I'm not a mom, so I can't answer that for you. Look," he says, grabbing a pen from the cup on the counter, then a napkin. He scribbles something down and shoves it my way. "I have to get to the arena, but take this."

"What is it?" I ask, picking up the napkin and looking at it. "A phone number?"

"Yeah." He nods. "Call that number. Ask for advice. She'll give it to you."

"Who is it?"

"Someone with a lot of experience going through what you are right now."

I stare down at the number he's scrawled. "Okay…"

"Call," he instructs, his voice stern. He sends a wave to Scout. "Lady Miller."

My sister giggles again, but I don't even have it in me to be annoyed this time. I'm too enamored with the mysterious phone number.

"Later, kid," I hear Greer say to Macie as he walks past her.

She watches him cross the parking lot to his car, all the while a longing gaze settling into her eyes. She wants to play hockey with him badly, and I want her to be happy…and safe.

Macie sits there watching the lot, not moving until I tell her it's time to go. She doesn't say anything on the car ride home or when we make it into our apartment. She doesn't speak through dinner or even attempt to turn on the game, which I know she knows is on because she's Macie, she loves hockey, and she has the Comets schedule memorized.

When she goes to bed without asking what the score is, I know she's truly bummed. I kiss her forehead, tuck her in for the night, and then make my way to the kitchen, where I pour a glass of wine before stepping out onto our small patio.

With a steadying breath, I punch in the number as best I can on my shattered screen and put the phone up to my ear. It rings twice before someone picks up.

"Hello?" A soft feminine voice comes over the line.

"Um…hi." I let out a long breath. "This is going to sound weird, but Greer gave me your number. See, my kid wants to learn to play hockey, and he's agreed to train her. Yesterday, though, on her first day, she fell. I freaked, and now my kid won't play. He said you may have some insight."

The woman chuckles. "Well, all right, then. What's your name, sweetheart?"

"Stevie."

"Nicks?"

"The one and only."

She laughs. "Look, Stevie, I've been in the same boat as you. I remember the first time Jacob took a spill on the ice. I threw a huge fit and made them stop practicing while I called an ambulance for him. He was fine, of course, just a little bruised, but it scared the shit out of me. Us moms never want to see our babies hurting, you know?" She sighs. "He told me afterward that he never wanted to play hockey again. At first, I was relieved. I loved the idea of my kid not getting hurt. But then I realized he didn't want to play because *I* scared him, not the game. He loved it. He belonged on that ice. It meant everything to him. My freak-out hurt him worse than falling ever did."

"What'd you do?"

"I took his scrawny little ass to the next practice and made him play."

I laugh. "I can't imagine him being scrawny."

Greer's so big now, easily topping six four. He's still lean, but if the way his shirts cling to him is anything to go off, it's all muscle.

"Oh, trust me, sweetheart. He was. A mouthy little shit, too, though he hasn't grown out of that yet."

She lets out another breathy laugh, and for some reason, I can just picture her sitting outside like me, but instead of a glass of wine in her hand, it's a cigarette. She's an older version of Greer, all dark hair and bright eyes, only instead of frowning at the entire world, she smiles constantly.

The image makes me giggle.

"What's that for?" she asks, not missing it.

"Sorry. I was just thinking about your son."

"Are you soft on him?"

"Excuse me?"

"My son. I assume you are if you're calling his mom."

"Oh. Um, I'm his date for your wedding. Congratulations, by the way. I'm really looking forward to it." I sincerely hope she doesn't have that weird *I know when I'm being lied to* thing moms seem to have.

"Aw, thanks, sugar. I'm sure my son isn't too happy to be attending yet another wedding of mine."

"That's not true. He's very excited."

She lets out another raucous laugh. "You don't need

to lie for him, but I appreciate it. Makes me like you more. You said you have a daughter? I'm surprised you're dating my son, then. He's not really fond of kids."

I want to correct her and tell her I'm definitely not dating her son, but I just let it go for now.

"He's great with Macie." I take a sip of my wine to swallow down the lie.

All right, so it's not a complete lie. They do seem to be getting along better now than before. They have a weird relationship, but if it means she's not calling him The Jackass every five minutes, I'll take it.

"Well, I'm glad. Maybe he's growing up some, settling down instead of being so stubborn about love. Though I'm sure I'm to blame for that one." She chuckles, but there's no sweetness to it like there was before. Instead, it's pure sadness. I want to reach through the phone and hug her. "Anyhoo, enough about me. We're talking about you and your kiddo. Tell me what happened."

So I do. I describe the fall Macie took and how my heart climbed into my throat and hasn't really left. How Macie is moping around, feeling down, and how helpless I feel about everything.

When I'm done, the woman sighs. "Oh, Stevie, sweetheart. It'll all be all right. I've been a hockey mom for a long time now. It's hard. I know that, but we have to let our kids figure their stuff out, you know? If she wants this—and it sounds like she does—you have to let her have it. She'll be okay. Goalies wear lots of gear, you know."

A weight that's been slowly settling onto my shoulders begins to lift as her words sink in. She's right. I know she is.

"I have to let her do this."

"You do, and I have full faith in you *and* her. If my son is willing to give up his free time to help her, he must see something in her."

I don't want to burst her bubble and tell her the only reason he agreed to train Macie was that I would be his date, so I don't.

"Yeah, he must."

"Well, listen, sweetheart, I'm going to get going. Us older ladies need all the beauty sleep we can get, and I'm sure you still have lots to think about tonight."

"Thank you for taking the time to talk to me… Well, shoot. I never even asked you your name."

"It's Loretta."

"Lynn?" I tease.

"The one and only." She gives me another one of those laughs that I'm really starting to love. "Good night, sweetheart."

"Good night, Loretta."

I hang up the phone, then set it on my belly, lifting my wineglass to my lips and taking the final sip. I stare at the moon while I do exactly what Loretta said I would—I worry. I mull over every word of our conversation, then replay Macie falling.

It's going to be tough letting my only baby do something that almost guarantees she's going to come home bruised or broken.

But…I know what I have to do.

Me: I want her to play.

Me: Call me tomorrow?

King of Hell: You got it.

CHAPTER 10

"Are you sure this is going to work?"

I sigh. "That's the fifth time you've asked me that when I should be asking *you* that. She's your kid."

"Yeah, but you two have some sort of hockey bond or something."

She has a point there. Sure, Macie is a ten-year-old with the attitude of a sixteen-year-old, but on some level, I understand her. I'm not really sure what that says about me, but I don't want to get into it now.

"If she sees you excited about it, she'll be game."

"You think?"

I pinch the bridge of my nose, trying my best to swallow down another sigh. "Yeah."

We've been standing here for the last ten minutes, and this is the third time we've had this same conversation. Stevie's nervous in a way I haven't seen before.

But…I get it. After seeing Macie go down like she did, there was even a part of me that didn't want her to play. I was surprised when we were standing in Doc's office and that feeling hit me. I never wanted to see that kid in that situation again.

And I don't mean any kid—I meant *her*. I didn't want Macie hurt. I really, really didn't.

I felt awful seeing her fall, but I looked at it as a hockey player. It was a soft tumble compared to some I've seen, so I wasn't too worried. But seeing her afterward lying in that bed with Stevie looking like she was about to throw up? I fucking hated it.

So, I left. I walked away.

Only I couldn't stop thinking about it. I needed to be sure she was okay, just like I needed to make sure she wasn't going to give up on the game over one bad fall. It was too clear how much she loves being on the ice for me to let that happen.

I'm glad I went to see Stevie, and I'm really damn glad I gave her my mom's number. Whatever she said to her worked because here we are, ready to pick up Macie from school and take her for her second training session.

"Your car is so extra."

I glare over at Stevie, who is glaring at my vehicle. "Be nice to my car, dammit."

"Or what? You'll frown at me some more?"

"Yes."

She rolls her eyes, but not before I see her lips tip up at the corners.

She's such a brat. I can't remember the last time I've been so annoyed by someone yet still couldn't stay away.

It's disconcerting, and if I never feel this way again, it will still be too soon.

"How much longer?" I ask, checking the time on my entirely too expensive watch.

I don't spend my money on much because I know this career isn't going to last forever, but after signing my extension contract with the Comets, the watch and the car were both gifts to myself.

"About five min—"

Her words are cut off by a yawn, and I glower at her. "Stop that."

"What?" She shrugs. "If someone hadn't woken me up with a phone call at five in the morning, maybe I wouldn't be yawning."

"How's it feel getting woken up?"

"You could have ignored my text, you know."

"Right." I snort. "Like you'd have let me."

"True." She grins, and it's an evil grin. "Are you sure she's going to—"

"Stevie, I swear," I say, shoving off my car with a huff, "if you ask me one more time if she's going to go along with this, I'm going to—"

She flinches.

Stevie fucking flinches, and it's enough to have me stumbling back, completely caught off guard by it. When it sinks in *why* she flinched, so does the anger. I'm pissed, so fucking mad I can't see straight. Not at her, though—I'm upset at what that flinch just implied.

"What was that?"

"What?"

"Why the hell..." I gnash my teeth together, chomping away the words that so desperately want to fly out of my mouth. "Why'd you flinch? Did..." I swallow. "Did someone hit you?"

She shakes her head. "It was nothing."

I seethe at her nonchalance, at her eagerness to brush it aside.

"That's not nothing, Stevie. Who did that to you?"

She raises her chin, meeting my heated stare. "It's none of your business, Greer."

It might not be any of my business, but I want it to be.

"Who."

Not a question. A demand.

"My ex. He would grab me...leave bruises. Pin me against the wall and yell in my face. But hitting me... It was only once." She rushes the words out quickly, like it only happening once somehow makes it okay.

"Once is enough for me to kill the man," I say, brushing past her.

I have no clue where I'm going, no clue what I'm doing. I just know I need to do *something*. Why I feel so fucking protective over her and her kid is beyond me, but I'm just so damn mad right now. I—

"Jacob."

It's the first time she's said my name, and I stop in my tracks when it tumbles off her lips.

I don't go by it. I never have, not even when I was

younger. The moment I knew I wanted to be a hockey player, I insisted I be called Greer. My mother is the only person to call me Jacob.

I turn back to Stevie. She's staring at me with trepidation in her eyes.

"Where are you going?" she asks quietly.

"To commit murder."

She lets out a soft laugh. "Stop. Please." She waves me back to her, and I reluctantly trudge to her side, taking a spot beside her. "You don't even know his name."

"I would have found out."

She grins. "I don't doubt that."

We sit there in silence for a moment. It's uncomfortable in a way that only having this conversation can be uncomfortable.

I hate this for her. I hate this for Macie.

Oh shit… "Macie…"

"Never," Stevie answers my unasked question. "*Never.*"

Thank fuck. I drop my head into my hands, scrubbing my face, trying to rid myself of the knowledge I never wanted to know.

I run a restless hand through my hair, then say, "I wasn't…I wasn't mad at you, and I wasn't coming at you. I'm sorry if that…"

"I know," she says, but I'm not sure she does.

If she knew, she would know that one time I caught my mother's second husband wrapping his hand around her throat, and I came unglued. I broke my hand fighting the asshole and had to miss a lot of good fucking hockey, but it was worth it, and I'd do it all over again.

"Never," I promise her.

"I believe you. Just…I spook easily sometimes. You seemed irritated, and you did that thing he always did when he was irritated." She mimics me pinching my nose. "It was kind of his tell. And then you had your fists clenched. Like that." She nods toward my fists.

And yep, they are clenched, but this time, it's because I'm pissed as fuck at the guy who dared to lay a hand on her. He needs to be dead, just like any other fucker out there who dares to touch a woman.

I shove off my car again, this time letting my hands fall to my sides in a relaxed position. Stevie doesn't flinch, and I'm grateful for it.

I stand in front of her, tucking my hand under her chin and lifting it up. I'm not surprised to see her blue gaze shining, but it doesn't mean I like it.

"I'm sorry." I don't take my eyes off her. "Thank you. For telling me, I mean."

She nods. "Thank you…for listening."

"What was that?" I cup my hand around my ear. "Not sure I heard you."

"Ugh." Stevie tosses her head back with a groan, shoving playfully at my chest. "You're the worst."

"No, that's not what you said. It was something else. Sounded like two words."

"Fu—"

I clamp my hand over her mouth before she can finish her sentence.

"Careful," I warn. "We're on school property, you know."

She glares at me, and I can feel her frown beneath my palm.

"Now, I'm going to remove my hand, and you're going to say two words I am very much owed, got it?"

She lifts her blue eyes skyward but nods.

"Good girl."

It's subtle, but there's a spark in her eyes when I say it.

Interesting.

I store that information away—for what, I don't know—then slowly remove my hand from her mouth. When she's no longer silenced, I stare at her, waiting for her to say something…anything. I don't know how much time passes before I finally see her mouth move.

"Thank you."

It's quiet, barely audible, but it's still somehow the sweetest thing I've ever heard.

"You're welcome."

Just as the words leave my lips, the bell rings. Five seconds later, kids begin filing out of the building.

I step away from Stevie, trying hard to ignore how much I miss her heat the second I do. I resume my spot next to her against my car, then wait.

Several kids stop and stare at us—mostly my car. A

few gawk at me in awe, probably recognizing me from their televisions.

One yells out a "HOLY CRAP!" then promptly gets in trouble for saying crap.

Moms do double takes and giggle. Dads look jealous.

Eventually I hear, "Mom? Greer?" Macie's pace slows, her mouth open at the sight of us. "What are you doing here? Whose car is that?"

"It's mine. Want to drive it?"

"Heck yes I do!"

"Greer!" Stevie reprimands me, and I hate my last name for the first time in a long time. "She's ten."

"Oh shit. Right."

"You can't say shit," Macie points out.

"Right. My bad."

The kid grins, her bright green and navy blue braces on display. I'm pleased to see they are still Comets colors.

"What are you doing here?" she asks, looking around at the kids who are all staring at her. Off to our right, a group of boys around Macie's age are whispering behind their hands. I wish I knew which little shit got into the shoving match with her so I could pummel him, but then I remind myself they're kids and that likely wouldn't go over well.

"Hockey," I tell her.

"Huh?"

"You have practice."

Elation steals over her face, but it's gone just as quickly as it came when she slides her eyes to her mother.

"I, uh, can't."

Stevie steps forward. "Yes, you can. I want you to play."

Macie's jaw drops again, her head tipping to the side. "I…I can? You do?"

Her mom nods. "Yes, I do. And we better hurry if we're going to get practice *and* ice cream in before bed."

"What? Are you kidding? I'M PLAYING HOCKEY!" She throws her hands into the air, spinning around in circles, her little backpack twirling right along with her.

She abruptly stops, then marches right up to the group of boys and says, "Suck it!" She darts to the car, but not before sticking her tongue out at them.

They glare at her, but the second they catch me shooting even sharper daggers their way, they stand up straight and run off.

Good. Little pricks.

"Come on," I tell Macie. "You can ride shotgun. Your mom will follow us."

"I get to ride in the fun car, not the minivan?"

"It's not a minivan—it's an SUV!"

"Same lame thing, Mom," Macie grumbles, pulling her door open.

"Yeah," I say to Stevie as I push off the car. "Same lame thing, Mom."

She looks like she wants to hurl some not-so-nice words at me right now, but when she takes a peek around and sees we're still being watched by just about everyone, she refrains.

"See you at the rink. And, Greer?"

"Hmm?" I ask her as I pop open my own door.

"Drive safe. You have precious cargo in that car."

"Yeah, I know. I got my gear in the back."

"Greer! I—"

But I don't hear the rest. I climb in and fire up the engine, giving it a few good revs to drown out her yelling.

I look over at Macie, all buckled up and smiling brightly.

"Five bucks says we beat her there."

Her smile widens. "You're on."

"Again!"

Macie drops to her knees, then maneuvers herself back to her feet.

"Again!"

She does it once more.

"Again!"

"Ugh! Seriously?" Her hands go to her hips, and she purses her lips like she just ate something sour.

"Yes, seriously." I tap her helmet. "How do the new skates feel?"

"Good."

"Better than those other ones?"

She nods several times. "Much better. Thank you again."

"Yeah, yeah," I say, brushing her off before she can latch on to my legs in a hug like she did earlier. "Again."

She groans but drops to her knees, then pushes up on her skates. She looks absolutely ridiculous in the goalie gear that's practically swallowing her, but she's catching on quickly.

We run through it twice more before moving on to the same thing, but this time holding her stick. She struggles a bit during the fourth one but pushes through it. We take a water break when we hit five, and she skates over to the bench with ease, like it's not just her fourth time on the ice. We've been skating together for a week now, and we do the same things at every practice: up-and-down drills, holding-the-stick drills, and skating. All the while, Stevie sits on the bench and reads or works on her laptop.

"Oh my gosh," she mutters, tipping her green squirt bottle back and squeezing water into her mouth. She misses, splashing herself in the face and letting out a loud yelp when it hits her eyes instead of her tongue, but she quickly recovers as if nothing happened and takes a drink.

I tried to warn her that she wasn't ready for the real goalie bottle, but she wouldn't listen. She was insistent on having her own squirt bottle.

After she takes a few long pulls of water, she hits the ice again, skating around in slow circles, still getting a feel for the surface. I was right about her—she's got fire. She's smart, pays attention, and is not afraid to ask questions. When she's struggling, she pushes through. When she's doing well, she pushes herself to do even better. She has all that hockey grit that makes a great player, and she's only ten. I'm betting she'll have a long career playing if she's willing to put the work in.

"How's she doing?" Stevie steps up beside me just as I squirt water into my mouth.

"Good," I say, dragging the back of my hand across my lips. "She's a natural, but even naturals have to work at their skills."

Stevie's face lights up. "Yeah?"

I nod. "Yeah."

"Good." She shimmies her shoulders with happiness. "Honestly, she's been so in love with the game for the last few years I was scared she was going to build this experience up in her head, and it wasn't going to be what she expected, and she'd hate it and lose interest. That's what I did when I said I wanted to learn ballet. I quit after a year."

"All that work, and you quit?"

"Well, yeah." She shrugs. "We had some family stuff going on, so it was rough."

"Is everything okay now?"

Stevie lets out a sad sigh. "Yes and no. My dad passed away a few years ago from cancer, so that part isn't good, but my other dad is finding a way to move on, so I guess that's a good thing. He's healing. He's rediscovering himself. It's…good."

"I'm sorry about your dad. I've never lost a parent, so I can't imagine how hard that is."

"It's not fun, that's for sure. I was about to ask something dumb like *Are your parents still married?* Then I remembered I'm your date to your mother's wedding."

"Fourth wedding," I correct.

"Does that bother you? Loretta being married so many times?"

"Yes, but probably not in the way many people think it would bother me. I'm bothered by it because it means she keeps giving away all the best parts of herself to douchebags who don't deserve her. I want her to be happy more than anything, but at what cost, you know? She's tried this so many times. What's it going to take to make it stick?"

"The right person. Trust me when I say that's hard as hell to find."

My jaw tightens at the mention of her failed marriage and the ex who mistreated her. "I could still kill him, you know."

Stevie grins up at me. "I appreciate that, but it's not necessary."

"Does Macie know him?"

She shakes her head. "Nope. She was only two when we left. She asks about him sometimes, but it's best that he's not in our lives. We think so, and so does he. He hasn't even tried to reach out since our divorce, which I am perfectly okay with. He didn't want Macie to begin with."

My blood boils. How could he turn either of these girls away? I mean, not that I'm mad about it given what I know about him, but still.

"He sounds like a prick."

"He is." She shakes her head like she's shaking away all thoughts of him. "Anyway, what about your father? Is he remarried?"

I laugh. "Oh yeah."

"Uh-oh. Stepmom troubles?"

"Nah. He only married one of them, then divorced her shortly after she had her second child. The rest he's never married."

"But he…"

"Had kids with them. I have six siblings."

Stevie's eyes widen. "That's…"

"I know," I tell her, understanding she's at a loss for words like a lot of people are when I tell them. "For what it's worth, he's a really good dad. Shitty husband for sure, but he's a present father."

"Well, that's something, at least. How long was he married to your mother?"

"That's the real kicker." I grin. "They never got married."

"Wait—they've both been married and have kids, but they never married each other?"

"Nope. Mom went on to be a serial bride, and Dad became a serial father. Match made in heaven if you ask me." I shrug. "Oh well. At least it gives me a better understanding of love. It's a—"

"Crock of shit?"

"Bingo."

I wink at her, and she rolls her eyes.

"Don't be that guy, Greer."

"What guy?"

"The guy who gives up on love before he ever has it because he's scared he's going to get hurt."

I scoff. "That's not what it is."

It's not.

At least, I don't think that's it.

Shit. Is that my problem?

I shake my head. *No, definitely not.*

"How about we stop with the psychological analysis and get back to hockey?"

"Oh goody, grumpy Greer is back." Another roll of her eyes.

"I'm not grumpy. I'm focused."

"Sure." She pats my shoulder. "Whatever you need to tell yourself."

She pulls her phone out of her pocket, and I see that the screen is completely shattered. I'm surprised she can even do anything on it it's so cracked.

"What happened?" I ask, nodding toward it.

"I dropped it in the truck last week." *Hmm.* "How much longer is this going to be?" she asks.

I try not to let my irritation at her line of questioning show. She's done this every practice, trying to rush things along. "Do you want her to play hockey or not?"

"I do, but I also want her to get her homework done and get to bed at a decent time. I also need to feed her dinner, you know."

"I'll buy dinner."

Her mouth opens in surprise. "What?"

"Dinner—I'll buy it."

I don't know why I say it. I haven't taken them to dinner before, but I'm not ready to go home yet, either. I'm tired, yet also wired. I need the distraction, or all I'm going to be doing is going over how I let that goal in last night. It went right over my glove, and I *never* miss on my glove side, especially not an easy shot like that.

"Greer, no," Stevie argues.

"Well, it's too bad. I'm buying, so pick a place." I point toward the ice. "We're going to run a few more drills, and then we'll go."

She calls after me, but I pretend I don't hear her, stepping onto the ice and taking off in full stride to catch up with Macie. We go over a few more things, practice her stopping and starting, and I show her how to hold her stick properly.

"All right," I tell her just after five. "I think we're good for the day."

"Really? That's it?"

I laugh. "Yeah, that's it. But we'll go again in a few days."

"A few days? I have to wait days?!"

"Well, not to skate, but to do other stuff, yeah." I point a finger at my chest. "Pro-hockey player, remember?"

"Someone likes to brag." She skates past me in a huff. "Mom! I'm hungry!"

"Well, good. We're going out tonight."

"Really? Where?!"

Stevie bounces on her heels gleefully. "It's a surprise."

Why do I not like the sound of that?

CHAPTER 11

If you had told me a few weeks ago that I'd be sitting down to have dinner with the goalie of the Carolina Comets, I would have laughed for multiple reasons.

One, there's no way I'd be hanging out with hockey players. That's my sister's thing, not mine.

Two, if I were with a player, it certainly wouldn't be the one who drives me basically insane.

But here we are.

"You know, when I said you could pick the place, I meant you could pick *anywhere*."

"I know. And I did pick."

"Yeah, but…" Greer curls his lips in disgust. "This?"

I shrug. "It's Macie's favorite, and quit acting like you're better than everyone else."

"I am better than everyone else, and that kid needs a better palate."

"Hey! My palate is just fine!" said kid argues.

"Do you even know what that means?" Greer asks her, brows raised.

"Duh. Of course I do." She huffs but doesn't elaborate. Instead, she shoves past him to the counter and lifts her head up high. "Hi. I want the McNuggets Happy Meal, please. Fries, barbeque sauce, and a big Coke for the drink."

I step in at that. "Make that a Sprite, please." The last thing she needs is to be all jacked up on caffeine.

"You get your own drinks." The kid presses a few buttons on the screen, never looking up. "What else?"

"I'll have a ten-piece McNuggets, small fry, water, and a chocolate shake," I tell him.

"Any dipping sauce?"

"Hmm. I'll do buffalo."

"Sure. Anything else?" the worker asks, finally looking up and directly at Greer. His eyes narrow for only a moment before he looks away.

Greer tugs his Comets hat down lower, then steps up to the counter. "I'll have two Big Macs with extra sauce, a ten-piece McNuggets, a large fry, and a Diet Coke."

"Any dipping sauce?" the kid asks in the same monotone voice he's been using.

"Ketchup."

"Ew!" Macie and I say at the same time.

Greer sends us a glare. "I didn't judge your order. Mind your business." He turns back to the kid. "Add an apple pie to that, too, will ya?"

"Sure. Your total is…"

He rattles off our final bill, and Greer taps his card on the screen with a sigh as Macie and I grab our cups.

We make our way to the soda fountain, and I have to stop Macie when she tries to go for the Coke. She frowns when I make her dump it out and refill it with Sprite.

I fill my water cup, then take a drink. I can feel Greer's eyes on me.

"Yes?" I ask when I find him staring at me in disbelief.

"Did you really just put water in your water cup?"

"Um, yeah?"

He shakes his head. "You're such a rule follower."

"It's a water cup. That's what it's for—water."

"Yeah, but nobody actually puts water in there. The people at the counter don't even expect you to put water in there."

I shrug. "I wanted water."

"Something making you extra thirsty this afternoon?" He bounces his brows up and down.

I roll my eyes at the implication that I could ever thirst after him. "No, but now that you mention it, my stomach is sort of upset."

"What's wrong, Mom?" Macie asks, completely oblivious to the second conversation Greer and I are having right now.

Us adults share a secret smile as we make our way to the back of the fast-food joint and find a seat.

I don't miss the way people shift to look at Greer. I'm sure even if he weren't an NHL player, he'd turn heads just on his height and build alone. I'm sure being panty-dropping hot doesn't hurt, either.

We file into the booth, Macie choosing to sit by Greer instead of me, then we wait. They wait for their food while I wait for the awkwardness to settle in.

Except it never comes. I don't feel weird sitting here with Greer and Macie. It feels…normal.

I watch as they talk animatedly about the upcoming game against St. Louis. Macie tells him he needs to keep his eyes on a certain player, and Greer laughs.

"Oh, don't worry. He's never scored against me."

Macie's jaw drops. "Ever?"

"Nope. I know him too well."

"How?"

"He's my brother."

"SHUT UP!"

"Macie! Don't tell people to shut up."

"Sorry, Mom." She sinks into her seat. "Sorry. But…" She looks up at Greer. "Are you for real?"

"Yep. He's about six years younger than me."

"That's so cool. What's it like having a sibling? I want one someday."

My head jerks back because this is the first time Macie has ever said anything about wanting a sibling.

"It's fine. We didn't grow up in the same house, but we're still really good friends."

"That's so cool," Macie says.

"It is really cool," Greer agrees. "He's a good player."

"Did you see his goal against Tampa? It was insane! Bet you couldn't have blocked that."

They argue back and forth about whether or not

Greer could have stopped the puck from crossing the line, but all I can think about is what Macie said.

Do I want another kid? I'd be lying if I said I hadn't thought about it. I bet it'd be amazing to see Macie in the role of older sister. I know I had a fun time being one.

But then I start thinking about how much of an age gap it would be between Macie and them. How, in just eight years, Macie will be off at college, and I'll have free time again. Do I want to have another kid and give that up again?

Maybe if I found the right guy and the timing was right, but I'm sure with the poor state of my love life currently, it will be years before that ever happens.

"Order number 12." Two people appear at the end of the table holding trays, and we make room for them to set everything down. They both disappear without another word, and I divvy up the food. Macie dives right into her nuggets, tearing open her barbeque sauce and plunging one after another in.

"Slow down, Mace," I tell her.

She holds her hand over her mouth, nodding her head. "Okay."

She chews a little slower, and I feel less concerned that she's going to choke, turning my attention to my food. I carefully lay out each nugget, then open my sauce cup and pour some onto each chunk of meat. I grab a few fries and pop them into my mouth. That's when I notice Greer staring at me.

"What?" I ask after I swallow.

"What the hell is that?" He nods toward my tray.

"My dinner?"

"Yeah, I can see that, but why did you dump the sauce *on* the nuggets?"

"It's weird, isn't it?" Macie says, still shoveling fries into her mouth. "She always does that."

"Mind your own business, Macie." Then I look at Greer. "You too. Isn't that what you said earlier? No judging."

"That deserves judging."

"Agreed."

I pick up a fry and toss it at my kid for that.

"Hey!" she yells before grabbing the fry and popping it into her mouth.

Greer shakes his head when I lift a sauce-covered nugget and take a bite. "Shameful."

"What? I want even sauce distribution. It's not weird. It's…it's…science!"

"Pretty sure that's a bunch of bull—"

I narrow my eyes, cutting off his almost curse.

"Doo-doo. That's bull doo-doo."

"Haha. Doo-doo." Macie giggles like a maniac, which makes Greer laugh too.

It's my turn to shake my head at them.

And he had the balls to call Macie and me two peas in a pod. Those two have more in common than he thinks.

I wish I could say we eat our dinner without any more fry-throwing incidents, but that would be a lie.

Greer lobs a handful at Macie when she steals one of his nuggets because she "can't bear the thought of the nugget going through ketchup abuse."

Greer empties our trays in the trash can while we don our coats.

"You girls ready?" he asks, shrugging his own jacket on and tugging his hat down lower.

Only it's fruitless.

"Um, hey, mister?" a small voice says.

We all look down to find a kid who probably isn't older than six holding a pen and a piece of paper that looks like a receipt. I glance over to see a smiling young couple watching their son stare up at Greer with wonder. They both look a little starstruck too.

Greer doesn't hesitate to drop down to his haunches, the widest and brightest grin I've ever seen from him stretching across his face.

"Hey, little man. How are you?"

"Are you…" The little boy swallows, the slip of paper shaking in his grasp. "Are you Mr. Greer? The goalie?"

"I sure am, buddy. What's your name?"

"Jonathan."

"No way! That's my dad's name."

"Really?" The boy's eyes light up. "That's so cool."

"It really is." Greer nods at the paper that's now crinkled in this kid's clutch. "Do you want me to sign that for you?"

Jonathan nods. "Please."

"How about I do you one better, huh?" He pulls the

hat off his head and reaches into his coat pocket, producing a silver marker. "You can have this hat."

"Wow!"

The kid—right along with me—watches in wonder as Greer scribbles his name and the number 29 on the bill, and my heart melts when he places the cap on the kid's tiny head. It's so big it immediately falls over his eyes, causing him to laugh.

"What do you say, Jonathan?" his mother prompts.

"Thank you, thank you, thank you!" He throws his arms around Greer's neck, and it takes the grumpy goalie a minute to realize what's happened, but he squeezes the boy back, patting him gently on the head.

"No problem." Greer pulls back. "Just make sure when you're watching our game tomorrow night, you're cheering for us. Got it?"

Jonathan nods. "Yes, sir!"

He runs away to his parents, who both give thanks to Greer as he stands, and he waves them off, muttering a *No problem* before turning back to Macie and me.

"Ready, ladies?"

He says it so casually like he didn't just give this kid a moment he's going to remember forever in the middle of a McDonald's.

"We're ready," I say, ushering Macie ahead of us but not able to take my eyes off Greer.

"What?" he asks, eyes falling to slits.

"Nothing," I murmur.

But it wasn't nothing. It was definitely something, and

I felt it somewhere I would never have expected, especially not when it comes to Greer.

My heart.

"It's so uncool that we had to ride in the lame-mobile when we have a perfectly awesome car we could have taken."

"I think one ride in the death machine is enough for now," I say to Macie, making eye contact with her in the rearview mirror.

She mutters something, but I don't catch it, which is probably a good thing for her.

"You know, I could have brought my orange Viper ACR instead. Now *that's* a death machine."

"You have not one, but two sports cars?"

"Three."

"Three?!" My eyes bulge at this news, and then I shake my head. "Freaking rich people, man."

Here I am, barely chugging along in the same car I was driving in high school, and he has three cars.

He laughs. "Hey, I work hard for my money, you know."

"You play a game."

"A game where I work hard. Do you have any idea how many players play with bruises and broken bones?"

"They do that?"

"Of course they do. Ask Miller about the time he

scored twice on Pittsburgh and then had his shoulder reset after the game because it had been popped out since the second period."

I slide my eyes toward him. "No way."

He nods. "Yes way."

"It's true, Mom. They all do it. They even put out a list of injuries at the end of the playoff runs. It's wild." Macie sits forward, gripping my seat and Greer's. "But don't worry, that won't happen to me. I won't be hurt—I'm a goalie."

I'm not stupid enough to think that's true. I've seen enough games over the last few years to witness the goalie get mowed over a few times. Heck, I even saw once where one had to be helped off the ice on a stretcher. It's a dangerous sport, and I still can't believe I'm letting her play it.

"Loretta told me about your first fall, you know."

"Oh man." Greer laughs. "She was so mad, made them stop the practice. Did she tell you she tried to do it again during my first game when someone bumped into me?"

"She didn't."

"She's got fire, that woman." The love in his voice is so clear. I want to tease him for being a total momma's boy, but it's hard when he's so sincere about her.

"She was really nice. Not sure what happened with you."

"Hey! I'm nice. I just gave that kid my hat."

I smile because he did just give that kid his hat, and it

might have been my favorite moment I've had with Greer in the two weeks we've been spending time together.

"Nice isn't the word I'd use to describe you."

He makes a noncommittal noise as we pull into the parking lot of the Comets practice arena. I don't know how much Greer is paying for us to use this space, and while I know I should ask to be prepared to pay him back, I don't have it in me just yet.

I learned two nights ago that my time at the law firm is coming to a quick close. They're going down to one secretary at the end of the month, which means I need to find a new full-time job if Scout doesn't have use for me at the donut truck.

I steer into a parking spot a few down from Greer's fancy sports car. I have no clue what it is because I don't know a thing about cars, but it just looks like it's fast.

"I could give you a ride in it, you know," he says when he catches me staring.

"What is it?"

"It's a ZR1."

"Which is…"

"Corvette."

"Ah. I thought it looked familiar. For years, my dad had a very outdated car calendar in the garage."

"Want a ride?" He raises his brows, and for a split second, I swear he's not talking about a ride in the car.

I give myself a shake because there is no way he means that…right?

No. Another shake.

"Guess that's a no," he says, pushing the car door open. "Later, kid."

"Bye, Greer!" she says cheerfully.

He nods at me, then disappears, closing the door softly behind him.

I watch him go, watch the way his coat stretches across his broad shoulders. The way he walks with authority like he's the boss and everyone else knows it. The way he commands attention, even when nobody is looking.

"Where are you going, Mom?"

"Huh?"

"Your door is open."

I look down, and she's right—my door is open. What am I doing?

"I'll be right back."

"Okay, but hurry. I want to watch some of the Minnesota game before bed."

I can only nod as I race from the car, chasing after Greer. He must hear me because he spins on his heel, his brows raised in question when I skid to a stop in front of him.

We're standing just a foot apart, staring at one another in the middle of a dark, nearly empty lot.

"Stevie?" Greer finally asks. "What are you doing?"

What am I doing? I've gone nuts. That's the only explanation I have.

"Yes!" I blurt out.

"Yes?"

"A ride."

His brows rise higher. "A ride?"

I nod. "Yes. A ride—in your car," I add quickly. "I think I'd like that."

A lazy grin pulls at his lips. "I think I'd like that too."

"Yeah?" He nods. "Good."

Because I've thrown all intelligent thoughts out the window, I push up on my toes and press my lips to his stubbled cheek. I let them linger, let the feel of the sharp prickles of his cheek brush against my lips and the way he smells like something spicy and warm wash over me.

We both know the amount of time I spend with my lips on him is inappropriate.

But we both let it happen anyway.

When I finally peel my lips away, I step back, only to find him staring down at me with a look I've never seen from him before.

"Good night, Jacob."

I swear I hear him mutter *Evil woman* as I walk back to the car.

"What are you smiling for?" Macie asks when I climb back inside.

"Nothing, baby. Nothing."

It's a lie because it's definitely something. I'm just not sure what yet.

CHAPTER 12

Stevie: Macie's not handling this well.

Greer: Me either.

Greer: Can't fucking believe we lost.

Stevie: I mean, the streak had to end at some point, right?

Greer: Yeah, but not like this. Not in a shootout against Arizona.

Stevie: I'm sorry.

. . .

Greer: Yeah, me too.

Greer: Is she changing her braces colors?

Stevie: She's already on the phone.

Stevie: Kidding. She hasn't moved from her spot on the couch since the horn went off.

Greer: If it makes her feel any better, I'm still sitting in the locker room.

Greer: I'm not ready to leave and face the press.

Stevie: That has to be hard, talking to them after a loss.

Greer: It's the fucking worst.

Greer: Shit. I have to go. Coach is yelling at me to get on the bus.

. . .

Greer: Tell Macie I'm sorry.

Stevie: I will.

Greer: Am I forgiven?

Stevie: After that win tonight? Yes, I believe so.

Stevie: She's already making plans to have the same breakfast, lunch, and dinner and wear her jersey for the game in two nights.

Stevie: Hockey players are so weirdly superstitious.

Greer: It's a curse we all bear.

Stevie: What's your weird superstition?

Greer: Peanut butter and banana toast.

. . .

Stevie: What?

Greer: I have to eat peanut butter and banana toast the morning of a game.

Stevie: That's so…

Greer: Weird?

Stevie: Old. My grandpa used to eat that.

Stevie: You're an old man in a hot body, aren't you?

Greer: You think my body is hot?

Stevie: You know you're attractive. Don't play stupid.

Greer: True. But it is nice to hear once in a while.

. . .

Stevie: Please. As if women don't tell you that all the time.

Greer: They do, but I still like hearing it.

Stevie: Gag me.

Greer: Already getting kinky with me? All right. I can get into that.

Stevie: Goodbye, Greer.

Greer: Wimp.

Stevie: Me?

Greer: Yes. You dip out just when the conversation gets good.

Stevie: I'm "dipping out" because I have a kid to take care of.

. . .

Greer: How convenient.

Stevie: *laughs in parent*

Greer: Tell the scrawny little shit I said she better be working on her stamina like I told her.

Stevie: I already took her to the track today so she could run.

Greer: Did you run with her?

Stevie: Oh yeah. Did a quick ten miles. No biggie.

Greer: That's what I start my morning with.

Stevie: You're kidding.

Greer: I'm not.

. . .

Stevie: That may be the most disgusting thing you've said to me yet.

Greer: What? Running is good for you!

Stevie: Yeah, and so is eating kale, but there is no way I'm touching that.

Greer: I like kale…

Stevie: Of course you do.

Stevie: I really do have to go. I have to tuck Macie in.

Stevie: But don't tell her I told you that. She'd kill me if she knew you know her mommy still tucks her in.

Greer: My lips are sealed.

. . .

Greer: Good night, Steve.

Stevie: Tell me about this wedding.

Greer: Well, when two people "love" each other, they get married.

Stevie: Greer.

Greer: Steve.

Stevie: I meant, what am I supposed to wear?

Greer: I think they'd prefer clothes.

Greer: Well, most people would. There will probably be a few old perverts who'd vote otherwise, though.

Stevie: I'm being serious!

. . .

Greer: Fine. I guess I also wouldn't mind seeing that.

Stevie: GREER

Greer: STEVE

Stevie: Help me. Please.

Greer: I have it taken care of.

Stevie: What the hell does that mean?

Greer: It means I have it taken care of.

Stevie: Yes. SO helpful.

Greer: I try to be.

Stevie: I was going to say something mean about you losing tonight, but then I remembered I'd have to deal with my daughter pouting, so GO TEAM.

Greer: Smart woman.

Stevie: Macie is bugging me about your next practice. Any ideas?

Greer: We're flying back tonight after the game. I have shit to do tomorrow, and we have the wedding Saturday. I have practice Sunday, then a game on Monday. We leave for a road trip on Tuesday, so…

Stevie: She's going to hate that non-answer, but I'll tell her.

Greer: Hey, being trained by an NHL player has its perks. It also has its drawbacks.

Stevie: I know, I know. Macie is so grateful too. There's no way I could ever afford training like this, so it really does mean the world.

. . .

Greer: Don't get all weepy and emotional on me now.

Stevie: Weepy? Emotional? All I'm doing is thanking you!

Greer: And it's weird.

Greer: Go back to hating me.

Stevie: I wish I could.

Greer: What's that supposed to mean?

Greer: Steve?

Greer: Ugh. I take back the weepy and emotional thing.

Greer: STEVIE?

Greer: Maybe you fell asleep. Good night.

CHAPTER 13

"What the hell are you doing here?"

I shove off my car, casually strolling toward the woman who is currently shooting daggers my way while holding a giant white box that's overflowing with stuff.

"Here, let me take that," I say, grabbing it from her before she has a chance to protest. My momma would be so proud of me in this moment, being a gentleman. "What is all this?"

"I'm not answering that until you tell me what you're doing here first." She looks around the almost empty parking lot. "How'd you know I worked here?"

I lift a shoulder. "I asked around."

"So you got information from Miller again?"

I don't answer her because the last thing I'm trying to do is get Miller into trouble for giving me information on Stevie, especially when he doesn't know what I'm doing when I ask him about her. He's so oblivious sometimes and gives up the information freely. It's comical.

"I thought you said you had stuff to do today," Stevie says.

"I said I had *shit* to do today, and this is it."

"You had to stalk me at work?" She crosses her arms over her chest, glaring up at me. She seems irritated, even more so than usual.

"No. I'm here to give you that ride you requested."

I don't miss the way her cheeks pinken at my words or the slight hitch to her breath. She reaches up and brushes her long dark hair over her shoulder.

"Oh," she mutters, sighing softly. "Today feels like a bad day for that."

"Why?" I jiggle her box, looking down into it to find a few picture frames, some pencils and pencil holders, several stacks of papers, and…*is that a corded phone?* I haven't seen one of those in years. "Does it have anything to do with this?"

She lets out another long sigh. "Yes. I, uh, I lost my job."

"Shit, Stevie. I'm sorry." No wonder she's upset. She has Macie to take care of, and this is a blow for her.

She waves her hand. "It's fine. I knew it was coming. Well, it was supposed to come next week, but here I am, jobless today."

"What happened?"

"They're merging firms, and they don't need two secretaries. I guess my skills weren't up to snuff, and they chose someone else."

Just then, the door behind her is shoved open, and a

woman with short red hair steps out wearing a skirt I'm pretty sure would show *everything* she has to offer if she bent over. Her legs are long and toned, her bright yellow heels drawing your eye just right. She's wearing a white blouse that shows her bright red bra underneath. She almost looks like a sexy cartoon character or something.

"Did you need any help with that, Ms. Thomas?" But she's not looking at Stevie when she asks. Instead, her eyes are trained on me, that same caught-you-staring grin I've seen time and time again pulling up one side of her mouth.

The brunette in front of me huffs. "No, Becky, I'm good."

"All right," the redhead says, not once taking her eyes off me.

She doesn't make a move to go back inside, which irritates Stevie even more. She doesn't have to say anything for me to know it; it's obvious in her protective posture and the way her fists are now clenched at her sides.

Stevie's eyes begin to fill with tears, and I hate it. I hate it so fucking much, more than I've ever hated anything before, and I've lost some well-fought games and been eliminated from the playoffs a few times. But this? Seeing Stevie so upset? It's so much worse.

I drop her box, not caring about the items inside, vowing to replace them if anything is broken.

"What are you—"

I kiss her.

I fucking kiss her.

It takes her a second to catch on to what's happening, but then she's kissing me back.

Stevie is kissing me back.

Her lips are soft and pliable. She tastes like caramel candies and feels like heaven pressed against me. I grip her waist, holding her to me, angling my head so I can get a better taste. I run my tongue along the seam of her lips, and she easily opens for me. I swallow the sigh that leaves her, tugging her closer because I can't get enough for the life of me.

I want more. I need more.

A throat clears, and it's enough to snap Stevie out of the moment. She shoves away from me, eyes now glassy with desire instead of tears. Her chest heaves up and down, her dress a mess from my hands pulling at her. Her lips are swollen, and her cheeks are stained red.

She looks fucking gorgeous, and it makes me want to kiss her all over again.

"You can leave now, Ms. Thomas."

Stevie tugs at her dress, righting the misaligned material, then grabs her box and marches past me.

I look the other woman right in the eyes and wink.

Then I chase after Stevie. I jog past her, popping open the trunk of my ZR1 and grabbing the box from her hands at the last moment. I try to catch her eyes to get a feel for what she's thinking, but she won't look at me. She just stares down at the ground as she turns and heads for the passenger door.

A soft gasp leaves her lips when she pulls it open.

"Greer…"

Finally, her summer sky blue eyes meet mine, and in that moment I'm not sure I've seen a more beautiful sight.

"What did you do?"

I reach around her into the car, retrieving the white box.

"Yours broke."

"I know, but—"

"No buts. Yours broke because of me, so I replaced it." I shove the iPhone box her way. "It's not the same model you had, but I think you'll like this upgrade just fine."

"Jacob…" she whispers, marveling at the device. "I can't accept this. It's too much."

"If you think that's too much, you're really going to hate the dress I sent over to your apartment today."

Her gaze snaps to mine, a bit of that fire she's so full of creeping back into her eyes. "The what? What dress?"

"I was only kidding about you going naked to the wedding." I lean down until my lips brush against her ear. "Though I wasn't kidding about me liking the idea of seeing you that way."

When she pulls back, her cheeks are brighter than I've ever seen them.

"Come on." I place a hand on her hip and nudge her toward the car. "Get in. We have plans."

"We do? Where are we going?"

"It's a surprise."

"I hate surprises."

I laugh. "You won't hate this one. Go. In."

This time, she doesn't argue. She slides into the car, still staring at the new phone in her hands. She doesn't look up until I've climbed into the seat next to her.

"You like it?" I ask, firing up the engine.

"This is a month's rent for me, you know."

"Is it?"

She nods. "Yes. I…" She slams her eyes closed and swallows thickly, her fingers running along the edges of the box. When she peels them back open, she looks over at me just as a single tear escapes down her cheek. It takes everything in me not to lean over and brush it away.

"Thank you, Jacob," she says quietly. "For *everything*."

She doesn't just mean the phone or the dress or the lessons.

She means the bar too.

"You're welcome, Stevie. For *everything*."

Another thick swallow. A nod.

She clears her throat, then looks down at the phone. "You might have to help me set this up."

"I think I can manage that. But first…fun."

I rev the engine a few times, and she laughs.

It's the sweetest sound I've ever heard.

"You can't be serious." Stevie stares out at the space before us. "I am not properly dressed for this."

"Hey, it's not my fault you wore a dress to work today."

"You saw the competition I had. I had to try everything possible."

I hate that she felt she needed to show some skin to save her job, but I don't think she'd be up for a lecture on that right now, so I say, "I have some extra stuff in my bag you can wear."

"That's not going to fit me at all."

"We can make it work." I shuffle toward the duffle I tossed onto the bench and unzip it, root around until I find something suitable, then hold it up. "Here. This should work."

She curls her lips at the clothes but accepts them anyway. "This is ridiculous."

"Sure, but it's going to be fun. I'll get to teach you *and* your kid how to skate."

"Except she was ready for this. I'm not."

"You'll do fine."

"You're not going to let me fall like you did her, are you?"

My heart drops into my stomach. "I didn't—"

"I'm kidding, Greer. I know it wasn't your fault."

I'm annoyed I'm back to being called Greer, but I don't say anything.

"If it's any consolation, I don't think I've ever felt so bad in my life, including when I went to the World

Juniors and lost the gold medal in OT and all of Canada was pissed at me."

"Wow. What a comparison, my kid to your hockey game."

"Hey! World Juniors is a big thing."

"Yeah, and so is my kid."

"Right." I clear my throat. "I am sorry."

"I know. I could see how upset you were. Not as upset as me, obviously."

"No. I think the only person topping you there was my mother when she had her freak-out over me."

"Be nice to your mother, Greer. She loves you."

"Yeah, yeah—whoa! What are you doing?"

She stops moving, her dress halfway up her body, leaving her bottom half in nothing but her underwear and red heels that I bet would look really fucking good wrapped around my waist.

"Uh, changing?"

"Here?"

She shrugs. "There's nobody here. What? Have you never seen a woman in her underwear before?" She gasps. "Oh my gosh, it was never Miller—you were the virgin all along!"

I glower at her. "As if."

"The '90s called—they want their Valley girl talk back."

I send her another glare, trying my best to keep my eyes trained on her face and not on her body as she peels the rest of the dress off. It's hard, and so am I just watching her. She's fucking beautiful, even with her mismatched baby blue bra and lacy black underwear.

"Laundry day?" I ask to distract myself.

"Nope. I'm just not fancy enough to match. Nor do I care—I'm not trying to impress anyone."

"Good."

She pauses for a moment, eyes focused on me and the very possessive-sounding word that just left my mouth. If she has something to say, she keeps it to herself. She just toes off her heels, grabs the pair of pants from the pile of clothes I gave her, and pulls them on.

I admit I'm sad when she slips the shirt over her head and lets it fall. It's too long on her, but she's got that covered, pulling the hair tie from her wrist and cinching the shirt to a wearable length.

I toss her a pair of socks, and she puts those on, then sits.

"Can you help?" she asks, batting her lashes and pointing to the skates.

It's subtle, but I hear the shift in her breath when I drop to my knees in front of her. I don't even have a witty one-liner to tease her with since she's clearly enjoying this. I'm too fucking busy trying to talk my dick down because something in me loves this scene entirely too much.

Visions of a naked Stevie spreading her legs for my assault do nothing helpful for the aching cock in my jeans, and I wish we were anywhere else right now so I could bring them to fruition. What I wouldn't give to slide my tongue along her pussy so I could hear her scream my name.

"Greer."

I snap my head up.

"I think they're tight enough."

I look down, and, yep, her skates are on and all tied up. She's ready to go.

I shove up to my feet, adjusting my cock as discreetly as I can, then plop down next to her and put on my own skates.

"You ready?" I ask once I'm all laced up.

"I guess." She wobbles a bit as she pushes to her feet.

"You look ridiculous." She does. But also seeing her in my clothes… I like it entirely too much.

"A good ridiculous?"

"Of course." I grab her hand to steady her, then lead her to the ice. "All right. We'll go slow at first, okay? I'll keep hold of you just like I did Macie."

"Sounds good," she says, walking onto the ice looking like Bambi, bumbling all over the place.

"Your kid is a lot better at this than you."

"Yeah, I guess so." She stares down at her feet as I tug her along.

We skate like that for several minutes before I ask, "Think you're ready to try it on your own?"

She nibbles on her bottom lip, looking up at me with wary eyes. "I think so."

"All right. Letting go in one…two…three."

I release her, ready to reach out and catch her because I fully expect her to go tumbling down.

But she doesn't. No, she takes off in a full stride, gliding across the ice like a fucking pro.

"What the…"

I watch in awe as she skates with ease, shifting her feet perfectly, skating backward, and even spinning in a circle. I stand there with my arms crossed over my chest, glaring at her.

"You were playing me."

She grins from across the way, her shoulder rising. "Maybe."

"Where'd you learn to skate like this?"

"Lowell."

I tip my head back. "Lowell, as in my captain Lowell?"

She nods, doing another twirl and adding a small jump this time. "Yep. We went to high school together and often hung out at the skating rink. We'd go after school and mess around."

I pull to a stop, my fists balling up at my sides. "Mess around as in…"

She rolls her eyes. "As in *skating around.* Nothing sexual. We weren't into each other like that. Well, except for that one time."

She sticks her tongue out, skating backward even farther away from me.

I chase after her, determined to make her pay for her so-not-funny joke. The thought of Stevie and Lowell together makes me furious. I know he's madly in love with Hollis and there's no chance of anything happening, but I hate the thought all the same.

I know I have no business hating it, which irritates me even more as I hunt Stevie down.

I'm much faster than she is and could easily catch her, but I'm enjoying our game of cat and mouse too much to let it end so soon. When I see she's running out of steam, I pounce.

Well, not really, but I do ease her against the boards, boxing her in, and she sucks in gulps of air.

"That wasn't a very funny joke." I grip her waist in one hand as I help to hold her steady.

"Aw, that's too bad. I was going to use it in my next standup routine."

"You do standup? You'll have to let me know when and where. I'll make sure to bring tomatoes."

"Nobody throws tomatoes anymore, Greer."

"Too bad. Some people could really use a good tomato to the head."

She laughs and loses her balance, letting out a little squeal as she starts to slip and reaches out for me, her hands curling around my biceps. It's a familiar position—her pressed against me and nearly out of breath. It's the same one we were in just an hour ago when I kissed her.

We haven't said a word about it, not even on the drive over to the rink. She spent that time talking to Macie on the phone as Scout drove her to Miller's place for a sleepover. I know she will be alone tonight, and that's the kind of information that could get me in trouble.

So much trouble.

It's just the kind of trouble I want to be in…the kind of trouble I want to be in with her. But if we're going to do this, I have to know we're on the same page.

"Steve."

"Greer," she responds, not even having it in her to admonish me for using her nickname. Her focus is entirely on my mouth, never wavering.

"I can't offer you love."

My words pull her out of her haze, and her eyes slide to mine.

She swallows once. Twice.

"I don't believe in it," I say.

"I know that," she whispers.

"So, this…"

"It's fun," she says.

"Fun?"

"Yeah. That's what we're supposed to be having, right?"

I hold her gaze with mine. If I look past the heat that's burning in her eyes, I can see something else, something I'm not sure I'm quite ready to see. There's a niggling feeling in the back of my mind that tells me something is wrong, says something isn't right about this and I should walk away. We had one kiss. It doesn't have to lead to more.

But I'm not sure I can walk away. Not now, not when

I know what she tastes like. Not when I know how perfectly she fits against me, like it was always meant to be.

I can't walk away, even though I should because I know there's no way I'm going to be able to give her what she's inevitably going to want.

It's stupid. It's dangerous.

Knowing all those things? It changes nothing.

I feel myself nod, and I hear myself say, "Yeah…fun."

Her tongue pokes out to wet her lips. "Okay."

"Okay."

We stare at each other for several moments, and I'm not sure either of us even blinks in that time. I want to be sure she understands what I'm telling her. I can't love her. It's not who I am. This, what's happening between us, it's purely physical. It's fun.

When she has no objections, when I don't see any second-guessing, I ask, "Can I kiss you now?"

"Oh, are you asking now? Because earlier, you weren't a gentleman at all. You just—"

I don't let her finish that sentence. I crash my lips to hers, stealing away her smartass comment and her breath.

This time she doesn't hesitate to kiss me back. She gives me everything she has in her as she throws her arms around my neck and tugs me closer.

It's still not enough.

I haul her up and into my arms, loving it when she

hooks her legs around my waist like it's right where they belong. It's a bad idea, holding her and kissing her like this on the ice, but dammit, I'm a professional hockey player who lives on the ice. I can handle this, especially for her.

She lets out a soft moan, pressing against me as I drop my hands to her ass. *It's just so I can get a better grip*, I tell myself. It's a lie, though. I can't resist touching her, can't deny how good she feels beneath my exploring palms.

This moment…it's fucking magical. I can't imagine a place I'd rather be, a person I'd rather be with.

Her. Her. Her.

It's all I want.

All I need.

I have no clue how long our tongues stroke together as we paw at one another, but it's long enough for her to begin shivering in my arms. I miss her touch the second I finally convince myself to pull away.

"How's that for being a gentleman?" I ask, setting her back down on her legs.

She wobbles a bit—something I really fucking love—and grins up at me. "You might be the most gentlemanly gentleman I know."

"That so?"

She nods. "Th-That's so."

I want to push her against the boards and kiss her again, but she's shaking right in front of me, and I want to shield her from that even more.

"Come on." I grab her and tug her back across the ice.

"Where are we going now?"

"My place."

"Greer." She tugs on my hand until I stop. "I can't just go home with you."

"Why not?"

"Um, because I have a kid."

"She's with your sister for the weekend."

I know because Miller was excited about the spa night he has planned for all of them, which I mercilessly teased him about earlier.

"I know, but…" Her tongue darts out to wet her lips. "I can't. I'd like to go home."

If I said those words didn't hurt like a puck to the nuts, I'd be a liar.

"Okay. I can take you home."

I turn back to keep going, but she tugs on me again.

"What?" I ask, turning back around, trying to mask the hurt I'm definitely feeling but have no right to.

"Come with me."

"What?"

"Home," she says. "Come home with me."

CHAPTER 14

This last month of my life has been the most insane.

First, the night out at the bar with other moms—the same ones who still haven't called to invite me out again. Then Greer showing up at the truck and guilting me into a date. Him training Macie. Me losing my job. Greer kissing me.

And now, he's in my apartment.

None of this was at all how I thought this month would pan out, but here we are.

Here we are, stepping into my apartment, Greer's eyes taking in the space around him. I'm sure it's not much to him, but it's home to Macie, Scout, and me.

"This is nice," he says, pulling his jacket off. "It's—"

"An absolute disaster? I know, but you'll have to excuse the mess. I have a ten-year-old."

Greer folds his jacket—one I'm sure cost as much as my rent—over his arm and lifts his dark brows. "I was going to say *cozy*. It's cozy. A lot more lived in than my apartment."

"Lived in is a nice way to say messy."

"No. It's a nice way to say my apartment is cold and unwelcoming. This isn't." His eyes move around the room, still surveying each part. "I don't spend much time at my place, especially during the season, so it feels a little bland. This one reminds me of my childhood home —lived in."

"Does your mother still live there?"

"No. She lives here, actually."

"Really?"

"Yep." He nods. "I moved her here a few years ago after her third divorce. She was in a rough place, and I figured a change might do her some good. Now her business is thriving, and she's getting married. So we're all happy, I guess."

"Yes, you sound positively elated when you talk about your mother's fourth marriage." I roll my eyes so he knows I'm being a complete smartass. I grab his coat, hanging it up on one of the empty hooks near the door, then toeing off my heels. I look ridiculous right now, still wearing Greer's clothes and my high heels, but I didn't feel like changing again after skating.

He grunts. "Sorry. It's just…"

"You don't believe in love. I know."

An arm curls around my waist, and I'm tugged back against him before I even know what's happening. He spins me around, pressing my back against the door and boxing me in. I'm out of breath as I stare up at him, my chest heaving, nearly brushing against him because that's how close he is.

"Steve," he whispers, his hand slipping down my side to my waist, his fingers curling into my skin, branding me as his.

"Greer." I grin despite my best efforts not to. I hate being called Steve, but the way it sounds coming out of his mouth…well, it makes me hate it a little less.

"Say my other name."

"Huh?"

"My first name." His grip on me tightens. "Say it."

"Jacob."

He inhales sharply, and a quick beat later, his mouth crashes against mine. I have no clue who reaches for the other first, but it doesn't matter now that we're fused together, pulling at each other like maniacs.

His hands slide under my shirt—or rather his shirt—and mine grip the edges of the tee that hugs him like a second skin. He shivers when my hands collide with his bare skin, and I nearly combust as the pad of his thumb outlines the wire of my bra. His hands are somehow soft and rough at the same time as he holds on to me like he's afraid I'm going to fade away at any moment.

There's no way there's a single thing in this world that's better than having his hands on me. It's not possible.

I'm not sure how long we make out like teens against the door, but it's long enough for me to need more.

"Jacob."

He pulls, taking one last nibble at my lips. "Yeah?"

"Can we—"

I can't even finish my sentence before he's dragging me through the tiny apartment and to the couch. He plops down, pulling me onto his lap and tugging me back down for another kiss.

I laugh at his urgency.

"Stop laughing," he says, not finding it as funny as me.

"Well, I can't help it. You're practically mauling me, tossing me around like a wild man or something."

"That's because I can't get enough." He sits forward, pressing his lips to my throat. "It's been too long."

"Since you last kissed me? Or since you last kissed anyone?"

He pulls back, his eyes narrowing. "Is that your way of asking me if I'm seeing anyone?"

Crap. Is it?

I lift a shoulder. "I guess it kind of is."

"No, Stevie. I'm not seeing anyone else. In fact, I haven't seen anyone else for months."

"Months?" I squeak out.

"Yes."

"Years."

"Years?"

I nod, looking down at my lap and where we're connected, not missing how well we seem to fit together. "I haven't been with anyone in years. Not since…"

He inhales sharply at this information. "Nobody?"

I shake my head. "Not even a kiss."

"Fuck, Stevie. If I had known that…"

He leans forward, one hand gripping my waist, the other sliding into my hair. His thumb caresses my cheek as he stares into my eyes like he never has before.

"I would have kissed you like this."

He presses his mouth to mine. It's a soft kiss, so much different than the others we've had, languid and sweet. There's nothing rushed as he coaxes my lips open and slips his tongue inside. It might be the gentlest side of Greer I've experienced yet, and somehow it gets me just as hot as the rougher version.

An involuntary whimper leaves me the moment he pulls away because I already miss him. He doesn't miss it.

His chest rumbles with a laugh. "Better?"

"Just as good," I tell him, because it's true.

"Hmm. Guess I'll have to do it again, then."

And he does, only this time, his gentle touches don't last. They turn quickly into the same rough, unfiltered, and impatient movements from earlier as he pulls at me, needing more.

I need more too.

I break the kiss, reaching for the hem of my shirt and pulling the material over my head. I let it fall to the floor somewhere behind me as I reach behind me and unhook my bra. I sit on his lap in nothing but a pair of pants that aren't even mine as I stare down at Greer and his hungry green eyes.

Unlike earlier at the rink, he doesn't try to pretend

he's not looking at me. This time he is doing so completely unabashedly. He takes me in, eyes tracking over every inch of me, from my eyes to my tits that aren't as perky as they once were, the faint stretch marks on my belly from my pregnancy and the loose skin I have there too. His eyes linger on the small scar from my C-section, then he drags them back to my face and starts all over again.

I feel like I'm supposed to do something like cover myself or be shy or embarrassed by my body, but I can't find it in me, not when he's looking at me like I'm the most beautiful woman he's ever laid eyes on.

He wants me, and I want him too.

He reaches a single finger out, and I shiver when his fingertip connects with my already hard nipple. He traces the puckered skin over and over, and it's annoying because it feels so good and like not enough all at the same time.

I squirm against him. "Greer, I—"

My complaints quickly transform into a gasp as his mouth closes around the same nipple he was tormenting, and my eyes drift closed with pleasure.

The moment they close, I hear him. "Eyes on me, Stevie."

His voice is rough and deep, and I want to obey his request so badly, but it's hard. Having his mouth on me feels too good.

I peel them back open, watching him as he kisses both my breasts, sucking and nipping at them only to swipe his tongue over the slight sting he leaves behind. He does it over and over again until I swear I'm about to come from this alone.

Then, without warning, he releases me.

"No!" I cry out, reaching for him.

He laughs darkly, grabbing my hands and halting my movements. "If you keep squirming like you are, I'm going to blow my load in my jeans, and that would be sad because I'd rather come down that pretty throat of yours."

My mouth waters at his words.

"Oh," he says. "You like that idea, huh?"

I nod.

"On your knees, then."

I scramble off his lap, dropping to the floor in front of him. He spreads his legs, and I relish the sting in my knees as I scoot closer to him.

"Take my cock out," he instructs.

I've never been happier to listen to someone than I am at this moment.

I reach for his belt, sliding the expensive leather through the buckle and undoing the clasp. I unsnap the button, then drag the zipper of his jeans down. He rises up just enough for me to tug his pants down while he pulls his shirt off.

He sits before me, his pants half off, no shirt. He looks like a king on his throne, and I'm happy to be his servant.

"Take it out," he instructs again, his voice gruffer than before.

I oblige, reaching into the black underwear and pulling his swollen cock free. I swallow thickly at the sight of him. He wraps his hand around himself, stroking slowly. I couldn't look away even if I tried.

"You want to taste me, don't you?"

I nod, unable to take my eyes off him.

"Do it. Put me in your mouth."

I don't waste another second, sliding my tongue against his shaft from base to tip. A deep growl leaves his throat, and it's like music to my ears, spurring me on. I close my mouth over the head of his cock, circling my tongue on the underside, paying special attention to the frenulum.

He hums his pleasure as I swallow more of him, letting my untrained mouth adjust to his size before taking more. He lets me go at my own pace, but I know he's holding back. I know he needs more.

I need more too.

I grab his hand and bring it to my head, looking up at him. His eyes are glassy and full of lust, but he understands what I want.

"Are you sure?" he asks. "Because I'm not so certain I can be gentle, Stevie. In fact, I don't *want* to be gentle. Do you understand?"

I nod.

I feel it the moment he lets go. His fingers close around a fistful of hair, and he ruts up into me, shoving his cock down my throat. I choke on the intrusion, which spurs him on even more, and he thrusts into me again. Tears spring to my eyes, a few spilling over nearly instantly. I can't breathe, yet I've never felt so alive before.

I feel like I should hate this, being used like this, but I realize I just don't care. It feels too good, too right having him in my mouth.

His grip on my head tightens, his other hand coming down to stroke away the tears that are now streaming down my face as he continues thrusting. I swallow around him, and he lets out a guttural sound.

"*Fuuuuuuck*," he moans. "You take me so well, Stevie. I swear your mouth was made for my cock."

I nod because I swear it too.

He drives himself into my mouth over and over, his body growing stiffer with each movement, his breathing getting sharper and sharper while mine gets weaker and weaker.

"I have to come," he mutters.

He tries to pull away, but I refuse, digging my nails into his thighs to halt his movements.

I deserve this. I deserve all of him.

He thrusts into me twice more, and that's when I feel the hotness of his cum hitting the back of my throat. I swallow everything he has to give me as his strokes slow while he comes down from his high.

When he's fully spent, I let him slide out of my mouth, then rest my head on his thigh, sucking in pulls of air for what feels like the first time in hours as Greer strokes my head and attempts to steady his own breaths.

How is it I didn't even come, and I feel spent like I just ran a marathon? Everything in my body aches, and I'm not sure I'll be able to move again.

"I should go."

His words are like a bucket of ice water.

They're enough to have me lifting my head and peering up at him. "Go?"

He nods. "Yeah. I have practice tomorrow morning."

"Oh."

It's a stupid thing to say. I know it is, but it's all I can muster. I just let him fuck my mouth, and he has to go because he has practice in the morning? I…

Well, I'm pissed.

And hurt.

And did I mention pissed?

I shove up to my feet, trying hard to ignore the sting in my knees when I stretch them out. I'm sure I'll have bruises tomorrow. If you had asked me about them just twenty seconds ago, I'd have said they were worth it, but now, staring down at Greer as he tugs his jeans back up and buckles his pants like nothing happened, I don't think that's the case at all.

I step back when he rises from the couch, crossing my arms over my chest to cover my naked breasts because I'm still practically nude as he tugs his shirt back on.

"Hey," he says softly, his fingers sliding under my chin and pulling it up to meet his eyes. "We good?"

I nod because right now, it's all I can do.

"Okay. I'll see you at four tomorrow."

My brows crush together. "Four?"

"The wedding. I'm the dude of honor, so we need to get there early."

"Oh. The wedding. Right."

A frown pulls at his lips, but it's gone as quickly as it appeared. He gently kisses my lips, then gives me a grin. "Good night, Steve."

"Night," I mutter.

Without a backward glance, he walks out of my apartment.

I don't remember the last time I felt this awful. I'm glad Macie isn't coming home tonight; there's no reason for her to see me upset like this.

I go to the kitchen and chug a glass of water, then say screw it and grab a bottle of wine. I unscrew the top as I make my way down the hall to my bedroom, coming to a screeching halt in the doorway when my eyes land on the box sitting atop my bed.

I want to ask Greer how he managed to get this in here, but then I remember he's not here. He's gone. He used me, and now he's gone.

I shove the box off the bed and crawl under the sheets, still wearing his pants and still holding on to my wine. I close my eyes, pushing out all thoughts of what just happened.

I have no idea how long it takes me to fall asleep. All I know is it's the worst night of rest I've ever had.

CHAPTER 15

I'm running late.

I fucking hate running late, and I really hate running late when it involves a beautiful woman.

"Listen, all I'm saying is, maybe things would have been different if JC was the one whose career took off and not Justin, you know? He was clearly the most talented member of the band, but no, we had noodle-hair boy plastered all over the cover of *Teen Bop* for years."

"Fucking hell." I pinch my nose between my finger and thumb, a headache settling in between my eyes. "Why are we talking about this again, Miller?"

"Because I was out grabbing pizzas for the girls, and I saw Justin on the cover of some magazine with an article about his perfect life with his perfect wife, and it just brought up some old feelings."

"So you called *me*? To chat about NSYNC?" I rub at that same spot again, the throbbing starting back up.

"Well, no. I called you to say you had better take

good care of Stevie tonight, but I saw the magazine and got sidetracked."

"You called me about Stevie? To…what? Threaten me if I don't take care of her?"

"Yep." He pops the P, shuffling the phone around, and I watch as he grabs a bag of chips and opens them right there in the aisle. "I know where you work. I know where you live. And I also happen to know all of the weak spots in your gear. So if you hurt her, I swear to God I'll make it look like nothing more than a freak hockey accident when I slit your throat."

"Jesus, Miller."

It's quite the visual he's painted, one I can see very clearly. That isn't the scariest part, though. It's how he tells me all this—with a grin on his face and sincerity in his eyes. Miller means what he says, and it makes me respect him.

It also pisses me off.

"I don't plan to hurt Stevie."

"Oh, I know you don't." His bright smile nearly blinds me even through the phone screen. "You act like a big tough grump, but deep down, you're a softy. I still have to let you know how it's going to be, though. Stevie's going to be my sister-in-law someday, so consider it my brotherly duty."

"Your warning has been heard." I roll my eyes, but he doesn't care. "Can I go now? I kind of have a wedding to get to, and I'm about to knock on my date's door."

I glance up at the 23C on the door, hoping like hell

Stevie can't hear this conversation on the other side of it. I wouldn't have usually answered Miller's call, but he never sends me video chat requests, so I was worried something was wrong with Macie.

Nope. Turns out he just wanted to chat boy bands and threaten me.

"You can go. Please tell Stevie I said she looks beautiful."

"You haven't even seen her." *I* haven't even seen her, though based on the dress I bought her, I have no doubt she looks incredible.

"Yeah, but she's always pretty. I mean, Scout's prettier, but still."

I really want to come back with something stupid about Stevie being the prettier one, but that would be super high school of me, and I don't have the time anyway.

"Good night, Miller."

"Night, Greer. And remember…"

"Yeah, yeah. Skate to the throat, big accident. I got it."

He grins. "Good boy."

I hit the red button before he can say anything else that's going to drive me nuts and slip my phone into my pocket. With a steadying breath, I rap my knuckles against the door. There's a soft shuffling on the other side before it's pulled open, and my breath is stolen from my lungs.

"Wow."

It's all I can think of to say when I take in the woman in front of me.

I was right to pick the dress I did. The blue matches her eyes perfectly, and the waist is flattering in all the right ways. Her tits—the ones I know taste so fucking sweet—are pushed up high, and she's showing just enough cleavage to make my cock ache inside my dress pants but not enough to make me embarrass myself. The buttery-soft material swishes against her legs, stopping just short of hitting her knees, which are still red from last night's activities. I'd be a fucking liar if I said I didn't love the sight.

"I feel entirely overdressed," Stevie says.

"Nonsense," I tell her, finally peeling my eyes from her body. Her dark hair is swept up into a bun. There are two braids, one on either side of her head, and a pair of earrings that perfectly match the necklace I got her dangle from her ears. "You look gorgeous."

Her cheeks pinken, something I'd normally find cute, but something seems off. *She* seems off.

"Everything okay?" I ask her.

She gives one curt nod. "Fine."

Except it sounds like nothing is fine at all. Just as I'm about to ask her to elaborate, my phone goes off once again. This time, I know the ringtone. I pull it from my pocket and don't even bother looking at the name on the screen when I hit the green button.

"Mom?"

"Jacob! Where are you? You were supposed to be here ten minutes ago."

"Calm down. We're on the way now."

"Boy." She tsks. "I swear, if you weren't so damned big, I'd bend you over my knee and whoop your ass for telling me to calm down on my wedding day."

I grin. "You've never spanked me."

"Well, don't make me start now. Just get here. I need my dude of honor."

"We're leaving now. Love you."

"But never as much as I love you. Drive safe," she rushes out quickly before ending the call.

I slip my phone back into my pocket.

"Is everything okay with your mom?" Stevie asks, her bottom lip tucked between her teeth.

"Oh yeah. Just her usual pre-wedding jitters. She does this every time. We're good."

Stevie gives me a small smile, and it's nothing like the smiles she's given me before. In fact, it reminds me entirely too much of the smiles she first gave me—forced and fake. I want to talk more about it, but we really are running out of time, so I hold my hand out to her.

"Ready?"

She nods, and instead of placing her hand in mine, she brushes past me like I'm not even there.

Between my mother and Stevie, I have a feeling it's going to be a long night.

"I now pronounce you husband and wife! You may kiss the bride!"

David wraps his arms around my mother and dips her backward, kissing her harder than I ever want to see my mother kissed. Everyone erupts into cheers, and I paste on my best smile and clap along too.

She did it. She married her fourth husband. This one has to stick, doesn't it?

They make their grand exit, and the bridal party follows suit. I catch Stevie's eye on the way out and don't miss when she swipes her fingers over her cheeks, brushing away tears.

Women and weddings, man. They always cry.

I don't think anything could top David sobbing through his vows, though. He really loves my mom, which is great. I wish him the best.

We take a few photos—why my mom needs any more wedding pictures is beyond me—then we're set free for the cocktail hour. I rented out the swankiest hotel the city has to offer as my wedding gift to my mother. She doesn't know I also got her tickets for a three-week trip to Ireland for their honeymoon. They leave tomorrow, and I'm letting David be the one to give her the news later.

I'm stopped no less than five times as I make my way through the reception hall in pursuit of Stevie. If I know my mother, she's placed us at the front table, which is where I'm hoping to find my date. After shaking hands with another of my mom's favorite clients, a break in the crowd lets me know I'm right.

I stop for a moment to admire her as she fingers the straw in her cocktail, her other hand under her chin. She looks sad but beautiful. The urge to sweep her into my arms and swing her around the dance floor so everyone can see she's mine is strong.

But I don't. Instead, I slip into the chair next to her, startling her as it scrapes across the floor.

"Sorry," I mutter, pressing a kiss to her cheek.

She stiffens under me for a moment before relaxing.

"You okay?" I ask her for what feels like the millionth time tonight.

She's been quiet since I showed up at her apartment. She didn't even make any comment on the red light I definitely ran on the way here. Something's bothering her, but I'm not sure what.

"Mhmm," she answers, lifting her drink to her lips. She takes a long pull, then another. And one more until her glass is empty. She pushes her chair back. "I'm going to get a refill."

I rise, ready to chase after her. "Stevie, wait. I—"

"There you are!" my mother calls out, shoving her way through the crowd. "My boy!"

In all her glory, my mother glides across the floor, her cream dress dragging behind her. I think of all the gowns I've seen her in, this one is my favorite. She looks beautiful with her gray-streaked hair twisted up in a bun and her makeup all done. She doesn't look a day over thirty when she's actually just two months shy of fifty.

"Hey, Mom."

She presses a kiss to my cheek, no doubt leaving behind a smudge of lipstick, and eyes Stevie. "Is this her?"

I nod. "Mom, this is Stevie. Stevie, meet my mother, Loretta."

"The famous Stevie Nicks!" Mom claps her hands together. "I'm so honored to meet you."

"You're honored to meet me?" Stevie grins. "I'm meeting Loretta Lynn—I'm the one who is honored."

They laugh and hug like they're old pals, and I'm incredibly curious why they're calling each other names that definitely belong to famous musicians.

"It's so wonderful to finally meet you," Stevie tells her. "I've heard so much about you from Greer."

"All good things, I hope." Mom winks, then nudges me. "I'm truly so happy you came. When this one told me he was bringing a real live date, I nearly fell out of my salon chair. He always causes a ruckus at weddings, and I was relieved he was going to have someone to keep him in line." My mother looks Stevie up and down. "I had no idea you'd be this gorgeous, though."

Stevie blushes. "Thank you. You look stunning."

"Oh, stop it." My mother waves her off, but I know she loves the compliment. "How are you, dear? How's your daughter adjusting to hockey?"

"She loves it. Greer's been a fantastic coach."

It's the nicest thing Stevie's said to me all evening, and I wish my mom would stick around so I could hear more compliments.

"Good. I'm so glad." Mom squeezes Stevie's hands. "You have my number, so if you ever need another pep talk, I'm just a call away."

"Thanks, Loretta."

"I better get back so we can make our grand entrance. I just had to come say hello to you first."

Mom pats her cheek, then turns to me. I bend down so she can wrap her arms around me.

"You really do look beautiful, Mom," I tell her, squeezing her tightly.

"I know I do." I laugh as she pulls away, setting her hands on my cheeks. "Take care of her." She lifts her brows. "You hear me?"

I nod. "I hear you."

"Good. Love you, baby."

"Not as much as I love you."

"Hey, that's my line!" She winks before gliding off into the crowd.

I turn back to Stevie, but she's gone. I move through the groups of guests, hoping I don't get stopped a million times before I reach the bar. I'm in luck because not a single soul stops me, but that high disappears when I see the scene in front of me.

Stevie's talking to some guy.

Some guy who is leaning in closely as she throws her head back laughing.

Some guy who is about two seconds away from being thrown over the bar and having a bottle broken over his head.

I march toward them, sliding up right behind Stevie, leaving no space at all between us. Her ass fits perfectly against my cock, and if I'm not mistaken, she presses back into me.

"Stevie," I say into her ear.

"Greer," she mutters back. She doesn't look away from the dead guy, but she does relax against me, and the dude doesn't miss it.

"Sorry. I didn't realize you were together."

"Well, we are," I tell him. "You can go now."

He lifts his hands, then scuttles away.

Stevie whirls around the moment he's gone, her baby blues full of fire.

"That was so rude, Greer."

"Stop calling me that."

"Would you rather I call you asshole, then?"

"What is your problem?"

She huffs, crossing her arms over her chest. "Nothing."

I'm about to call her on her shit when the deejay comes over the speakers.

"Would everyone please make their way to their seats so we can introduce the newlyweds?"

Stevie shoves past me, heading back to the table. I wish it were anyone but my mother getting married right now so I could haul Stevie off to some coat closet and demand she tells me what's wrong, but I can't do that to my mom.

Instead, I follow my date and slide into the chair next

to her. We clap and cheer as my mother and David are introduced, and I swear I catch Stevie wiping away another tear as they have their first dance. We sit through the speeches—my mother spares me from making one—and the dinner, not once talking to one another.

It's not until the deejay announces that the members of the wedding party should kick off the dancing for the night that we even look at each other.

I rise and hold my hand out to my date. She looks at it for a moment, clearly considering leaving me in the dust, but eventually she slides her palm against mine.

I tug her against me as the music begins to play, relishing the way she feels pressed against me. She may be upset with me, but I don't care. I can't not touch her right now, not when she looks as gorgeous as she does, pouty lip and all.

"You know, everyone in this room can see that you're upset with me," I say softly. She grunts. "I just wish you'd tell me what I did wrong so I can fix it."

She pulls back, looking up at me with raised brows. "Are you serious right now?"

"Yes, I'm serious. I don't understand what's going on."

"Dammit, Greer."

"Stop calling me that."

"No."

I grit my teeth, my patience growing thinner by the second. "What did I do?"

She tries to pull away and run, but I don't let her. If anything, I tug her even closer.

"No running. Talk to me."

"You left!"

Now it's my turn to pull back. "What?"

"Last night. You just left, after…"

"After my cock was in your mouth?"

Her cheeks darken. "Y-Yes. I thought…" She exhales a steadying breath. "I thought I was okay at first, fine with you leaving and me feeling used—but then I wasn't. I wasn't okay with it. I'm still not okay with it."

"Stevie, I—"

"No, Greer." She shakes her head, pushing out of my arms and backing away from me. I glance around. We're definitely being watched by just about everyone in the room, including my mother, who has her brows raised in silent question.

I grab Stevie's wrist, tugging her off the dance floor to go somewhere more private where this conversation is better had. The moment we're alone, she yanks free of my grasp, her arms coming up to cover her chest. Her shoulders are hunched, and she looks sad…broken.

I hate it, and I hate even more that I caused it.

"I'm not that girl. You can't just expect me to do…*that* and be okay. That's not who I am."

"I know that." I take a tentative step toward her.

She moves away. "Really? Because you just left."

"I know," I say, moving closer again. She retreats once more. "But—"

"No buts, Greer. I—"

"Goddammit, Stevie, I couldn't stay!"

Her eyes widen at my outburst, but they quickly fall to slits. "Really? That's your big excuse? You *couldn't stay*? Why not?"

"Because if I had stayed, I wouldn't have been able to control myself." I prowl toward her.

She takes one step back for every step I take forward until she hits a wall. She's trapped. She has nowhere to go. I lean down until my eyes are boring into hers.

"I would have fucked you, Stevie, and you weren't ready for that."

Her eyes are wider than I've ever seen them as she blinks up at me in surprise.

"I couldn't stay. It's been a long time for you, and you deserved better than what I could have given you last night. You deserve what I want to give you tonight."

"To…night?"

I nod. "I got us a room here."

"You did?"

"Yes, and I plan to make very, very good use of it and the time we have together."

She swallows. "Oh."

I reach out, running the pad of my thumb along her cheek. "I'm sorry I just left. I should have said something. I should have…" I shake my head. "I'm not good with this stuff, Stevie. I don't do *this*. I don't…"

"Have fun?"

My brows wrinkle at her words. It's what we said at

the rink yesterday, and just like then, it feels wrong. It's not the word I want to use to describe this thing between us, but it's all I have.

"Yeah."

"Oh," she says again. "Okay."

"Okay?"

She nods. "Okay. I'm sorry I got upset. That was stupid, I just—"

"No. Don't apologize. I'm the dick—you were right to be upset. I should have explained things better, but I didn't, and I'm sorry for that. I'm just… I'm not used to having to explain myself to someone. I'm not used to… well, caring about the person I'm with."

The truth is, last night, seeing Stevie on her knees for me…it awakened something inside of me. I don't know what, but something just felt different. I've been in the same position before with a beautiful woman on her knees, but none of it felt familiar.

It was special. *She* was special. I knew if we were going to go any further, I had to make it something she was going to remember.

When that hit me, I knew I had to leave. I had to make this something better. So, I made arrangements for tonight and planned out all the things I want to do to her…if she'll let me, of course.

"I liked last Greer. Before you left, I liked it. I… I was okay with what was happening. It was special enough."

"It was?"

"Yes. It *really* was."

I roll my tongue across the bottom of my lip, taking that in. "Do you want to go back to the wedding?"

She shakes her head. "No."

"Do you want to go home?"

"No."

"Then what?"

She lifts her eyes, her long lashes casting shadows across her cheeks. Her tongue darts out to wet her lips, and she sucks in a breath. Lets out a deep exhale.

"I'd like to see that room now, please."

CHAPTER 16

Greer's eyes flash with heat at my words.

Words I can't even believe I've just spoken, not after last night. I'm still upset with him, but I also understand. I'd literally just told him it had been years since I'd had sex, and the last person I'd been with had abused me. He wanted to make it special for me, and I can't really fault him for that.

Besides, up until the moment he left, I liked it. I *wanted* it. And if we had kept going, I would have liked that too.

I like that he didn't treat me gently, like I was some hurt and broken woman. I felt good. I felt strong. And I knew that if I ever wanted to stop, he would have in a heartbeat.

He reaches into his suit pocket and produces a key card, holding it my way. "It's the suite on the top floor. Go."

"By myself?"

"Yes. I have to explain to my mother that I'm leaving."

Oh god. I hadn't even thought of that. "What are you going to tell her?"

"That you have a headache, and I'm taking you upstairs to lie down. I'll be up in five minutes."

I nod, taking the card. I notice then that my hands are shaking.

I'm nervous. I don't know why I'm nervous. It's Greer, and I trust him. But I suppose that doesn't erase the fact that I haven't had sex in nearly a decade, and it feels like I'm doing this for the first time all over again.

I suck in a steadying breath, then slip past Greer. I'm a few steps away when he calls my name.

"Yes?" I turn to look at him.

"I want you naked on your knees waiting for me."

I gulp, then race toward the elevators. My knees shake as I press the button for the top floor, holding the card up to the talking machine when it yells at me that I need a key card for access.

Holy shit, holy shit, holy shit.

I'm doing this.

I am having sex with Greer.

If last night is anything to go off of, I'm having hot, rough sex with Greer—and I cannot fucking wait.

The elevator feels like it takes days to reach the top floor, but when it does, it spits me out into a small hall with a door at the end. It's a big door. A dark door. A foreboding door. A door that, once I open it, I can't close.

Am I ready for this?

Yes.

I slide the key into the slot and push into the room. It's dim inside, the lights turned down, casting a soft, hazy glow. Soft music plays from a speaker somewhere, creating a more romantic atmosphere. There's an ice bucket sitting on the coffee table. Inside is a bottle of champagne—probably something expensive—and two glasses sit off to the side. There's a tray of chocolates that I can't resist. I pop one into my mouth and grin when I realize it's my favorite—caramel.

I resist the urge to grab another, knowing I must be running out of time. I check my phone.

Two minutes.

I let out a squeak. *Oh god, oh god, oh god.*

I try to stay focused and not fixate on how hard my hands shake as I reach behind me and pull at the zipper of my dress. I do my best to regulate my breathing as I let the material slide down my legs, and when I unclasp my bra and slip off my underwear, I ignore how my knees knock together. I fold my clothes and gently lay them on the chaise lounge, then toe off the last item I'm wearing—my heels.

I can't believe I'm doing this. There's no way I'm doing this. I'm Stevie Thomas, divorcée and mother of a ten-year-old. I'm not the hook-up-with-a-hot-hockey-player kind of girl, and I'm really not the kinky-sex kind of girl.

But none of that matters when my knees hit the floor and I hear the elevator chime.

This is it.

The door to the room clicks open with a soft *snick*. Greer's dress shoes bounce off the floor in the entryway with sharp clacks.

Then, he's there. He's standing before me, his green eyes taking me in as I stare up at him.

I'm wet, like embarrassingly so, but I can't help it. There's something so hot about the way he's looking at me, like he's proud of me. I want to make him proud.

"You're beautiful," he mutters, walking deeper into the room. He strips off his jacket, setting it on the back of a chair, then tugs at the collar of his shirt. He undoes the top two buttons, then moves to the sleeves, unbuttoning them and shoving them up his forearms.

I don't think he's ever looked better than he does at this moment.

He stalks toward me, his hands going to his belt. This feels familiar, yet I'm eagerly anticipating it like it's the first time.

"Take my cock out, Stevie."

Like last night, I undo his buckle and shove his pants and boxer briefs down his legs. His cock springs free, and I reach for it, the desire to have my mouth full of him strong. I might have felt awful last night after he left, but it doesn't erase how good it felt in the moment. My mouth waters just thinking about it again.

"No," he says, stopping my efforts. "Open."

I slacken my jaw, and he sets his cock just inside my mouth. The weight of him is heavy, and I love it. A bit of pre-cum leaks onto my tongue, and it takes everything in me not to react and lick at him.

"I'm going to come down your throat like I did before. After, I'm going to bury my face between your legs until you're screaming my name, but you won't come —not until I say you can. Then, when I've had my fill of you, I'm going to fuck you. Only then can you come. Understand?"

I nod.

"Good girl." He reaches out with two fingers, running them along my jaw. "Now, relax."

Slowly, he slides his cock into my mouth, dragging it back and forth against my tongue inch by tedious inch. He takes his time teasing and toying with me. I hate it and love it all the same.

By the time his cock reaches the back of my throat, my jaw is tired and my knees are killing me, but I don't care. Having him inside of me like this feels like coming home.

"So good," he mutters, watching as I swallow around his cock. "Are you ready?"

I nod.

And he lets go.

Just like last night, he fucks into me without one iota of gentleness, and just like last night, I'm in heaven. He's using me again, but I know the score this time, and I welcome it. I squeeze my thighs together as he has his way with my mouth, and he doesn't miss it.

"You want to touch yourself, don't you?" he asks as I

can barely breathe around him. There's no way my mascara isn't running down my cheeks, no way my eyeshadow isn't a wreck, but I don't care.

He's right, though. My pussy is throbbing, and I want to touch myself badly right now. I've never felt an ache like this before.

"Do it," he instructs, reading my mind. "Touch your cunt."

My hand goes between my legs, and I sigh in relief the second my fingers brush over my clit. He must feel the same because not seconds later, he's emptying himself down my throat.

Unlike last night, I'm unable to keep it all in this time, and some dribbles out. Greer reaches down and swipes the mess away, shoving his cum-soaked thumb into my mouth, silently instructing me to suck it off.

I do so with glee.

"So proud of you," he mutters, and a wave of pleasure washes through me at his praise.

Then I'm being hauled to my feet. My legs are numb from kneeling for so long, but it's not a problem for Greer. He drags me to the chaise lounge, swiping the clothes I carefully folded and laid there onto the floor. He sets me on the seat, and this time, it's him who drops to his knees.

He's still wearing his dress clothes, which I don't think is fair, but I can't complain, especially when he puts his hands on my legs and pushes my thighs open.

There's no preamble, no teasing like before. He's

there in an instant, his tongue on my pussy as he licks and sucks at me like a starved man.

I don't dare close my eyes, not wanting to miss a moment. Not like he'd let me anyway. I remember the rule.

He sucks my clit into his mouth, and I've never been so close to an orgasm so fast. I groan, torn between wanting to come so badly and wanting to please him at the same time. My legs shake as I try to hold it off, and Greer laughs.

He *laughs*.

He eases his ministrations, and my impending orgasm fades, but Greer isn't satisfied with that. He eats at me, bringing me to the brink again, then backs off. He does it two more times until I can feel sweat sliding down my back, and my legs shake around his head as I try to stave off the wave that so desperately wants to hit me.

"Do you want me to stop?" he asks, eyes glistening like he's the one getting off on this.

I want to nod, but it somehow comes out as a headshake. There's no way I can keep going. If his tongue touches me again, I'm a goner, but I don't want to stop. I don't want to disappoint him. I want to be good for him.

He lets out another dark chuckle, then kisses his way up my body, paying extra attention to the marks on my stomach, and he takes a turn kissing each of my breasts before planting his lips over mine. I should probably be grossed out, kissing him after he just spent so much time between my legs, but I'm not. I like the way I taste on his lips.

He kisses my mouth, then my nose, my cheek, all the way to my ear, where he makes the sweetest promise I've ever heard.

"I'm going to fuck you now, Stevie."

A whimper claws its way out of my throat.

"Do you want that?" He pulls back, running a finger over my cheek as he stares into my eyes. "Do you want to see how well you take my cock?"

I nod.

"Say it."

I slide my tongue over my lips. "Please, Greer. I want your cock."

"Such a good girl," he murmurs. Then he shoves away, holding his hand out to me. "Come."

I let him pull me up, then steer me toward the bedroom, his hands running over my body the entire time. He spins me around when I reach the bed, capturing my mouth with his and kissing me hard enough to leave a bruise.

I'm out of breath when he finally relents, giving me a gentle shove onto the mattress. I fall backward, watching as he unbuttons his dress shirt, then peels it off his shoulders. He removes his undershirt, his belt. He shoves his pants and boxer briefs down his legs, kicking them off somewhere to the side.

Finally, he's naked before me, and holy hell is it a sight worth waiting for. He's lean but full of muscles. His shoulders are broad, his abs defined, his thighs rock solid.

He's beautiful.

He laughs. "Thank you."

"Oh shit, I said that out loud, didn't I?"

"You did."

I blush, and he doesn't miss it.

"Don't be embarrassed, Stevie. I work hard for my body. I'm glad you enjoy it. I enjoy yours too." He sets a knee on the bed, his hand wrapping around my ankle as he drags his eyes over me. "You're gorgeous."

"Stop," I mutter, starting to feel shy, which is ridiculous considering everything else tonight.

"I mean it. You're stunning, and I want to worship your body properly if you'll let me."

"Oh yeah?"

A sinister smile tugs at his lips. "Not tonight, though. Tonight, I'm going to fuck you hard."

Without warning, he climbs into the bed, grabbing my legs and yanking me toward him. He fits himself between my thighs like it's right where he belongs.

He runs his nose along my neck, pressing kisses to my throat. "You smell incredible. Like caramel candies."

"I always have them in my purse. They're my favorite."

"They're my favorite now too."

He kisses my neck again, and I giggle, but it quickly turns into a sigh when I feel his cock press against the part of me that hasn't seen action in far too long. He feels foreign and familiar all at once, sliding along my pussy, teasing at my entrance.

"I need..."

"What, Stevie? What do you need?"

I grab his face, pulling it to mine. I look him right in the eyes and say, "Fuck me, Greer. *Please.*"

He doesn't waste a moment, slamming himself home. I let out a loud yelp, the sting of not being fucked for so long making it hurt, but the pain is gone in seconds, replaced by nothing but pleasure as Greer rocks into me.

"Fucking hell," he curses as he buries himself until he has nothing left to give. "You're..." He huffs out a labored breath. "Incredible. You feel fucking incredible."

I feel incredible? *He* feels incredible. I don't think anything could ever get better than this moment.

Slowly, he rocks into me, and I lied—*this* moment is better. His cock drags along every right spot, and I can already feel myself getting close to the orgasm that's been just out of reach all night.

"More," I tell him.

He growls out his approval, and before I know it, I'm flipped onto my stomach and dragged to my knees, where Greer pounds into me again at the same time his hand comes down on my ass. It stings, but I welcome it. He swats at me again, and I'm almost embarrassed by the moan that escapes me.

"My handprint looks good on you. Maybe one day, you'll let me spank you properly."

Goose bumps rise on my skin at the thought of Greer bending me over his knee and paddling my ass.

One hand kneading the red mark he's just made and the other fisting my hair in a tight hold that borders on painful, Greer folds himself over, rutting into me as he kisses the back of my neck. His mouth is such a sharp contrast to what his hands and his cock are doing, and I like them all equally.

"Whose pussy is this, Stevie?"

A shiver races down my spine at his words. "Yours."

"Whose?" he growls into my ear again.

"Yours!"

"That's right. Mine, mine, mine." Each word is enunciated with a hard thrust as his hand moves from my hair to my throat. He presses lightly just on either side of my esophagus, testing the waters, but I'm good. I trust him. I trust *this*.

He doesn't relent as he pounds into me so hard there's no way I'm not going to feel this tomorrow. I'm glad because I *want* to feel it tomorrow. I want to feel this always. I want this moment seared into my brain, into my body. I want to be ruined by him…if I'm not already.

I squeeze my eyes tightly together as he fucks into me, my orgasm so, so close but just out of reach.

That's when I feel it. Something warm slides down my back and into my ass. It's his spit; I know it is. Something hot and heavy presses against the hole that hasn't been explored before, and Greer's thrusts slow when he realizes I've tensed up.

"Relax," he says softly, and I do. "That's my girl," he murmurs as he presses his thumb into me, massaging my throat at the same time.

It's uncomfortable at first, but I don't hate it. I feel him spit again, his thumb pushing in deeper.

"God, I can't wait to fuck you here," he says, the pace of his movements picking up. "Your ass is going to stretch around my cock so beautifully."

I moan at the thought. It's not something I've ever wanted before, but with Greer, it sounds like paradise.

"Oh, you like that, huh?" I nod. "Next time, I'll come prepared, and this ass is going to be mine."

"Yours," I echo.

"Do you want to come?" he asks, still sliding his thumb in and out of my ass with his thrusts.

"Please," I beg, my body literally shaking with the need for a release.

"Put your hand on your pussy, beautiful, and come for me like the good little girl you are."

I slip my fingers between my legs, and it takes all of two touches to my clit before I fall over the edge. Wave after wave hits me, each one enunciated by Greer's thrusts.

"So perfect," he groans. "So…fucking…perfect."

He stills, emptying himself into me, and at that moment I realize what just happened.

We didn't use a condom.

"Fuck," he murmurs like he's just realized too. "Stevie, I—"

I shake my head. "It's okay. I'm on birth control."

"I get tested every month," he says.

"I trust you."

He sighs, holding on to my hips as he slips out of me. I can feel him leaking out between my thighs as he turns me over, and I relish the mess we've made.

Greer slides off the bed, and I hear him pad out of the bedroom as I lie there, trying to catch my breath. I'm exhausted. I think the last time I felt this worn out was when I was lying in the hospital bed after I gave birth to Macie.

I jump at the sudden intrusion between my legs.

"Sorry," he mutters, dragging a wet washcloth over me, cleaning away everything we just did.

He tosses it aside, then climbs into the bed next to me, tugging me to him until I'm practically on top of him. His heartbeat is erratic under my ear, thumping away in record time, and it's the sweetest melody I've ever heard, lulling me into slumber.

"Sleep, Stevie," he whispers, brushing a kiss to my forehead. "Sleep."

It's the most restful night I've had in ages.

CHAPTER 17

I'm alone when I wake up. I know it before I even reach over to find the spot beside me empty and cold.

Did I dream last night?

I roll over, and the ache in my body tells me there's no way it was a dream.

I slept with Stevie. Not only did I sleep with her, it was the best sex I've ever had in my life.

There's a clatter from somewhere in the room, and then I hear the shower kick on.

She's still here.

I don't know why I'm so relieved by that. If this were any other person on any other night, it would be me who'd snuck out.

I toss the sheet off me, climb out of bed, and make my way to the bathroom. The door is cracked, and I peek inside. Thank God for glass shower doors because it gives me the perfect view as Stevie stands under the spray of water, her head tossed back as it cascades over her body.

Fuck me, she's so gorgeous. I don't know how I've stayed away as long as I have, especially now, knowing how well her body responds to me.

I was scared she would tell me to get lost when I told her I wanted her on her knees for me, scared she would tell me to screw off when I denied her orgasm after orgasm. I thought for certain she'd run when I said I wanted to spank her with something other than my hand or she'd bolt when I said I wanted to fuck her ass, but she did none of those things. She welcomed them all.

I push on the door, and her eyes spring open.

"Greer." She says my name softly like a prayer.

I pad deeper into the bathroom, lifting the toilet seat.

"What are you doing?"

I peek at her over my shoulder. "Taking a leak."

"I'm showering."

"I can see that. I'm taking a leak."

"But I'm showering."

"And I'm still taking a damn leak."

"You can't be in here," she argues. "I'm showering!"

I sigh, finishing up, then shutting the lid and flushing.

"I had my tongue in your pussy last night, Stevie," I tell her as I wash my hands. "You rode my cock like a fucking cowgirl rides a bull at the rodeo. I'm pretty sure seeing you in the shower isn't a big deal."

Her cheeks flush. "That was…different."

I cross my arms over my chest, then lean against the doorjamb. "Was it?"

She nods. "Yes. That was…in the heat of the moment."

"Hmm."

"Ugh!" She groans. "Why did I sleep with you?"

"I didn't hear you complaining about it last night. Actually, it sounded a lot like praise. No, wait—that was me doing all the praising and you coming from my words alone."

"I hate you."

I smirk. "Liar."

"I was drunk."

"You were stone-cold sober."

"It was a late-night mistake, like eating a pint of ice cream at midnight."

"Pretty sure that was much more satisfying than a pint of ice cream."

She glowers at me. "Hate. You."

I shove off the wall and stalk toward her, ready to punish her for her words.

"What are you doing?" she squeaks as I pull the shower door open.

"Getting annoyed with how long you're taking because I have practice."

"In like two hours!" she tosses back as I close the door.

"True. But I also have plans for you."

"Greer, I—"

Her weak protests are silenced when I slant my mouth over hers, crowding her against the wall as the water splashes against my back. Our tongues tangle together so long the water begins to turn cold, but I don't care, and it doesn't seem like Stevie does either.

Not when she wraps her legs around my waist, and certainly not when I slide my cock inside of her.

Not when I slowly thrust into her, and not when I draw circles over her clit, making her fall apart around me, only for me to follow shortly after.

I kiss her through her aftershocks, not wanting to let this moment go so quickly. It's different than last night. Softer. Slower. Yet, it's still somehow just as good.

"Better than ice cream?" I ask when I finally drag my mouth from hers.

"Y-Yes." She shivers. "Sorry," she says through chattering teeth. "I'm cold."

I reach over, shutting off the water, then I carry her out of the shower. I don't bother to grab either of us towels—I'm taking her right back to bed.

"You didn't even shower."

"I rinsed off," I tell her, pulling the blanket up over us. Her eyes are already drifting closed.

"Practice," she mutters.

"I know."

"Macie."

"I'll make sure she's fine," I promise.

She slips back into sleep, and I sit there watching her for a while. It's long enough for my phone to buzz against the nightstand, telling me I need to get up and head out for practice.

Trying my damnedest not to wake her, I ease out of the bed and pull on the clothes I packed for today. I also grab the spare toothbrush and toothpaste I brought, along with the clothes for Stevie. I wasn't sure if she would want to stay the night, but I came prepared just in case.

She doesn't move a muscle the entire time I walk around the room, getting ready to leave. I glance at the clock. I don't want to leave her, but I really need to go.

I grab a pen off the dresser, scribble a note, then press a kiss to her forehead and slip out the door. I pull my phone up to my ear as soon as I'm in the elevator, tugging my overnight bag higher up my shoulder.

"What's up?"

"Tell Coach I'm going to be a few minutes late."

"No shit?" Miller says on the other end of the line. "You're never late to practice."

"Yeah, well, it's a slow start this morning."

"He's not going to like it."

"I know. But tell him."

"All right, I will."

"Thanks."

"Sure."

I'm about to hang up when I remember. "Miller!"

"Hmm?"

"How's Macie?"

He pauses, then I hear him laugh. "She's good, Dad. We had a great time last night."

"I'm not…" I pinch my nose, shaking my head. "Whatever. Just tell Coach. Bye, Miller."

He cackles as I end the call.

"Fucker," I mutter to nobody.

I'm not the kid's dad, and I'm not trying to act like it, either. I'm just doing a favor for Stevie, checking on her kid. I don't care if she's okay or not.

Okay, fine, I do care—but so what? We've bonded since I've been training her. That's all it is. Nothing else.

I keep telling myself this as the doors slide open to the hotel lobby. I make my way to the front counter, letting them know they can add another day to my card and that my guest will leave whenever she's ready.

"Of course, Mr. Greer. Anything you need," the clerk says. "Can we help with your bags?"

"No. Just bring my car around, please."

"Right away, sir." The employee disappears into the back room.

I hike my bag higher up on my shoulder, then head for the front door to wait outside.

"Jacob!"

I come to a halt just as I'm about to walk through.

"Did you really think you could just sneak away this morning without saying goodbye to your mother?"

"Sorry, Mom," I mutter, turning around to find her hustling through the lobby. She's wearing head-to-toe velvet in the form of a jogging suit. I'd bet a hundred bucks the back of her jacket says *Bride* and poor David—

who is wearing a matching outfit—has *Groom* on the back of his.

He's a better man than me because there's no way in hell I would ever be caught dead wearing something like that, not even for Stevie.

Whoa. Where did that come from? I'm looking at the new bride and groom, and I automatically think of Stevie.

I shake away the thoughts. I'm just tired from last night and then waking up early. That has to be it.

"How's Stevie feeling?" My mother comes to a stop in front of me as David tries to catch up. She's short, but man, can she walk fast. I'm sure the four bags her husband has slung over his shoulders aren't doing him any favors in the speed department, though. "I hope her headache is better."

"She's feeling much better."

"Oh good. I really liked her, you know. I wish I could have spent more time with her, but the little that I did, she was lovely. She feels like an old friend or something."

"She was just my date, Mom."

The words taste sour as they fall out of my mouth, mostly because they don't feel true.

"Maybe, but a mom can hope for more, you know."

"Sure." I give her a tight smile. "Wait—don't you two need to get to the airport for your flight?"

"You mean the flight you booked for the trip you bought me?" Her eyes narrow. "That's too much to spend on me, Jacob. You've already done enough."

"I could spend a million dollars on you, and it still wouldn't even touch how much I love you."

She sighs, patting my cheek. "Oh, Jacob. One day you're going to make someone very happy with the sweet words that come out of your mouth."

Stevie's face flashes in my mind, her expression when I told her I wanted to worship her coming front and center.

Fuck. Why am I thinking about her again?

"We'd better get going," my mom says, pulling me back to the present. "I'm sure security is going to be a pain."

"I have practice to get to anyway." I press a kiss to my mother's cheek. "Have fun on your trip. Don't do anything too wild, and keep your hands off the Irish men."

"With that accent? There's no way. I'll have my fifth husband picked out before we leave."

"Mom…"

She swats at me. "I'm kidding. I have David now, and I'm madly in love with him."

"Good. I'm happy for you, you know."

She grins. "I'm happy for me too."

"I love you."

"But never as much as I love you."

I give her one last kiss, then wave goodbye to David and head outside just as the valet brings my ZR1 around. I slide behind the wheel and gun it to try to make it to practice on time.

I only think about Stevie for nine and a half of the ten minutes it takes me to get there.

I'm not sure I remember the last time I was so eager for practice to be over.

I love being on the ice. Playing hockey means everything to me. Practice is one of my favorite things because it means I get to work on getting better at the game, and I always want to get better. I want to be the best, and you do that by practicing.

But today…today I want to be done with this so fucking badly.

"Optional skate tomorrow morning, boys. Wright and Fitz, Doc wants to see you," Coach says before skating off the ice.

Finally, it's over. We're dismissed.

I skate off in a hustle.

"Damn, dude. What's the rush?" Hayes asks, catching up to me down the tunnel.

"No rush," I say.

It's a lie, though. I'm always the last to leave the ice, but not today.

"Uh-huh. Clearly."

I ignore the rookie, making my way to the dressing room, already stripping my gear off.

"How was your mom's wedding?" Lowell asks. "Good?"

"Yep. She's all married and off to Ireland on her honeymoon."

"Ireland for a honeymoon? With those accents?" Miller shakes his head. "Her husband is a brave man."

I agree, but not for the reason he's referring to.

I pull off my gear as fast as I can without making it seem like I'm rushing. The last thing I want is more questions thrown my way. I grab a quick shower, then scoop up my bag and race to my car.

If anyone notices me hustling away, they don't say anything. I'm grateful too because all I want is to get to Stevie. I want to talk to her and see how she feels after everything.

When I pull into the parking lot of Scout's Sweets, it's packed. There's a line of at least ten people, and I can see Stevie bustling back and forth inside with Rosie. Macie's sitting at one of the picnic tables, her head in a book like usual.

I'm not sure how long I sit there watching them like a creeper, but I really don't want to get out when there are still so many people showing up. Maybe it was a bad idea to come here. Maybe I should just leave.

I'm set on driving away when there's a knock at my window.

"What the—"

I look up to see a toothless, grinning Fitz. He waves, and I shove the door open. He barely jumps out of the way.

"What."

It's not really a question. I'm annoyed he's bothering me. I'm more annoyed, though, that he caught me sitting here like a weirdo.

"Why are you just sitting in your car?"

I gesture toward the chaotic line. "Do you want to deal with that shit?"

He shrugs. "It's not so bad. I've seen worse."

I huff. I forgot he's a people person and perfectly fine with standing in line and being bothered by fans.

I'm not really in the mood for it, but he already has me out of my car, so I might as well. I pop the door back open and pull out a ball cap, tugging it down low, hoping and praying it'll help keep people away.

"Greer!"

Well, there goes that plan.

"Hey, kid," I say to Macie, taking a seat at the table with her as Fitz plops down beside me. "Whatcha reading there?"

She holds up the book. "*This Team Is Ruining My Life (But I Love Them)* by Steve 'Dangle' Glynn. This is how I feel about the Comets, by the way."

Fitz snickers. "Noted."

I'm used to her shit-talking, so I ignore her. "You have a good time with Scout this weekend?"

"I did. Miller let me paint his toenails."

Fitz grimaces. "You touched Miller's feet? Ew."

Macie laughs. "I did, but I made them prettier." She looks at me. "Mom said you guys had fun at the wedding. Did you dance with her? She loves to dance. I assume you did because she smiled so much when she picked me up from Aunt Scout's."

I like the idea that it was me who made Stevie smile so much.

"We danced," I tell Macie, but my eyes are somewhere else.

Stevie's staring at me from the donut truck, a sly grin tugging at her lips. Is it possible she got even prettier in the few hours we've been apart?

"I'm going to grab a coffee," I announce to the table, rising to my feet and heading for the truck.

"I'll take one, too," Fitz calls after me.

I lift my hand in acknowledgment, continuing my prowl. I bypass the line, not caring about the few people who call out their protest. I don't stop until I'm on the side of the truck. Then, I wait.

I watch as Stevie bustles around, slinging coffee and donuts with a smile on her face. Every minute or two, her eyes slide to me, and that same knowing grin curves her lips. When just a few people are left in the line, she reaches behind her back and undoes her apron.

"I'm taking my ten, Rosie."

The baker bounces her brows a few times. "Have fun."

Stevie takes a glance at Macie, who is deep in a paper football competition with Fitz, then meets me at the end of the truck.

"Hi," she says softly…shyly.

I grab her hand and haul her around back, pushing her back against the bright blue metal and boxing her in.

"Hi." I grin down at her. "How's your day so far?"

"You know, it's not too bad. I woke up kind of early, took a shower, then crawled back in bed and went to sleep in a big comfy hotel bed, where I wasn't bothered by anyone for the next two hours. It was nice."

"Nice, huh?"

She grins. "I'd say more than nice." She pushes up on her toes and presses a soft kiss to my lips. "I'd go as far as to say it was spectacular."

"Spectacular, huh? That must have been some shower."

She giggles, and I love how flirty she is right now. I wish more than anything we were alone so I could slide my hands under her ass and haul her into my arms and then carry her to one of those picnic tables and eat her for lunch.

But unfortunately, we're not. We're surrounded by people, including her kid.

"Soo..." she starts, dragging out the word. "Last night."

"Spectacular?"

She nods. "And then some. I... It might have been the best *fun* I've ever had."

The word twists around in my gut, leaving a sour feeling that I don't like.

"It was the best I've had too."

"Really? I wasn't…rusty? It's been a minute, you know."

I drop my lips to her ear. "I'd say based on the way you swallowed my cum, there was nothing rusty about you."

When I pull back, her cheeks are bright red.

"You can't say things like that to me right now, Greer. It's not fair."

Fair? She wants to talk fair? I'm the one standing here with my cock pressed against my zipper.

I crowd against her, letting her feel what just being near her is doing to me.

"So you mean I can't tell you how I was just fantasizing about tossing you onto a table and spreading your legs to take a look at that pretty pink cunt of yours?" She lets out a soft gasp, her eyes sparking with fire at my words. "How, if we were alone, I would bury my cock inside of you for hours? How I so, so badly want to run my tongue over every inch of your body until you're begging for me to stop, just so I can start all over again? We can't talk about any of that?"

Her lips part, breaths coming in sharp as she stares up at me like she's debating taking me up on everything I just said.

"You're mean."

I laugh. "Oh, baby. You haven't seen me be mean yet."

I capture her lips with mine, kissing her hard and fast because I know we could get interrupted at any moment, and I don't want to waste another second not touching her.

"Mom?"

Stevie shoves at my chest, wrenching her mouth from mine and sliding out from under my arms. She tugs at her shirt, pulling it down, then runs a hand through her hair just as Macie rounds the corner.

"There you are," she says, barely casting a glance my way. "Rosie said she's out of half-and-half and needs you to go grab some."

"Yeah," Stevie says, rushing toward her daughter. "I can do that." She doesn't spare me a backward glance as she disappears into the truck.

Macie, on the other hand, can't take her eyes off me. They're shrewd like she knows I was just kissing her mom, but if she suspects anything, she doesn't say.

All she asks is, "When's our next practice?"

I've never been so relieved to talk about hockey before.

"I'm not sure, kid. We have a road trip."

"I know, but I was hoping we could practice at least once before then."

"I might not have time. I'm sorry."

She nods. "It's okay. Maybe we can do an extra practice or something when you get back? I can finally wear *all* the gear this time."

I chuckle because she's been on my case about wearing all the goalie gear for the last week. "Sounds like a plan."

"Macie!" Stevie calls out, rounding the back of the truck. "I'm heading to the store. Are you staying or going?" Her eyes slide my way when she says this, and I know it's a question for me too.

"I can stay here with Greer," the kid says.

"I'm sure he has plenty of other things to do today."

"I don't," I say, even though it's a lie. I have shit to get done at home and stuff to set up so my cleaners can stop by while I'm gone, but I don't tell them that. "She can stay with me."

Stevie's brows rise. "Are you sure?"

I nod. "I'm sure. Come on, Macie. Let's go see how many straws Fitz can fit in his missing tooth hole."

"Yes!" Macie pumps her arms up and down, racing around the front of the truck.

I follow behind her, stopping next to Stevie, who is looking at me in surprise.

"What?" I ask.

She shakes her head. "Nothing." Then, after a quick look around, she rises up and presses a quick kiss to my lips. "I'll be right back."

I stand there grinning like an idiot as she walks away, wishing like hell she'd come back.

"Greer, come on! He already has two in there!" Macie calls. "You're missing it!"

I laugh. "Coming!"

Guess I'm spending my day here.

CHAPTER 18

Greer: You know, I always thought Miller was the worst guy to sit next to on a plane, but I'm really starting to think it's Lowell.

Stevie: Why is that?

Greer: I've seen no less than fifty pictures of his kid today. FIFTY!

Greer: I swear every photo looked the exact same too. The kid was wearing spaghetti sauce as a beard in all of them.

Stevie: It's a parent thing. Totally normal.

. . .

Greer: Right, but why do *I* have to be subjected to this torture?

Stevie: Because he's proud of his baby.

Greer: Babies—gross.

Stevie: You really do hate kids, huh?

Greer: No. I like Macie just fine, but other kids? No, thanks.

Stevie: I take it that means you don't want any of your own?

Stevie: Not that I'm asking you to get me pregnant or anything. I mean, we've only had sex twice.

Greer: Once is all it takes from what I hear.

. . .

Stevie: That's true.

Stevie: But I'm not. Just so we're clear.

Greer: Chill. I know what you were asking.

Greer: Honestly, I've never seen myself being a parent. I just don't think it's for me.

Greer: Do you want more kids?

Stevie: Sometimes, but sometimes not, too. Maybe if I meet the right person, I will.

Stevie: Greer?

Stevie: I guess you fell asleep after the long flight.

Stevie: Sweet dreams, Greer.

Stevie: That last save was incredible!

Greer: I should have never had to make it. That was a sloppy play on our end.

Stevie: That's what Macie said, but it doesn't make it any less amazing.

Stevie: You disappeared yesterday. Is everything okay?

Greer: Yeah, sorry. I got busy.

Stevie: Oh.

Stevie: Well, that was a great game.

Greer: Thanks.

Greer: Steve?

. . .

Stevie: Yes?

Greer: I wasn't busy. I just didn't like the idea of you with someone else.

Stevie: SHE GOT THE LEAD ROLE!

Greer: Huh?

Stevie: Macie! She got the lead role in the spring fundraiser play that's in April.

Stevie: I mean, it's not a real play, just a little musical the kids put on to raise money for a class trip at the end of the year, but there are a few talking scenes, and Macie's the lead character.

Greer: Well, damn. Good for her.

Stevie: I'm so proud of her.

. . .

Stevie: She says it'll be good to practice her public speaking for her aftergame interviews. I can't believe how much she's grown. It's hard to think I was just nineteen when I found out I was pregnant with her.

Greer: Is that how old you were when you got married?

Stevie: Yes. We eloped when I was five months pregnant "for the right reasons."

Stevie: I regretted it almost instantly.

Greer: How long were you married?

Stevie: Two years too many.

Greer: What was his name again?

Stevie: Ha-ha. Nice try.

. . .

Greer: Dammit.

Stevie: You can't play hockey from prison, you know.

Greer: There must be one prison out there with a hockey team.

Stevie: Yes, because they're going to give murderers sharp weapons.

Greer: Good point.

Greer: It'd be worth it, though. Not playing, I mean.

Stevie: It was a long time ago.

Greer: Doesn't make me want to kill him any less.

Stevie: I'm deleting these texts, just in case.

. . .

Greer: Good call because I will find out his name one day.

Stevie: I promise to bring you plenty of cigarettes when I visit.

Greer: Good girl.

Greer: Be honest…did you just clench your thighs together?

Stevie: Go to bed, Greer.

Greer: Fine, fine.

Greer: But I'm taking that as a yes.

Stevie: Noted.

Greer: When I tell you I'm ready for this road trip to be over…

Stevie: I'm sorry you guys lost. It sucks.

Greer: It does.

Greer: I wish I were there.

Stevie: Me too.

Greer: Yeah? How badly?

Stevie: So, so badly. Macie misses you.

Greer: Just Macie, huh?

Stevie: Yeah. Definitely nobody else.

. . .

Greer: Not you?

Stevie: Nah. I'm a strong independent woman.

Greer: I know you are. It's badass.

Stevie: That so?

Greer: A total turn-on.

Greer: Well, if I'm being honest, just about everything about you turns me on.

Stevie: Everything?

Greer: Yep.

Stevie: What if I told you I shave my toes?

. . .

Greer: What are you, a hobbit?

Stevie: Yes, you got me. I'm a tiny little woodland creature.

Greer: Hobbits aren't woodland creatures. They live in the sides of hills in the beautiful Shire, not in the woods.

Stevie: Sorry, sorry. I didn't mean to get your nerd terminology wrong.

Greer: It's not nerdy. It's a classic.

Stevie: Right. Sure. Whatever you need to tell yourself.

Greer: I tell myself it's a classic because it is.

Stevie: Mmhmm.

Greer: Just wait until I get home, Steve. You'll pay for this.

. . .

Stevie: In kisses?

Greer: In spankings.

Stevie: Promises, promises.

CHAPTER 19

I haven't seen Greer in over a week, and it's slowly driving me insane.

Not just because Macie won't stop asking when he's going to be able to practice with her next, but because I lied before—I do miss him.

A lot.

Probably a lot more than I should, if I'm being honest. We've spent so much time together between Macie's lessons and him stopping by the truck over the last month that it's strange having him gone.

And maybe I'd like a repeat of our time at the hotel too. I swear I can still feel his hands around my throat and the weight of him between my legs. There was no way that night was ever going to be enough.

"Whatcha daydreaming about over there?" Rosie asks as she rolls out some dough.

"Huh? I'm not daydreaming."

"No? Then why did you mix the red sprinkles with the black ones?"

"I didn't. I—shit!" I quickly stop pouring, trying to catch as many as I can before any more red ones fall into the black bin. "I'm sorry."

She shrugs. "No biggie. We'll use them anyway. We can make donut holes with them or something. They'll be our oopsie batch."

I know it's fine, but it's still frustrating. I've been helping in the truck since Scout set this place up, but it's not my favorite thing. Scout and Rosie are the ones who belong in the kitchen, not me. This isn't what I'm meant to do.

Granted, working at the law firm wasn't what I wanted to do either, but it was better than this. This I'm just a mess at, a point proven by my mixing the sprinkles.

"It's Greer, isn't it?"

"What's Greer?" I ask, closing the lid on the red sprinkles so I don't accidentally knock them over or something—which I've already done twice since I started working here full-time. After the law firm let me go, I begged Scout for more hours, and she was happy to give them to me. I'm not sure I want to stay here long-term, but it's better than nothing in the meantime.

"That's who you're daydreaming about, isn't it?"

My face feels like it's on fire as I stop screwing the lid on and slowly look over at Rosie. "I have no idea what you're talking about."

She grins. "Liar."

"It's not a lie," I lie, focusing back on the sprinkles. "I was just—"

"Daydreaming about Greer and all that hot sex you two had at the wedding?"

I whirl around, my mouth ajar. "How did you know about that?"

"Well, I didn't officially until now." She winks. "But I know an *I just got laid* look when I see one, and you definitely had that look the morning after the wedding."

"I… We… Oh, screw it. We had sex."

"Ha!" She points at me. "I knew it!" She sets aside the dough she's working on making into cinnamon sugar twisted donuts and gives me her full attention. "Tell me everything."

So, I do.

Well, not everything. I leave out the kinky stuff, but I share enough for her to get the picture.

"So you're saying he's as hot in bed as you'd expect?"

I nod. "So hot."

"Ahh!" She claps her hands together, bouncing on her heels. "I'm so happy for you! And totally jealous, by the way. I could really go for some steamy hot sex with a hockey god." She fans herself, no doubt thinking about Fitz, who she's been crushing on since he was traded from Vancouver.

"Do you think everyone else knows?" I ask, worrying my lip.

"You mean, do I think your sister knows? No, probably not. She's not been around much lately, plugging away on her book, so she hasn't seen you two together. But the moment she does, I'm sure she'll pick up on it." Rosie's mouth twists. "Why haven't you told her?"

I lift a shoulder. "I'm not sure. I haven't told anybody. Maybe because it's just something casual and fun. I don't need to get anyone else mixed up in it, you know?"

She nods slowly, but it's that kind of nod people do when they have something to say but don't want to say it for fear of pissing you off. I should ask Rosie what she's thinking, but I don't because I don't want to be pissed off. I want to keep this good mood I have going.

Greer comes home tonight, meaning I should see him tomorrow. That's all I want to focus on right now.

My phone buzzes against the table, and I glance over to look at the screen. *Hmm.* I slip my gloves off, then hit the green button, bringing the phone to my ear.

"Hello?"

"Stevie!" Bianca's loud voice rings over the line. "How are you?"

"I'm doing well, Bianca. How are you?"

I haven't talked to her since the night at the bar, not only because I've been busy but because she hasn't called. You'd think when someone leaves so suddenly like I did, the people you were out with would call to check up, but not one of them did. It really cemented the fact that even though we may have something in common like our kids going to the same school, we aren't going to be friends anytime soon.

"Oh, you know, the usual—running around like a chicken with my head cut off, taxiing the kids around."

She laughs loudly; it sounds so fake and forced it makes me feel sick. "I'm calling to run something by you. Do you have a moment?"

I look out at the empty lot. We should have a good half hour before there's any sort of midday pickup.

"Sure. What's going on?"

"Well, you know how the kids are doing the fundraiser thing, right?"

"Of course. Macie has the lead speaking role."

"Oh. That's lovely." It doesn't sound like she thinks it's lovely at all. "Okay, I was wondering if, since you know all those guys, you could get some of the Comets to come?"

"Oh, um, I'm not—"

"I heard about you showing up at school with Greer. All the kids are still talking about it, and I think he would be a great pick. He could really bring a lot of the parents out, and maybe they'll spend some more money."

I hadn't realized Greer showing up there was still such a hot topic. Sure, the kids were buzzing about it for a few days after—hell, even Macie couldn't stop talking about it—but that was weeks ago. Surely there's something else for them to talk about by now, not to mention I really don't feel comfortable asking Greer for favors like that. He's already done so much for Macie and me. I can't ask him for more.

"Bianca, I—"

"This fundraiser is just so important. It's for the kids, you know?"

Ugh. She just had to throw that in my face, didn't she?

I mean, there's no harm in asking, right? For the kids and all.

"I can ask him."

"Oh, wonderful! That's so great."

"I'm not sure he'll say yes."

"Nonsense. I'm sure he'd love to help the children too."

I roll my eyes because she really doesn't know Greer at all.

"Well, listen, I have to run. Thanks for getting this done. Us busy moms on the PTA really appreciate it."

I try not to react to the subtle dig about me not joining any school activities and force cheeriness into my voice. "Sure thing."

"Toodles!"

The line goes dead, and I make a promise to myself to ignore her calls in the future.

"Everything okay?" Rosie asks when I let out a long sigh and rub at my temples.

"Yep. Just parental politics."

She crinkles her nose. "Hard pass on that."

I laugh. "You're telling me." I point behind her. "Can you pass me that pink icing?"

She hands it over, and I turn away, pulling on new gloves and getting to work on refilling the piping bag she'll need in a bit. We work in silence for a bit, me refilling the decorating station and her twisting dough together. After probably thirty minutes, she's the one to break the silence.

"For what it's worth, I think you and Greer being together is good. He's a different guy with you, a better guy. You could be really amazing for each other."

I've tried hard not to think about us together because we said it was fun and that was it.

But if I really let myself think about it…I believe she could be right.

I've spent two hours trying to fall asleep, but it's just not happening. I tried reading, I tried watching TV. Hell, I even did all the yoga poses I know. I mean, sure, it was only two, but it should have helped, right?

Either way, nothing is working. I'm wide awake, and I think I know why.

Greer's home. He's back. Right here in North Carolina, and he's just a few miles away.

I want to see him so badly, but I can't. I have to wait until tomorrow…or maybe even the next day, I don't know. We haven't made any plans, something that's killing me too, not that I'd admit that to him or anything. It's just—

Ting!

What the hell?

I stop moving around in bed and hold my breath, waiting to see if any other noises pop up.

Nothing. Must have been a neighbor or the old pipes in the building making a noise.

I punch at my pillow for the twentieth time tonight, then flop back onto the mattress. I close my eyes and try to convince myself this is the time I'm actually going to fall asleep.

Ting!

My eyes fly open. It's the same noise as before, that same high-pitched *ting*.

I sit up, listening closely. Is Macie awake? That's not likely—the kid sleeps like the dead.

I wait. Nothing.

Ting!

I look to my right.

The window.

I crawl out of bed and tiptoe my way over to it, my heart hammering in my chest. We're up on the third floor, so there's no way there's someone there, but that doesn't mean I'm not scared to look.

Ting!

I let out a loud yelp, slamming my hand over my mouth.

"Fuck!" It's one word, but it's enough for me to recognize the deep timbre.

I yank open the curtain and look down, my heart hammering in my chest for a totally different reason.

Greer.

I scramble to the bedside table and grab my phone,

going to my recent calls and swiping on his name. It barely rings before I hear him pick up.

"Did I scare you?" he whispers, though I don't know why. He's the one outside throwing rocks at windows. It's not like he's trying to be quiet.

"Yes. What are you doing?"

"Throwing rocks at your window."

"I know that, but why?"

"Because."

"Because why?"

"Because I'm home."

"You're home."

He clears his throat. "Can I come up? I can't sleep."

"I'll meet you at the door."

"I was going to knock, but I didn't want to wake Macie. That's why I didn't call either. I wasn't sure if you had your volume on. I know she has school tomorrow."

"That kid could sleep through a hurricane," I tell him as I make my way out of my bedroom toward the front door. "In fact, she has before."

"Impressive." I can hear him climbing the stairs.

"That she is." I look through the hole in the door, watching and waiting for him to appear. "So, how many times did you hit the wrong window?"

"Twice. Did you know your neighbor sleeps naked? He manscapes, you know. Like *completely* manscapes."

"That is way more than I ever wanted to know about Mr. Henry."

"It's more than *I* wanted to know about him too."

I laugh, but it's cut short when I see him striding down the hall. I pull the door open, not caring that I'm wearing my nightgown and there could be anyone else out here prowling about.

Greer stops about fifty feet away, his eyes raking over my body, narrowing only slightly when he sees what I'm wearing.

"You're practically naked."

"I am not. I have a nightgown on."

"A silky, slinky, pink nightgown. I can see your nipples from here."

"It's cold out."

"Or you're glad to see me."

"It's cold out," I argue, though we both know it's pointless. It's him, and we both know it.

The point is proven even more when my whole body starts to hum as he takes me in from head to toe. I lose my breath just from the way he's looking at me, like I'm something to eat and he hasn't been fed in days.

"What are you doing?" I ask, my chest heaving.

"Trying to decide if I should rip your gown off or be a gentleman."

"Well, considering I paid good money for this, I vote the latter."

"But the former is so much more fun."

I squeeze my thighs together at the thought of him literally ripping my dress from my body. He doesn't miss it.

"Tell me something, Steve…"

"Yes?"

"Did you miss me?"

So much. So damn much it almost hurts. Much more than I'm ready to admit, and more than he's ready to hear, I'm sure.

So I don't say anything at all. I just nod.

"Say it," he instructs.

"I missed you, Greer."

Even from here, I can see the way his eyes darken at my words, and before I know it, he's closed the distance between us, and his mouth is on mine. He crashes his hands through my hair as he tips my head, kissing me roughly like he'll never get enough. I have no idea what happened to my phone or to his; all I know is how good it feels to be back in his arms, and it's really, really fucking good.

I'm not sure how long we stand there kissing, but it's well past appropriate. When he finally drags his lips from mine, they feel swollen, and I miss him all over again.

"Hi," he whispers against my mouth.

"Hi."

"Can I come in?"

"Yes."

He pushes the door shut behind him, his hand still on my waist. That's where it stays as he steers me through the apartment like he's been here a thousand times before. He doesn't stop until we're tucked away in my bedroom, the door softly closing behind us.

"How'd you know which bedroom is mine?" I ask as he strips his suit jacket off.

I didn't notice at first that he's still wearing his fancy clothes. That must mean he came straight here from the plane.

I like that he came straight from the plane.

"Well, one door is closed, and the other says *Macie's Room, Keep Out or Else* on it, so I took a shot in the dark."

I laugh. "Good detective skills."

"I'm a regular ol' Sherlock."

He sets his jacket on the small chair I have at my vanity, then peruses the room.

I try to see the space through his eyes, but all I come up with is messiness. Aside from the yoga mat in the middle of the floor, I have a pile of clothes I need to fold sitting in a basket in the corner, and three pairs of shoes sit in front of the closet instead of inside it. There are photos of Macie and me up on my dresser and a few of my favorite drawings she's done taped to my mirror.

Other than that, there's not much. It's plain and small and nothing special at all.

"This is exactly what I pictured your room would look like."

"Really?" I ask. "This tiny?"

"This *cozy*."

"There's that word again."

"What? My place is cold and barely lived in. This feels like someone actually sleeps here."

"Someone does actually sleep here."

His eyes fall to the yoga mat, and I laugh.

"All right, fine. You caught me. I couldn't sleep, so I was trying some yoga."

"How'd that go?"

"Well, I fell on my face twice and am still awake."

"Twice, huh?" He stalks toward me.

"Uh-huh."

"Did you hurt yourself?" He rakes his eyes over me again. "Anything I should check out?"

I roll my lips together, tucking away the smile that's threatening. "Maybe."

"Show me."

I'm not sure what's come over me, no clue where the real Stevie has gone. The real me, the one who is just a single mom who works tirelessly to make a good home for her daughter? Well, she'd never stand in front of a man with hungry eyes, pull her nightgown up, and point to her pussy.

"Here."

His eyes slide to the place between my legs. "Is that so?"

"Yes. I think…I think it needs a kiss."

"Hmm," he says. "I think I have a remedy for that."

"You do?"

He nods. "But you're going to have to be very, very quiet. Can you be a good girl and do that?"

I trap my bottom lip between my teeth and nod.

"Good. On the bed."

I do as I'm told, and he follows behind me, grabbing

my hips and flipping me around when I move too slowly for him. I let out a loud yelp, and he slaps his hand over my mouth.

"Shh! You said you'd be quiet. No noise, got it?" I bob my head up and down. "Good."

He slowly pulls his hand away, replacing it with his lips. He kisses me senseless until I'm writhing beneath him, begging for any kind of friction I can get.

He laughs darkly. "Someone's eager."

"I told you—I missed you."

"You missed my cock," he comments, kissing his way down my neck and over my chest. He sucks a hard nipple into his mouth through my silk gown, and I sigh with relief. He does the same to my other breast before making his way down my stomach, and he doesn't stop until he's shoving my dress up higher and pressing kisses to my mound. He rubs his nose against me, inhaling me with a growl.

It shouldn't be hot. I shouldn't be turned on by this. But I am.

"God, I fucking missed this pussy. Did this pussy miss me too?"

I nod, afraid to make a noise.

"You can answer me, Stevie."

"Yes," I whisper. "Yes."

He hums his approval, the vibrations rocking through me. "I'm going to lick your cunt now. I'm going to eat at you until you're squeezing my tongue, and you're not going to make a single noise. Do you understand?"

I nod again.

"Good."

Then, he makes good on his word.

He drives his tongue into my already wet pussy, licking and sucking at me like he's never going to get enough. He spreads my legs open, wrapping my thighs around his head like they're his favorite accessory, and plunges his tongue inside of me. I nearly let out a scream as he sucks my clit into his mouth, but I bite down on my lip just in time.

It's hard to keep quiet, especially when it feels so good, but I do. In fact, I don't make a single peep as my orgasm races through me, letting my shudders and shaking legs speak for themselves.

When the last of my aftershocks shoot through me, Greer gives me one last lick before pressing a soft kiss to my clit and sitting up on his knees as I work to catch my breath. His face is shiny with my release, his hair a mess from my hands running through it, and somehow, he still looks incredible.

"You good?" he asks, the cockiness leaking out of every word.

I nod, and he laughs.

He crawls over me, pressing his lips to mine in a brief kiss. "You did so good."

I melt at his words and reach for the buckle on his pants, but he grabs my hands, stopping me. I look up at him, brows furrowed.

"Not tonight."

My bottom lip juts out. "But…"

"Trust me, that was as good as any orgasm you could give me."

"Are you sure?"

"I'm sure." He presses a kiss to my head. "Bathroom?"

I point toward the dresser. "Other side of the hall."

He climbs off the bed, then disappears out of the room. I fix my dress while he's gone, brushing my hands through my hair.

When he returns, he clicks the bedroom light off. The moon shines in through the sheer curtains, and I watch as he pulls off his shirt and pants, folding them nicely and setting them on the chair along with his jacket. He grabs his phone, hitting a few buttons on the screen before he pads across the room and pulls the blanket back, sliding in next to me.

He opens his arms, inviting me to curl up next to him, and I accept the invitation. I rest my head on his chest, letting my fingers dance through his smattering of chest hair. I let them run over his abs and down, down, down, right to the waistband of his underwear.

He grabs my hand, stopping me.

"No."

"But…"

"Sleep."

I sigh, only a little upset I can't reciprocate. "Yes, sir."

The sting comes out of nowhere, his hand landing hard against my ass.

“Don’t tease, Stevie. Sleep.” He kisses my head. “Good night.”

“Night, Jacob.”

For the first time tonight, I have no problem falling asleep.

CHAPTER 20

"I hear you're training a kid," Hayes says, dropping into the stall next to me. It's not even his usual place, but he doesn't seem to care.

"Yep," I answer, stripping off my water-soaked jersey.

Practice was brutal today. Coach Heller had us running drills for nearly an hour after our loss last night. He wants us to be back to where we were, no fuckups, so we can go back on the road with a win under our belt.

"How's that going?"

"Well, she's upright on the ice, so I guess good."

"Goalie, right?" he asks.

"Yeah, but she seems interested in all the positions, so it might not stick."

Hayes nods, removing his own gear. "It's the donut truck girl, yeah?"

"What?"

"The kid you're training—she belongs to the donut truck girl, right?"

"Stevie."

"That's the kid?"

I shake my head. "No, that's the mom. Macie is the kid."

"Right." Hayes nods again. "Same one from the bar, yeah?"

My eyes narrow as I grow agitated with his line of questioning. "Yes."

"Hmm."

I stop removing my gear and sit up, staring over at him. It takes him a second to realize I'm looking his way.

"What?" he asks, but I see the fucker's lip twitch.

"Don't *what* me. Why the fuck are you asking?"

"I'm just curious."

"Why?"

"Huh?"

I clench my jaw. "Why are you asking?"

"You've just been spending a lot of time with her is all."

"Because I'm helping her kid."

"Right, and you helped her, didn't you? That night, I mean."

That's right; he was there. I didn't think he was paying attention, but I guess I was wrong.

"Yes. She went to my mother's wedding with me."

His reddish brows shoot up. "Hmm."

It's his second *hmm* of the conversation, and I'm officially fed up.

"Just fucking say whatever it is you're going to say."

He holds his hands up. "Nothing, man. Just interesting."

"How so?"

"Well, for starters, you hate people and kids."

"Ugh." I groan. "I don't fucking hate kids. Why does everyone say that?"

"Because you literally ran away when Lowell tried to hand you his, and that's the cutest damn baby I've ever laid my eyes on."

"She was crying. I don't do crying babies."

"She was not crying. She was being her usual cute self."

"Yeah, with snot running out of her nose." I shudder. "No-fucking-thanks."

The other guys start piling into the room, some of them stripping out of their own gear, a few just sitting there trying to catch their breath.

"What are we talking about?" Miller asks, running a towel across the back of his neck.

"Greer's training some kid."

"No shit?" Rhodes asks, his own brows raised.

"You hate kids," Lowell chimes in. "You literally ran away from mine. Really rude considering Freddie is the cutest child I've ever seen."

"See?" Hayes says, bumping his shoulder against mine.

I shove him away, and he laughs.

"Who are you training?" our captain asks.

"Scout's niece," Miller answers. "She's ten and loves hockey. I'm her favorite player." He grins proudly.

"Pretty sure after I let her sit behind the wheel of my ZR1 *and* I'm giving her free hockey lessons, I'm her favorite," I tell him, elated to burst his bubble.

He flips me off, and I pretend to catch it, kiss it, and send it right back to him.

"So everything's all good after her fall?" Wright asks.

"Wait—you knew about this and didn't tell me?" Rhodes looks at his fellow defenseman like he just kicked his puppy or something.

"I'm sorry. I didn't know you'd care. I—wait, Rhodes, hang on." Wright pushes off the bench, chasing after his best friend like he's a boyfriend who just got in trouble.

Everyone laughs, shaking their heads at them, totally used to the best friends and their dramatics.

"Don't you have, like, no spare time at all?" Lowell asks, going into full captain mode. "I mean, we're in a good spot right now and the post-season starts soon, but this is the time we need to be most focused."

"I have it covered."

"You sure?"

I sigh. "Yes, Dad. I'm good. It won't affect my game."

He nods. "Good. We don't need any distractions this year."

"You have two distractions at home—that kid and your woman. Am I not allowed to have anyone?"

He tips his head. "Is that what they are to you? Your woman and your kid?"

"Can we not call them women? Seems a bit misogynist," Fitz mutters.

"Scout loves it when I call her woman," Miller comments, a goofy grin on his face.

"Greer?"

"What?" I bite out.

"Is that what they are to you?" Hayes asks thoughtfully.

"No. But even if they were, who cares?"

This raises a few brows in the room, and I don't miss it.

It's annoying. It's none of their business if I'm spending time with Stevie and Macie. They all have their own lives too. I can have mine. Besides, they aren't interfering with my game, and that's all that matters, right? I'm still playing and still winning. Who cares that I'm having fun in my free time?

My stomach cramps, and I rub at it, trying to get rid of the sudden pain.

"They're nobody to me," I declare, pushing the ache aside. "Just a friend and her kid. That's it."

"Hmm."

This from Fitz this time.

I flip him off, just about as annoyed with him as I am with Hayes and all his stupid questions. He just shrugs it off.

"They mean nothing," I insist, but the statement isn't as strong as it should be.

This time, nobody says a thing, and I get the feeling

they don't believe me either.

If you'd told me a month ago I'd be willingly going to some fundraiser at a school, I'd have laughed in your face.

It's true what everyone says—I don't really like kids. Most of the time, they're loud and obnoxious and drive me insane. But when Stevie asked if I'd consider stopping by to help them raise money for their yearly field trip, I couldn't say no.

So, here I am, at a damn school surrounded by snot-nosed little shits.

The truth is, though, I don't entirely hate it. In fact, they're kind of…cute. They're all full of questions, and their eyes are wide with wonder.

We're standing in the middle of the hallway as parents and teachers mill around, looking at all the tables spread out, each littered with baskets and other things up for auction. The kids will sing some songs and tell us facts about the overnight aquarium trip they want to take, and we're supposed to bid on everything afterward to raise money for the trip and the touch tank experience.

What nobody knows is I've already cut a check to the school to cover the entire thing, so any leftover money is going to a special experience where they get to feed a shark.

"Tell us about the time you made that save on Connor McDavid, Greer."

"I grabbed the puck out of the air."

"Wow!" three of them say in unison, and I've never felt cooler.

"That's so cool," says a little boy with oversized, Coke-bottle-lensed glasses. "I want to be just like you when I grow up."

"You can't—*I'm* going to be just like him when I grow up," Macie says, her chest all puffed out. "I'm going to be the next great goaltender for the Comets."

"You're a girl!" another boy says, his nose all scrunched up. "Girls can't play hockey!"

"Hey." I point a finger at the little shit. "Girls can play hockey all they want. I know some incredible female hockey players, actually. Hell, some are better goalies than me. So don't tell her she can't do something, got it?"

The kid nods frantically, his eyes wide with fear.

Someone pulls on my shirt, and I turn to find a little boy with an off-center tie staring up at me. He crooks a finger, and I bend down to hear him.

"You said *hell*," he whispers.

"Sorry," I whisper back. "I meant *heck*."

"I won't tell," he promises.

I do everything I can to nod solemnly and not laugh. "Thank you. I appreciate that." I push back up to my feet, tucking my hands into my pockets as the kids continue to lob questions at me.

"What's it like playing with the Beast? Is he really as mean as he looks?"

"Did you meet Sign Girl?"

"Are you friends with Fitzgerald?"

"Was it hard to move to the US from Canada?"

"Greer!"

The last voice is the one that sticks out to me the most, and I spin on my heel to see Stevie barreling down the hallway, an older man trailing not too far behind her.

"Hey," I say as she approaches.

She takes in the scene around me, all the kids staring up at me like a god, and she grins.

"Having fun?"

"Loads," I reply, but it doesn't have that same sarcasm it usually does. "Where have you been?"

Her phone rang about ten minutes ago, and she left me to fend for myself.

"Greer," she says, waving at the man behind her, "this is my father, Cliff. Dad, this is Jacob Greer."

Holy shit. Her dad is here.

I didn't know I'd be meeting him. I mean, sure, she's met my mother, but that was different. It was her wedding.

Stevie clears her throat, bringing me back to the moment, and I realize her father's holding his hand out to me.

"Sorry," I say, finally shaking it. "It's nice to meet you, Cliff."

His eyes narrow at the same time the grip he has on

my hand tightens. "I wasn't aware Stevie was seeing someone."

"Oh, no, Dad. We're not dating. He's just here to support Macie. He's been coaching her."

"That so?" her father says, and I can tell he doesn't believe a word she says about us not dating.

I'm not sure I believe it either because as much as I hate to admit it, what we're doing *is* starting to feel a lot like dating. I've been thinking about it frequently since the other day when the guys were giving me shit in the locker room. I *am* spending a lot of time with Stevie and Macie; practically every moment I'm not in the rink, I'm with them. We're either working on Macie's goaltending, always going to grab dinner afterward, or I'm finding excuses to stop by the donut truck—not to mention every night I've been home, I've snuck over to Stevie's place in the late evening after Macie's gone to bed. We text or video-chat every day when I'm away, and she's all I can think about whenever it comes time to go home.

We're still just labeling it as fun but…what if it's not anymore? What if this is something else? Something more? Something…real?

I give myself a shake, bringing my attention back to the man who is still looking at me with uncertain eyes. I'm sure he's wondering why his daughter is lying to him for my sake. I know if the roles were reversed and my daughter told me she wasn't dating someone when that didn't seem to be the case, I'd have many questions, such as *Why are you stringing my kid along? Is she not good enough for you to settle down with? Are you using her?*

I'd bet a thousand bucks that's what's going through his mind right now. That same sour feeling from before settles into my stomach, but I swallow it down because now isn't the time to deal with it.

"Your granddaughter is doing great," I tell the gray-haired man, forcing a smile. "She's a natural out on the ice. I'm sure with some more training after she gets a few games under her belt, she'll be starting goalie in no time."

For the first time since he walked over here, he grins. "That's good. I'm glad to hear it. My late husband would be thrilled. He loved hockey." He peers down at his daughter with sad eyes. "I'm bummed he can't see her on the ice."

"Me too, Dad." Stevie pats his shoulder. "We should probably get in there and grab our seats. The play is going to be starting soon." She looks at the kids. "Kids, go on in. I'm sure your teachers are wondering where the hell you are."

She shoos them away, and they disappear reluctantly, all of them looking back at me, some even waving.

"We should head in too. After you, Dad."

Stevie lets her father lead us into the small auditorium, and we follow closely behind him.

"You know…" I rest my hand on the small of her back, dropping my lips near her ear. "You can't say *hell* in front of the kids."

"Is that so?" she asks as we take our seats.

"Yep. You see that one with the crooked tie?" I point to the stage where the kids are lining up on platforms, and she nods. "I got in trouble with him earlier."

She tucks her lips together, stifling a laugh. "He yelled at you?"

"Nah. Just gave me a stern talking-to. I was shaking in my boots."

She giggles, and I love the sound of it. It's quickly become my favorite thing she does.

A few people turn to look at us; the lights are dimmed and the show is clearly about to start. I don't care, though. I could watch her laugh all day long.

"Shh!" I tell her. "The show's starting."

She mimics zipping her lips and throwing away the key, but they're still pulled into a grin.

Out of the corner of my eye, I catch her father staring at me over her head. He looks between me and Stevie, a slow grin curling his lips. Oh, he's definitely not buying the *just friends* line she fed him.

And I'm not sure I'm buying it anymore, either.

"You did great, kid!" Stevie says, wrapping her daughter in a hug and pressing a loud, smacking kiss to her cheek after the show.

"Ew, gross, Mom!" She wriggles out of her mom's hold and wipes off the kiss. "Don't embarrass me."

"You let me kiss you every night before bed."

"Mom!" Her eyes widen. "Oh my gosh! Not in front of…" Macie slides her eyes my way.

I shrug. "My mom still kisses me."

"Really?"

I nod. "Yep, and I let her because one day she's not going to be here anymore, and I'll want those embarrassing kisses more than anything."

"Oh." Macie looks up at her mom. "All right, you can kiss me—but not when you're wearing that gross lipstick that I swear I am never wearing."

I chuckle, knowing there have been many times in my life I've walked around with a lipstick stain on my cheek, all thanks to my mother.

"Can we go? I'm hungry."

"Of course," Stevie says. "Do you want to grab McDonald's on the way home?"

"What? No! It's Thursday. It's mac and cheese night!"

"Mac and cheese night?" I ask.

"Every Thursday," Macie says. "And *I* make it."

"Yeah? I love mac and cheese."

"You should come. Mom, can Greer come for dinner? Grandpa too?"

"Of course I'll come," Cliff says, smiling down at his granddaughter. He looks at me. "Greer?"

I glance over at Stevie, unsure if she wants me to intrude on her evening with her family, but she doesn't seem to be giving any indication that she wants me to say no.

"Sure. Why not?"

Stevie grabs Macie's shoulders. "Come on. Let's get going."

We get stopped a few times leaving the school, and I do my best to greet each kid with a smile but also hurry up because I know Macie is dying for food.

"Can I ride home with Greer?" she asks once we hit the parking lot. "I was the star of the show, so I should be able to ride in the cool car and not the lame minivan."

"It's an SUV!" Stevie argues, though Macie doesn't pay her any attention, already skipping toward my ZR1, which I'm glad I drove instead of the Viper.

"Damn." Cliff whistles. "That's a nice car. I love Corvettes."

"That's what Stevie said. Want a ride?"

"What? No! I already called dibs, Grandpa!" Macie yells.

Cliff laughs. "Maybe next time."

I follow behind Stevie and her father, ensuring I drive the speed limit and not a mile over with the precious cargo beside me.

"You did well tonight," I tell Macie when we pull into their apartment complex. "Even I got excited about going to the aquarium."

"Me too. I love animals. If I didn't already have plans to play hockey, I would do something with animals when I grow up, maybe be a marine biologist or something."

"I already knew I wanted to play hockey when I was

your age too, but I thought about becoming a veterinarian for a while."

"Do you have any animals?"

I shake my head. "No. Being away on the road makes it too hard since I don't have anyone to take care of them at my place."

"We can," she says. "My mom and me can stop by and take care of them for you."

She says it so innocently like she has no clue the weight her words carry, and I suppose she doesn't. She doesn't realize her words have knocked the breath out of my lungs just thinking about them in my apartment, images of them playing with puppies and opening presents on Christmas morning playing like a movie in my head.

And, to my complete surprise, it doesn't sound bad or scary at all.

"Mom and I," I correct as I shut off the engine. "We're here."

She's out of the car before I can even get the words out, racing for her mother.

"Geez, someone's excited for mac and cheese," Stevie comments as Macie races up the stairs, her grandpa right behind her. She sashays over to me, her hands tucked into her back pockets. "You really don't have to stay for dinner, you know. I'm sure you have a lot of other things going on."

"Do you want me to stay?"

She peers up at me, her bright blue eyes as gorgeous as ever. “I do.”

“Then I’ll stay, Stevie.”

She grins. “Good. Come on, then. We better get up there before she tries to put corn in the pasta again.”

“Corn?” I wrinkle my nose, following her up the stairs.

“Oh yeah. We get really wild in the Thomas house on Thursdays.”

“What the hell did I get myself into with you girls?”

Stevie looks at me over her shoulder. “Heck.” She winks, running just out of my reach before I can swat her ass.

“You’ll pay for that later,” I call out, trudging behind her.

“That’s the plan!”

I shake my head, following her inside.

What the hell *did* I get myself into?

CHAPTER 21

"Come on, come on! We're going to miss warmups!" Macie grabs my hand, pulling me from the team store toward the ice.

I let her drag me along, knowing full well we're doing fine on time, and she's just excited about another hockey game. We're using the last of Miller's tickets tonight, and since I'm not sure when we'll be able to come to another game, I made sure we stopped by the Comets store for a splurge. I really shouldn't be buying such expensive stuff right now with my job situation, but I couldn't help it. I'll deal with my credit card later.

We make our way to our incredible seats, flopping down into them. Well, I sit; Macie stands, her eyes wide as she looks out at the ice in wonder like she's seeing it for the first time. I hope she never loses this joy with hockey.

"Put your jersey on, Mom. They're about to come out of the tunnel."

"All right, all right." I dig into the Comets-branded bag and pull my new purchase free. It was entirely too expensive, but Macie insisted I buy it to represent her new favorite player.

And fine, I wanted it too. I want to show him I'm here for him just as much as I'm here for Macie.

"Come on! Let's go to the glass!"

She takes off down the aisle, and I pull the jersey over my head, following behind her. Just as we press our noses against the cool glass, the music swells and the guys come barreling onto the ice, the goalie leading the pack.

He skates around half the rink, doing a few laps and hitting pucks at the net on each pass. He stops in front of his bench and grabs hold of that familiar green bottle, squirting water into his mouth to spit it back out. He does it four times, then switches to another bottle to start all over. This must be one of his superstitions.

He takes two more laps before stopping in front of his bench again and dropping down on his knees. He kicks his feet out to the sides, moving them back and forth like he's a frog. He's just inches from his nether regions touching the ice, and I've never seen anyone so flexible in person before. The way he's able to move like that is insanity. He does this several times, jutting his feet up before dropping back down again, stretching out in ways that shouldn't be possible. It's oddly satisfying to watch.

"Crazy, right?"

I look over to find Wright's wife, Harper, standing beside me. Next to her are Ryan and her sister, Hollis, who is holding her daughter up to the glass so she can watch her dad skate around.

"I didn't know you were all going to be here tonight!" I squeeze my arms around Harper.

"Yeah, we decided last minute to come. Sometimes it's hard to get all of us here, and when our schedules aligned, we said screw it." She hugs me back, then pinches my jersey. "Nice threads."

My cheeks warm. "Thanks. Macie insisted."

"Uh-huh. I'm sure." Harper winks, and I know the red on my cheeks deepens. "Where's Scout?"

"She's on a deadline. No Emilia tonight either?"

"No. That brat is working like always," Hollis answers for her best friend. "Rude, if you ask me."

I laugh. I'm sure she has her hands full trying to keep the program's media running. Her boyfriend, Smith, used to play for the team, but now that he's retired, he works as a video coach. I'm sure he's around here somewhere too.

"I seriously don't know how he does that. It looks like it hurts."

I follow Ryan's eyes to Greer, who is now in front of the goal, stretching once again.

"I bet it comes in handy, though," Hollis comments, waggling her brows.

I don't say anything, smiling to myself with my little secret that it does come in handy.

The team fires pucks at Greer, and he blocks every shot that comes his way. He looks good out there, strong and steady.

"It's going to be a good night," Macie comments, her eyes not leaving him either. "He looks focused."

He really does, which is why I'm surprised when he shoves up from the ice and skates right over to us, coming up beside Lowell, who is making faces at his daughter and kissing the glass.

I can't see his mouth, but there's no mistaking the spark of joy in Greer's eyes as he looks at me. I smile at him, and his eyes dip down to my jersey. I spin around, showing him his number on the back. When I turn back, the look on his face is something entirely different than joy—it's lust. Pure, unfiltered lust. He likes the sight of me wearing the number 29, and dammit, I like wearing it.

He taps his stick against the glass three times, and I have no doubt it's his way of saying, *I can't wait to take that off you later.*

I clench my thighs together, thinking about what's in store for me. He leaves tonight for another short two-game road trip, and this will be the last time I get to see him before he goes. It's only four days, but I already know it's going to feel like a lifetime.

Greer looks down at Macie, then holds up a puck, and she nods enthusiastically. He tosses it over the glass for her, and she catches it, jumping up and down as he skates away.

"Wow. I've never seen Greer be nice to a kid before."

"Me either," Ryan says, echoing Harper.

"He literally ran away from Freddie," Hollis says,

holding her baby up. The chunky little kid looks so adorable with her headphones on and her dad's number on her shirt. "How can you run away from something so cute?"

I laugh. "You should have seen him at the school fundraiser. The kids were all over him, and he was eating up the attention."

"He went to a school fundraiser?" Harper asks. "*Greer?*"

"Yes. He even funded the entire trip they were trying to raise money for."

The girls all exchange a look, which I don't miss, but nobody says anything.

Rhodes and Wright skate over, each saying hi to their wife and tossing Macie a puck before skating off. Warmups come to a close, and Macie bounces back to her seat with three pucks in her hands and a huge grin on her face. We follow her, taking our seats and settling in for a hockey night.

"So," Harper says, and just the tone of her voice has me on edge. "Anyone else sad the guys are going on a road trip? I mean, it's short, but man, I'm going to miss Collin." She sighs longingly.

"I hate it when Adrian leaves." Ryan sticks her bottom lip out. "It makes that big house of ours feel extra empty, you know?"

"Oooh! We should do a girls' night, a big sleepover or something. All of us, plus Emilia and Scout. Macie can come too. It'll be fun," Hollis suggests.

"And Greer."

Everyone looks over at my daughter, whose focus is on the bag of goodies I got for her in the team store, not even realizing we're all staring at her.

"Greer?" Harper asks.

"Yep," Macie says. "He stays over at our place all the time. Maybe he can come to the slumber party too. He loves them."

My heart feels like it's about to burst out of my chest, and despite the cold coming off the ice, my face is hotter than it's ever been before.

"He never stays for breakfast, though, which makes me sad. My mom makes really good French toast, and I think he'd love it too if he stayed."

I can just *feel* the stares from the other ladies burning into the side of my head, but that's not where my attention is. It's on my daughter.

"Macie, how do you know Greer has been staying the night?"

Oh god. She hasn't heard us, has she? I haven't scarred my daughter for life, right?

"I just do."

"Macie."

She finally pulls her face out of the bag, looking up at me. "What?"

"How do you know Greer has been staying the night?"

"I just do." She lifts her shoulders. "I've seen his jacket by the door. One time his hat was on the counter.

And because you're *so* happy in the mornings. It's the same kind of happy you are after we spend time with him."

She says it so matter-of-fact like it's the most obvious answer in the world, like she's not blowing my mind right now.

"Was I not supposed to know?" she asks, her brows drawn tightly.

"No, you can know."

"Oh. Okay. Good, because I like him. I mean, I didn't at first because he was a jackass, but now he's not so bad."

I smile at her. "No, he's not bad at all."

She goes back to digging around in the bag, and I sit back in my seat, completely stunned. When did he leave his jacket by the door? When was his hat sitting out for her to see? And am I really happier with Greer around?

Yes.

I am happier with Greer, happier than I've ever been before, and it's not just the sex, either. It's *him*. Sure, he's grumpy sometimes, but he's also sweet. He loves his mother and treats her like a queen, and he does the same with Macie, even putting up with her weird mac and cheese nights.

And then there's the way he treats me—like I'm the only person in the room who matters.

I like him. A lot. And I like spending time with him.

"Well," Harper whispers, leaning over to me. "That was…something."

I give her a weak smile. "Yeah, it was."

"Are you two together?"

"Kind of? I mean…"

Her eyes light up. "Oh."

"Yeah. It's been…*amazing*."

"Eeeek!" She lets out a high-pitched sound. "That's… Oh, I am *so* happy for you. And him. It's about time he found someone."

"We're keeping it casual," I tell her as my eyes sling toward Hollis and Ryan, who are listening intently to our hushed conversation.

"That's what Collin and I said too, but look at us now." She flashes her wedding ring. "We're far from casual."

"Yeah, but Greer doesn't believe in love."

Harper snorts out a laugh. "Oh, honey, I didn't either. But when you find the right person, weird things happen."

"Yes, they truly do," Ryan chimes in, and I know for a fact she's speaking from experience after marrying Rhodes on a drunken night in Vegas and then staying married to him.

"Trust me," Hollis says, "sometimes things don't happen the way you plan, but they turn out really amazing anyway." She presses a kiss to her daughter's head, the daughter she wasn't planning to have, especially not with Lowell, but did anyway.

"If it's meant to be, it'll work out." Harper squeezes my hand.

I give her a small smile just as the lights dim, and the announcer begins to read the starting lineup. I turn my attention to the ice, but it's a fruitless effort. All I can think about is Greer.

Am I being foolish by playing this game with him?

He's been honest from the start about his disdain for love. He doesn't believe in it, and I'm not stupid enough to think *I'm* going to be the one to change his mind, not to mention I have a daughter, and he doesn't like kids. He might have been successful with them at the fundraiser, but that's entirely different from stepping into a parental role.

Am I insane to keep doing this, knowing I'm getting attached to him? Knowing Macie is getting attached too?

Yes.

I swallow at the truth behind that answer. It's dangerous, completely reckless, for Macie and for me. I should be protecting her from the inevitable heartbreak that will come when Greer decides we're too much for him.

"Look!" Macie calls, pointing toward the ice. "There he is!"

Greer skates out, pointing his goal stick right at us. A few heads turn our way, and I try not to die under their curious stares.

The puck is dropped, and the game is underway. The first period is mostly uneventful, neither team scoring, but there is a lot of pushing and shoving around the net, and even Greer gets involved in it. Macie goes with Ryan for snacks during intermission and comes back with her arms loaded down with pretzels, nachos, and a slushie.

"Ryan!" I hiss at her.

"What?" She shrugs, her gorgeous blonde curls bouncing with the movement. "It's a special night."

I shake my head, laughing at how easily Ryan was duped into buying Macie everything that caught her eye.

The second period starts off with a bang—literally. Rhodes bounces the puck off the crossbar, the sound echoing around the arena.

"BEASSSST!" Macie shouts in a deep voice, making everyone around us laugh.

I tug her back into her chair by her jersey.

"You're having entirely too much fun," I tell her, booping her nose.

A collective gasp spreads through the crowd, and people jump to their feet, their hands over their mouths as a hushed quiet falls over the arena.

"What's going on?" I mutter, rising.

Macie gasps, pointing at the ice. "Mom! He's hurt!"

She's up on her tiptoes, trying to see around the people standing in front of us. It's the same thing I'm doing, and I'm struggling just as much as she is.

"Who? Who is hurt?"

"Greer!"

The moment she says his name, the crowd in front of us parts, and I see him crumpled on the ice, not moving. Everything in my body is on high alert as I watch him lying there, a player from the other team on top of him.

The player is dragged away by Rhodes, who hauls him to his feet and slams him against the boards. The two of them start fighting and everyone goes nuts around us, but I'm not paying any attention to that. All I can focus on is Greer, who is still down.

Miller helps a trainer to the ice, skating him to the net to attend to Greer. He drops to his knees, talking to the unmoving goaltender. I see Greer nod then the trainer frowns.

Rhodes and the other player get pulled apart, and Wright skates over to tap his defense partner on the head as he heads to the penalty box. Lowell is out there too, helping lift Greer out of the net. Miller grabs him on the other side, and they get him to his feet. Everyone cheers, glad to see him making it off mostly of his own accord. He disappears down the tunnel, and my heart is still sitting in my throat as I fall back into my seat.

"Is he okay, Mom?"

"I don't know."

"But he got up. That means he has to be okay, right?"

"I don't know, Macie."

I want to reassure her, want to tell her everything is going to be all right and Greer is just going off for protocol and will be back to the bench soon, but I don't.

I can't take my eyes off the tunnel he went down. He's back there, hurt and probably scared. I wish I were with him.

"You can be," Harper says.

"Huh?" I ask her.

"You can go back there. I've done it before with Collin. Come on. I'll take you." She grabs my hand, pulling me from my seat.

"Mom!" Macie calls after me.

"I'll be right back," I tell her.

Ryan grabs her shoulder. "Greer's tough as nails. He's going to be just fine. Let's watch the game."

Macie's worried eyes follow me as I trail behind Harper up the stairs, but she eventually turns her attention back to the ice.

Harper leads me through the arena, only stopping when she steps up to some very official-looking people. She whispers something to them, and they nod.

"Of course," the older woman says. "Right this way, Mrs. Wright."

We're escorted through a door and handed off to another arena worker, then led through a few different hallways. I have no clue where we are, but I can tell we're going deeper into the building because it's getting quieter the farther we go.

We stop in front of a door, and I already know it's where Greer is. I can feel it.

"I'll wait out here," Harper says, a soft hand on my back pushing me toward the room.

I take a calming breath, then shove the door open.

"Excuse me, we're—"

"It's fine, Doc."

He dips his head. "I'll give you two a moment."

My eyes snap to Greer, and I nearly break at the sight

of him. He looks so defeated sitting under the bright lights.

I rush toward him, throwing my arms around him. He winces the moment I touch his right shoulder.

"Sorry," I murmur, stepping back. "Are you okay?"

"No."

His voice is gruff. Stern.

"What…" I swallow the lump in my throat, then run my tongue over my lips. "What happened?"

His jaw is set tightly, and I hear the bed creak as he tightens his grip on the edge of the table. "That fucker barreled over me."

"I—"

A couple of different instruments go flying across the room. It happens so fast I don't even realize it's Greer who threw them until I look back at him, his nostrils flaring and his breathing heavy. I've seen this crazed look before, and I think I hate it even more now than I did then.

"He just fucking mowed me over, didn't even try to pull up and go another way. Ran right fucking into me."

His voice grows louder with each word, his chest heaving, his usually bright green eyes turning darker by the second.

"Why would he—"

"Because he's a fucking idiot!" Greer yells, and I flinch at the outburst. He's so deep in his anger that I don't think he sees it. "My fucking shoulder had to be reset, and I'm out at least two weeks. Two fucking weeks!"

He punctuates each word with a gnash of his teeth. He's upset, and I get why, but it doesn't make it any easier to see him like this—so out of control with his emotions, so angry. It's hard to watch because it reminds me so much of everything I left behind all those years ago.

"Why are you back here?" he barks.

I hate that he's even asking me that question like I don't have a right to know he's okay after everything between us. It feels like a knife to my gut because all it does is solidify that this thing between us really does mean nothing.

I'm just the girl he's screwing, and that's it.

I blink away the tears threatening and clear my throat. "I wanted to make sure you were okay. Macie was—"

"I'm not okay," he interrupts, so much ire in his voice. "My goddamn shoulder is hurting like a motherfucker. I'm sitting in here with *you* and not out on the ice like I want to be."

I don't know what to say to him, not when he's like this, so I don't say anything at all. I just stand there, staring at him as he seethes at the ground, his shoulders rising and falling in rapid succession as he sucks in breath after breath.

I hate seeing him like this, not just because of my past but because I don't want him to be hurt. I don't want his season to be jeopardized, especially not when he's doing so well. He lives for hockey, and I want him to have that for a long time.

I stand there for a while, probably longer than I should, given how he's spoken to me since I walked in, but I can't seem to move. The doctor comes back into the room, pulling both of our attention.

"I need to check him out some more," he says, a clear dismissal of me.

"I'll leave."

"Wait."

I turn back to Greer, slowly lifting my eyes to his, afraid of what I'm going to see, afraid of what he's going to say.

"Stevie, I'm…"

He trails off, not saying any more, and I don't wait around for him to gather his words. I spin on my heel and breeze out the door, barely able to hold back the tears threatening to spill once I cross the threshold.

"Hey!" Harper calls out, racing to catch up to me as I speed-walk down the hall. "Is he okay?"

I nod. "He'll be fine."

"Hey…" She grabs my wrist, pulling me to a stop. "What's wrong?"

"It's his shoulder."

"No." She shakes her head. "I mean with you. Are you okay?"

It's such a simple question, one that shouldn't have

any effect on me, but it does. It's all it takes for the dam to break and the tears to tumble down my cheeks.

"Oh, Stevie," Harper hums, pulling me into her arms. "It's okay. It'll be okay."

"He didn't even want me there."

"Shh." She rubs my back. "He did. He's just upset. Give him time to cool down. It'll be okay."

For the first time in a while, it really doesn't feel like it might be okay.

CHAPTER 22

I fucked up.

I know I did. I knew it the moment she walked out of the doc's office. She was hurt, and I was the one who did the hurting.

I wasn't upset with her—*never* her, but I handled it like I was. I treated her like shit, just like her ex did. She didn't deserve it then, and she definitely doesn't deserve it now.

"Hey," Miller says, dropping into the spot next to me. "I heard the news. You good?"

I nod, even though I'm not good at all, not just because of the injury that still really pisses me off. I'm not good because I hurt Stevie. I need to make it right, but we're leaving for a road trip tonight because we have a game tomorrow. I don't have time to fix it.

The guys move around the locker room with sullen faces, and I can't say I blame them after we ended up losing. It's always rough to hit the road after a loss, and tonight it's even worse knowing I'm going to be out.

Sure, we're in a good place in the standings, but it's not just about that. It's about losing momentum and team spirit. This isn't just a blow for me. It's a blow for them too.

"If that fucking linesman didn't pull me off him, I swear I would have put his face through that glass," Rhodes promises. "Fucking shithead. He knew what he was doing."

I'm mad at the guy who ran me over, but sometimes a play just goes bad. I have to believe that's what happened tonight and it wasn't malicious. It's the only thing keeping me on this bench and not going after that dude.

Coach Heller bursts into the room, making eye contact with me first. His jaw tightens when he sees my shoulder in a sling. He's just as pissed about it as I am.

"Get showered," he says to the room. "We'll talk tomorrow morning."

Then he's gone again.

A few guys pat me on the head as they walk by, heading for the showers. Everyone moves around me, stripping off their gear and getting ready to hit the bus.

I take my own quick shower as best as I can, given the state of my shoulder, then put my bag in a pile with all the others before heading for the bus. I'm one of the first ones on, and I find my favorite seat at the back, drop down onto the cushion, and rest my head against the window while I wait for everyone else to arrive.

I don't need surgery, just rest. That's the best part

about this situation. The doc thinks I could be ready to go in as little as two weeks, but he doesn't want me to get my hopes up just in case.

It could be worse, I tell myself. *It could be during playoffs.*

I close my eyes, instantly hit with the memory of Stevie's expression when I threw the tools. She looked terrified, and I knew in the moment it was wrong, but I couldn't stop. The rage had taken over, and I was lost in it.

I need to fix it. I need to ensure she knows I'm an ass and I wasn't mad at her.

My phone buzzes against my leg, and I fish it out, hoping like hell it's Stevie so I can apologize, but my hopes are dashed when I look at the screen.

"Hello?"

"Hello? HELLO?! That's all I get?" My mother's shrill voice rings in my ear.

I sigh, going to rub at my temple, then remembering I can't. I'm trapped in the damn sling.

"Hey, Mom."

"Hey?!" My head throbs at her volume. "I swear, Jacob, I am going to whoop your ass."

"You'd beat up a broken man?"

She gasps. "Oh god—what's broken?"

"Well, technically nothing, but I am in a sling."

"Oh, honey." She sighs. "What's going on?"

"Shoulder."

"Surgery?"

"No."

"Time?"

"Two weeks minimum."

She exhales slowly. "Thank god. It could have been…"

"So much worse, I know."

She's quiet for a moment, probably needing a second to come to terms with the fact that I've been injured yet again in my career and she had to see it on television.

My teammates start piling onto the bus, a few of them nodding at me as they take their seats.

"How's Stevie handling it?" my mother asks.

"What do you mean?"

She laughs. "Don't play me, kid. I'm your mother—I know when something is going on, and it was very obvious to me and everyone else at my wedding that you and Stevie are head over heels for one another."

It's my turn to laugh. "We're not in love, Mom. I don't believe in love."

She tsks. "Don't be like that, Jacob."

"Why not? It's not like I've seen it work out much in my life." I know my words hurt her the moment I let them fall from my lips. "Shit. I'm sorry, Mom. That wasn't fair to you."

"You're right, it wasn't, but I guess it wasn't fair for you to see me fail at finding my person so many times. That is why you don't believe in love, isn't it? Because of me?"

I swallow thickly. "I mean…"

She lets out a long sigh. "I'm sorry, Jacob. I'm sorry

you had to witness my heartbreak over and over again, but this life is too long to be so lonely. I couldn't stop trying just because it didn't work out a few times."

"Four times, Mom. Four."

"I don't need a reminder of my failed relationships, son."

I clear my throat. "Sorry."

"I am too. I'm sorry I made you feel this way about love. I'm sorry you feel as if you can't have it just because I couldn't make it work. It shouldn't be like that. It's not fair to you, and it's not fair to Stevie."

"Mom..." I groan. "I told you, we're not in love."

She laughs. "You poor, poor delusional boy."

My brows pinch together, annoyed by her words. "I'm telling you, I—"

"And I'm telling you you're wrong. If you'd just let yourself put aside your silly beliefs and actually *listen* to your heart, you'd find that you're wrong. You love her."

"I..." But my words of denial die on my tongue.

Is my mother right? Do I love Stevie? I like spending time with her more than pretty much anything else. If I'm not at the rink, I want to be near her, and hell, I like her kid, too. Macie is funny and whip-smart with a mountain of spirit.

But love?

I'm not sure.

"Do me a favor, Jacob. Close your eyes."

"What?"

"Can you listen to your mother for one second of your life?"

I chuckle. "All right. I'm closing my eyes." I do, shuffling down into my seat more.

"Now, I want you to picture yourself lifting the Stanley Cup over your head. You're happy. You just won the trophy of a lifetime, and you can't wait to celebrate. After you take your skate with the Cup, who is the next person you want to see?"

"Probably Miller. He's the one who is likely to score the game-winner, not that I'd tell him that."

"Jacob…" She sounds as tired as I feel as the bus driver closes the door and we start to move. "Please."

I want to roll my eyes, but she'd probably know. Instead, I shift in my seat and squeeze my eyes tighter, firing up the picture she's just painted.

I see it, me holding the Cup. That part is easy to conjure—it's something I've been dreaming about since I was a kid. I see myself skating around with a long, scraggly playoff beard, yelling at my teammates with glee. I see Wright is smiling, and, shit, even Rhodes has a grin on his face. Miller's down on one knee proposing to Scout, and Fitz is standing there next to a blonde. Lowell's holding Freddie in one arm and Hollis in the other.

Then, the crowd parts, and I see her.

Stevie.

She's standing on the ice with Macie next to her, the kid bouncing on her heels with excitement, stretching her neck trying to find me in the sea of Comets jerseys. They're there for me because they're *my* girls.

My eyes fly open, and I sit up.

Holy shit. They're my girls.

"Jacob?" my mother says softly in my ear.

"They're my girls."

I swear I can *hear* her smile. "Yeah, they are."

"It's her, Mom. It's *them.*"

"I know, son. I know it is."

"I… How? When the hell did it happen?"

"Well, I'm guessing Stevie's headache really cemented it."

She laughs, and this time, I do roll my eyes. There was no fooling her with that excuse, huh?

"So, now you've realized it. What are you going to do about it?"

"I'm going to fix it."

"*Fix* it? What is there to fix?"

I groan. "I kind of…got upset earlier. Not at Stevie. It was my arm, but I…shit, Mom. I messed up. I got mad, and I let her see it. I took it out on her, and she didn't deserve it."

"You're damn right she didn't." She huffs. "I raised you better than that."

"I know…I know."

"You'd better make it right with her and soon. There's no reason to let her sit there thinking she's done something wrong when you're just a jackass."

I smile at her name-calling because it reminds me of

Macie.

"I know. I'll make it right."

"Good. *If* you're lucky, she'll forgive you. But if she doesn't, remind me to send her flowers as an apology for raising such a shithead."

Hell, I'll send her my own flowers. She should get them anyway after dealing with me.

"Listen, David and I are pulling back up to the house. We were out when I got the notification, but I want you to call me tomorrow morning, okay?"

"I can do that."

"Good. And, Jacob?"

"Yeah?"

"Fix it with Stevie, then tell that girl you love her."

"I will. Love you, Mom."

"But never as much as I love you."

The line goes dead, and I settle back into my seat, feeling exhausted on so many levels—physically and emotionally.

I love Stevie.

I love Stevie.

I love *Stevie*. The woman who wanted nothing to do with me the first time I met her. The woman who lets her daughter call me a jackass. The woman who is smart and kind and gorgeous and perfect in every way.

I love her.

And I need to tell her.

Now.

"Stop the bus!"

Every head turns my way as I shove up out of my seat, racing to the front.

"Stop the bus," I repeat to the driver.

"Greer, what the hell are you doing?" Coach Heller says, rising to stand.

"I need to stop the bus."

His brows crush together. "What for, son?"

"I'm in love."

Those same brows rise high. "Okay."

"Like really, really in love, and I need to tell her."

"You need to get off the bus because you need to tell a woman you love her?" His hand lands on my shoulder. "You okay? You'd tell me if you were having problems, yeah?"

I shake off his touch. "The only problem I have is that I need to stop this bus. I need to get to Stevie."

"Stevie?"

"Scout's sister, Coach," Miller says, rising to his feet, his eyes boring into me. "You love her?"

I nod. "I do."

He watches me, looking for any sign of deceit, I'm sure, but there is no sign because I'm not lying.

I fucking love Stevie Thomas, and I want to tell her before it's too late.

"Please, Coach," I say, stepping closer to him. "I messed up tonight, and I need to tell her I love her, and I can't say it for the first time over the phone. I have to fix this before we leave…before it's too late."

"Greer, I—"

"Stop the bus, Coach," Wright says, standing up too.

"Stop the bus," Rhodes echoes.

Lowell pushes to his feet. "I'm with them."

"Me too," Fitz agrees, also rising.

Several other players get up out of their seats, showing their support.

With his hands on his hips, Coach looks around, taking in nearly every person standing.

"Surely you can't keep the bus going if we're all standing, right?" Miller looks at Heller. "Stop the bus, Coach."

"You fucking boys…" he mutters. He runs a hand over his face, scrubbing at it several times before pinning his hard eyes on me again. "You know this means you can't go on the trip, right? It could mean consequences like missing more games."

I nod once. "I know."

"And you're sure?"

"Hockey means a lot to me. This team means a lot to me, and I want to see us win. But her…*them*…they mean everything, Coach. *Everything*."

He sighs, hanging his head, shaking it. I swear he mutters something about what idiots we all are, but I don't quite catch it.

What I do catch is him clearly saying to the driver, "Stop the bus."

I stand in front of the familiar dark door, staring at it like an idiot.

I need to knock, I know that, but I can't because what am I even supposed to say to her? Do I start with sorry, or do I just blurt out that I love her? What if she doesn't love me back? What if she tells me to get lost and slams the door in my face? What the hell am I going to do then? Do I wait? Do I give up? Do I try to convince her to give me another shot or just respect her wishes?

I have no clue because I've never done this before.

Just knock, Greer. Just knock on the damn door.

With a steadying breath, I lift my hand, poised and ready to knock.

Here goes nothing.

I swing my wrist forward, but there's no sound because my hand never connects with the door. It's pulled open before I can even knock.

"You've got some real nerve showing your face here."

I look down and nearly take a step back when I see the look on Macie's face. She's glaring at me harder than she ever has, her little arms crossed and her lips scrunched up with disgust.

"What do you want, *jackass*?"

"Hey, kid," I say softly.

Her eyes tighten.

Right. Okay.

"Is, uh, is your mom here?" I ask, looking into the apartment. I don't see Stevie anywhere or even a sign of life in there other than her.

"No," Macie answers, and I have half a mind to tell her she should never tell someone her parent isn't home, but I have a really strong feeling she's not being honest with me right now.

"Do you know where she is?"

"Nope. Even if I did, I wouldn't tell you."

Her eyes flit to my shoulder just briefly. There's a hint of sadness in her gaze, but it's gone as quickly as it comes, replaced with ire.

"Are you mad at me?"

She snorts. "Of course I am. You made my mom cry."

"Stevie cried?"

"Yep. When she came back from seeing you, she was crying. She let me stay until the end of the game, but I didn't even enjoy it, and not just because you guys lost."

I briefly wonder if this means she's going to get her braces colors changed, but now isn't the time to ask.

"I didn't know she was crying."

"Well, she was."

Her little chin wobbles like *she's* about to cry just thinking about it. I don't want her to cry. I never want her to cry. I want this kid to have everything good in the world, and I'll lay my life on the line to make that happen.

"I'm sorry, Macie. Truly. I didn't mean to make her cry. I was…"

"A jackass?" she supplies helpfully.

My lips twitch at her tenacity. "Yeah, I was a jackass."

She lifts her chin a bit, and her shoulders slump just slightly like she's starting to come around.

"Is your mom really not here?"

"No."

"Who's here with you, then?"

"Aunt Scout. She's in the bathroom."

"Good. That's good." I nod. "Can you tell me where your mom is?"

Her eyes fall to slits again. "No."

"Macie, please. I just want to talk to her. I want to apologize."

Her arms drop to her sides, and she worries her bottom lip between her teeth, contemplating what I've just said.

She does this for several moments before saying, "You really want to apologize to her?"

"Yes. I really, really do."

"Why?" she asks.

"Because I hurt her."

"Why else?"

"I…" I exhale sharply, running my tongue over my suddenly dry lips. "I love her. I love *you*. You girls…you mean everything to me. I want your mom to know that too."

My words chip away at her hard stare, the anger slowly disappearing. We stand there, me waiting for her to say something, her just staring at me.

Then, after a solid, silent minute, she sighs. "She's at Slapshots."

"The bar?"

Macie nods. "She's with Harper and Ryan."

"Okay, okay. That's good. Thank you." I spin on my heel, taking off back toward the stairs.

I'm just about to them when I hear a small voice.

"Hey, Greer?"

I come to a halt, looking over my shoulder. "Yeah, kid?"

"I love you too."

CHAPTER 23

When Harper suggested we go out to Slapshots after the game, I wanted to tell her no. I had Macie with me, and I needed to be getting home. It'd been a long night, and all I wanted to do was curl up in my bed and sleep.

But here I am anyway, sitting at a high-top table with Harper and Ryan. Macie's at home with Scout, who promised to put her straight to bed, and Hollis went home with baby Freddie.

I finger the straw in my tequila sunrise. I didn't know what to order and said the first thing that came to mind. The funny part is I hate tequila, but I guess it's fitting for the night I've had.

I can't stop thinking about Greer and the way he threw those tools across the room, can't stop picturing the angry look on his face as he yelled about his arm. He was hurt, and I understand that, but him being hurt doesn't mean he gets a pass to hurt me too. I'm not putting up with that anymore, not for anyone, even if I am madly in love with them.

And I am in love with Greer. So, so deeply in love with him. I think I have been for a few weeks now, but I've been too scared to admit it to myself until tonight. Seeing him lying there on the ice and not moving…well, it was terrifying. The only other person who gets my heart in my throat like that is Macie.

I knew then that Greer meant the same to me that she does. I knew my heart…it beats for him too.

I just hope it's enough.

"Hey," Harper says, bumping her shoulder against mine. "You're supposed to be drinking your tequila, not playing with it."

"I hate tequila," I tell her.

"Amen," Ryan says, shuddering. "It only leads to bad decisions."

"I'm not sure you're allowed to say that when you're madly in love with your last 'bad decision,'" Harper tells her.

"True." Ryan giggles. "Best bad decision of my life, even when he drives me crazy, which he often does."

"You two are complete opposites, but it works. The beauty to his Beast."

A dreamy look crosses Ryan's face. "Yeah. It works." She groans. "Ugh, why do they have to leave tonight? Why can't they fly out tomorrow?"

"Acclimation," Harper says. "Playing in Colorado is a wreck on their lungs."

"I know, I know. It still sucks."

"Amen."

They clink their drinks together, each of them taking a sip. I want to participate, but I can't find the energy. Maybe it's because they're talking about husbands, and I'm over here with a heart that's slowly breaking. Maybe it's because I'm tired from the long week at the donut truck.

Or maybe it's because I wish I never went down to that damn room and saw the mess that was Greer.

I have no clue. All I know is I shouldn't be here right now.

"I think I'm going to head out," I announce.

They both frown at me.

"Are you sure?" Ryan asks. "We can get you something other than tequila."

"Yeah. How about whiskey?"

I crinkle my nose, shaking my head. "No, I'm good. I should get back to Macie."

"Okay." Ryan huffs. "We should probably head out too."

"No, no. Don't leave on my account." I hold my hands up. "Stay. Have fun."

"If I stay, all I'm going to do is drink more and drunk-call my husband, who is going to be very angry that I'm out without him," Ryan says. She tips her head. "Though, that doesn't sound all that bad. I do love getting him riled up when he's too far away to do anything about it."

Harper laughs. "You're so mean to him."

Her best friend shrugs. "He's so easy to mess with. All

grumpy ones are. Stevie knows all about that, though. Greer's the grumpiest of them all."

Just hearing his name has my heart aching. How is it possible to be hurt, mad, and missing someone at the same time?

Harper throws me a glance, her lips pulling into a frown. "Maybe we should all head out..."

"All right. Fine." Ryan jumps off her stool, her fingers flying over her phone screen. "I'm going to run to the restroom first. I just got an Uber. It's a silver Honda, pretty redhead inside."

"I'll come with you," Harper says.

"I don't need to go. I'll be outside."

They both nod, heading toward the back of the sports bar while I pull my crossbody purse over my head and head for the door without finishing my drink.

The cool air hitting my face is enough to sober me up instantly, not that I had much to drink anyway. I close my eyes, letting the fresh air wash over me.

"What a day," I mutter.

"You can say that again."

I let out a loud yelp, stumbling backward at the sudden intrusion. I mean, I'm in the middle of the sidewalk, so I'm not exactly expecting to be alone, but I didn't think anyone else was out here.

Especially not him.

I turn to my right to find Greer leaning against the wall, and my eyes go right to the sling that's holding his arm in place. My heart aches for him and his injury, but just as much as it hurts *for* him, it hurts *because* of him.

I fold my arms over my chest. Not because I'm cold, but because I'm scared. I'm scared I'm about to get my heart broken, and I want to protect it as much as possible.

"What are you doing here? You're supposed to be on a plane."

"I'm not."

"I can see that."

He shoves off the wall, taking a step toward me.

I take one back.

He doesn't miss it, rolling his lips together, his dark brows wrinkling as his eyes fall to the ground in front of him.

We stand there in silence for several minutes, long enough for the door of Slapshots to swing open again.

"Oh," I hear Harper say.

"What? Is—oh," Ryan echoes.

They step to either side of me, almost like they're protecting me.

"Everything okay?" Harper asks.

"Yeah, are we all good out here?" Ryan adds.

They're asking me, not Greer. We all know that.

The Uber Ryan called pulls up to the curb, waiting for us.

"That's our car," she says.

"But we can get another if we need to," Harper offers.

"Go," I tell them, my eyes still on Greer, who looks like he's seen better days. "I'm good."

"You're sure?" This from Harper.

I nod. "I'm sure."

She gives me a side hug, Ryan squeezes my arm, and then they both crawl into the Uber, their heads together as they whisper, no doubt about us.

The car pulls off, leaving just me and Greer on the sidewalk. There are so many questions running through my head, so many things I want to say to him, but I don't know where to start, and I don't know if any of them are even worth saying anymore.

It doesn't matter, though, because he's the first to speak.

"I stopped by your place."

"You did?"

He nods. "Macie answered the door." *Dammit. She's supposed to be in bed.* "I figured she'd be in bed by now since she usually is, but she wasn't."

"Scout must have let her stay up later."

"Yeah. Must have." He nods, then takes another step toward me. "We, uh, had a talk."

"About?"

"Something important."

"What's so important that it couldn't wait until you got back from your road trip?"

I know there's no way he's not going to be facing consequences for missing the bus, so whatever it is, it has to be big.

"I just had some things I needed to say to her."

He takes another step closer, that familiar scent of his washing over me. I want to close my eyes and breathe him in, but I can't, not when he's staring at me like he is…like I'm his and he's mine.

"Like what, Greer?" I ask quietly.

He exhales a shaky breath as he takes another step. He's so close now I can feel the heat coming off his body. It wraps around me like a warm jacket on a cold winter night.

"Like I'm sorry for making her mother cry."

I close my eyes at his words, warding off the tears that spring to life. I really don't want to cry again.

His fingers find their way under my chin, tipping it up toward him.

"That I'm sorry for being a complete and total jackass."

That makes me grin.

"And that I'm madly and completely in love with you."

My eyes fly open along with my mouth.

Did he just…

"Did I just say I'm in love with you?" He nods, closing my mouth gently. "Yeah, I did." He steps even closer, and I can feel him pressed against me this time. "I love you, Stevie."

I part my lips, but he shakes his head.

"I love you and Macie too. You're my people. You're

that thing I've been missing, that thing I've been waiting on. It's you, and it's her."

I can't even process what I'm hearing right now.

Greer loves me? Mr. Doesn't Believe in Love loves *me*? And my daughter? How?

"Greer, I—"

"I'm not done, okay?"

I nod, swallowing down the lump that's formed in my throat.

"I fucked up tonight. Big-time. Like really, truly messed everything up. I didn't..." He shakes his head. "I didn't think. I just acted. I was pissed about my shoulder, about losing so many games when we were doing so well. Hockey is life to me, you know? The thought of losing it terrifies me. When I was faced with that fear tonight, I reacted like a complete dickwad. I shouldn't have yelled, I really shouldn't have thrown anything, and I really, really shouldn't have let you walk out of that room letting you think for a single second that I didn't want you there. I always want you there, Stevie. Hockey? It might have been my everything at one time, but now...now it's you. *You're* my everything. You and Macie." He sinks his teeth into his bottom lip. "If you'll still have me, I mean."

My head is swimming, so many thoughts running through it that I don't even know where to begin, so I say the first thing that comes to mind.

"I'm mad at you."

Greer sighs, hanging his head. "I know."

"Like really, really mad. I've been through that

before. I've been with an angry guy who took it out on me, and I won't be with someone like that again."

"I understand. I—"

"But I know you're not really that guy, Greer. I know it's not you. You're not him, and you'll never be him. I know that because I know the person you truly are."

He gulps. "But..."

"No buts." I shake my head. "I don't have any."

He closes his eyes, relief settling into his shoulders.

And I don't. I don't have anything else except... "I love you."

His eyes pop back open. "You..."

"I love you. In fact, I am madly and completely in love with you, Jacob."

"Yeah?"

I nod. "Yeah."

Then his mouth is on mine, and he's kissing me like he's never kissed me before. It's different because we've never kissed while knowing we're in love with each other.

I don't know how long his lips dance against mine or how long we stand there, but when we finally part, everything feels different.

"I'm so sorry, Stevie." He drops his forehead to mine. "So, so sorry. I swear, it won't ever happen again."

"I know," I tell him. "I know it won't because you know I won't stand for it."

"Good. Don't ever let me or anyone treat you like that again."

I won't, I promise myself.

"I think I might have loved you the first time I saw you," Greer says. "Or maybe when Macie first called me a jackass."

I laugh. "She's feisty."

"That she is. I was scared as hell when she opened that door tonight. I was certain she was going to kick me in the nuts."

"You'd have deserved it."

He chuckles. "Yeah. Yeah, I would have." He presses another quick kiss to my lips. "Say it again. Please."

"I love you."

"No. Say *all* of it again."

"I love you, Jacob."

He sighs. "I'm not sure I'll ever get used to that."

"I'll tell you every day if it'll help."

"Every morning?"

"And night."

"For the next eighty years." Another kiss. "Because that's how long I plan to love you, Stevie. Until the last breath in my lungs gives out and then some."

"Come on, Greer. Don't get all weepy and emotional on me now."

He laughs. "I can't help it. I'm a man in love."

"Weird."

"So weird." Another kiss. "And so, so right."

EPILOGUE

"I knew it," I mutter, watching my cock disappear into Stevie's ass. "You take me so well, baby girl. Your ass looks so beautiful stretched around me."

She whimpers with delight as I push into her, and the sound is music to my fucking ears.

I love nothing more than the sounds she makes during sex.

"Jacob…" she moans my name. "So good."

We've been working up to this moment for months. She's been such a good girl, wearing plugs and letting me stretch her with my tongue and fingers. Now, she's finally taking my cock, and it's as heavenly as I suspected it would be.

"God, I love how you feel," I tell her, palming her cheeks, watching as I disappear inside her.

She lets out another pleased groan, pushing back and begging for more.

"You want more?"

She nods. "P-Please."

I land a hard smack to her ass, causing her whole body to shudder with pleasure.

I do it again.

Pause.

Smack!

Pause.

Smack!

Her ass is red and warm and looks fucking delectable wearing my handprint.

"Say it again."

"*Please.*"

"Please *what?*"

"Please fuck me, Jacob."

I lean forward, cupping her throat with my hand and applying the amount of pressure I know drives her wild and really let loose.

She moans beneath me as I pound into her. The sounds we're making are carnal and raw, and I love every single minute of it.

"Fuck, baby. You take me so well."

"Yours," she mutters. "All yours."

I slam into her once, twice, three more times, and my orgasm races through me. I pull out just in time, coating her back, loving the way she looks covered in my cum.

Mine.

I flip her onto her back, not caring about the mess on my sheets, and settle into my favorite place—between her legs. She sighs when my tongue touches her already soaking pussy.

I lick and suck and feast on her until her legs are clamped together like vise grips around my head, and I have to physically pry them off as she comes down from her high. Shudders rage through her as I crawl my way back up her body, slamming my mouth to hers.

I love that she never cares when I kiss her after I've gone down on her.

I love that she lets me use her however I like in bed, never complaining about it.

But most of all, I love the way she loves me—madly and completely.

I lift her from my bed with ease, carry her into the bathroom, then right into the shower. I crank the hot water, so glad the water never takes long to get warm. I pull her under the water when it's ready, letting it crash over us.

I grab her loofah, squirt body wash into it, then hand it her way. I do the same with mine, dragging the pouf over my body quickly before tossing it aside to deal with later. My attention is solely on the image in front of me. It's so stupid and so silly to love watching her shower, but it's my favorite. I love watching the water rivulets run down her body. Love the soft sighs that leave her lips when the hot water hits an extra sore spot. I could watch her forever and never get tired.

I'm happy. Happier than I've ever been in my entire life. It doesn't even matter that the Comets took yet another first-round exit. I'm still mad about it, sure, but I know things are going to be okay.

I have Stevie, and I have Macie. It's all I need. *They* are all I need.

Whenever I'm not on the ice, I've spent almost every waking moment with them over the last eight months. If I'm not running Macie to school functions, I'm taking her to hockey practice while Stevie attends night courses at the local college. If I'm not taking Stevie out on the town for a romantic night, then we're all curled up on the couch, watching a movie, and starting pillow fights.

I won't ever tell the guys this, but this team that Stevie and I have built? I love it more than the Comets.

And if it ever came down to it, I'd pick Stevie over hockey any damn day.

I want her. Not just now when she's standing naked in front of me. I want her every day, through the highs and lows. I want it all and more.

"Move in with me."

She stops her washing, and her mouth drops open, her eyes widening. She doesn't say anything, and my words hang between us like a thick cloud of uncertainty.

Finally, I break the silence.

"Is my request really that surprising?"

She lets out a loud laugh. "Yes!"

"What? Why? We've been together for eight months now. I… I thought we might be on the same page with it."

"Greer. You just fucked me in the ass, spread your cum all over my back, then ate me out for ten minutes, and the first thing you say to me is, *move in with me*?"

"Oh." I chuckle. "Fine. I guess my timing wasn't the best."

"No. No, it really wasn't."

I press a quick kiss to her nose. "I mean it. I want you girls to move in with me."

She clamps her teeth down on her bottom lip, chewing on it. "You do?"

"Of course I do. I love you. I love Macie. We should live together."

"It's a big step, Greer. It's…" She trails off, nibbling heavily at her lip still.

I capture her mouth, kissing the spot she was chewing on.

"If you don't want to or feel ready, tell me no, and I promise to listen. I don't want to pressure you if this isn't what you want."

"It is what I want," she tells me.

"Is it Macie? Because I really thought our relationship was getting better. She likes me now… I think."

Stevie laughs, then hangs her loofah back on the wall. "Are you kidding me? She *loves* you. Sometimes I think more than me."

"Nah. Not possible."

She grins. "True."

"So, then…"

"Then…" She sighs. "Here?"

"Huh?"

"You want us to move in here?"

"Well, yes. No offense, but I can fit three of your apartments in my kitchen and living room alone. Plus, I have heated floors in here, and you love those."

"No offense taken because that's true, and I love the heated bathroom floors, but… Have you thought about moving somewhere else?"

"I mean, I kind of play hockey here, so…"

She laughs. "I meant, like, maybe moving out of an apartment."

"Stevie Thomas, are you proposing we buy a house together?"

Her cheeks pinken, and she gives me a slow nod. "Yes. I mean, if you're ready for that, of course."

"It's a big step, Stevie. It's…"

She shoves at me when she realizes I'm teasing her, but I grab her hands, sliding them above her head and lacing my fingers with hers as I press her back against the cool tile. She shivers, and I'm almost certain it's not just because of the tile.

"You're mean." She pouts.

"But you love me."

"So much."

"Good, because I really don't want to buy a house with someone who doesn't love me."

"Does that mean…"

"Yes, I want to buy a house with you, Stevie."

"I'd clap right now, but someone's holding me hostage."

"As if you don't love it," I say, rolling my hips against

hers. A soft sigh leaves her when my cock brushes against her clit. "You love it when I take control."

"So much," she murmurs.

I plant my lips on her neck, kissing and sucking at the skin as I continue to rub against her. I love the sounds that leave her as I bring her to the brink of orgasm.

Even more, I love the groan that leaves her when I back away just as I think she's about to come.

I laugh darkly.

"Mean."

"And proud of it."

"Are you going to be this mean when we live together?"

"Are you kidding? I'm going to be *meaner.*"

She growls, and I laugh, dragging my cock against her wet pussy once again.

"You're going to have to learn to be quiet, you know."

"Hey, I think I've proved I can be quiet."

"Sure. Now. But what happens when I'm meaner…*rougher.* Can you be quiet then?"

"I guess we'll just have to see, won't we?"

"Or—and hear me out here—we could build a nice, pretty little soundproof room, and I can use it to do anything I want to you."

Her skin ignites with goose bumps as a shudder runs through her.

I grin. "You like that idea?"

She nods. "Very much so. We're going to need a hot tub too."

"A hot tub?"

"Yeah, I've always wanted to have sex in a hot tub."

I laugh. "Fine. We'll get you a hot tub."

"And—"

"Steve?"

"Yes?" she mutters, so lost in me rubbing against her that she doesn't even realize I've just called her Steve.

"Would you rather we just *build* a house?"

Her eyes fly open. "Are you nuts?"

"Possibly. But if we build, we could get everything we want."

"But your contracts… What happens if you move? I—"

"Then we'll figure it out later."

"Are we going to stay together if you move teams?"

"Do *you* want to stay together if I move teams?"

"I…" She runs her tongue over her bottom lip. "Is it going to freak you out if I say yes?"

"Not a chance. In fact, I want you to say yes."

"You do?"

"Of course I do. In case you haven't realized it yet, Stevie, I'm kind of crazy about you."

"Is that so?"

"That's so. I am madly and completely in love with you."

She sighs. "Good. Because I'm kind of crazy about you too."

"Yeah?"

"Madly *and* completely, Jacob."

Then I kiss her, and I don't stop until we're both trembling under the cold water.

After that, I start all over again.

If I never win another hockey game, I'll be okay.

I already played the best game ever…and won.

EPILOGUE

I never in my life thought I'd be where I am now, standing on a stage and ready to accept my diploma.

When Greer suggested I go back to school, I thought he was nuts. I had a job, a kid, and a life. I didn't have the time to go back to school to figure out what I wanted to do. But he promised he would help and take care of everything I couldn't. And somehow, even with his crazy schedule, he did.

There isn't a single doubt in my mind that he's the reason I'm walking across this stage right now.

"Congratulations," the dean says, shaking my hand.

"Thank you," I mutter, already feeling my cheeks get hot under all the attention.

Greer and Macie yell from across the auditorium, but they aren't even the loudest. It's all the other Comets players making noise that really sticks out to me.

Aside from Smith and Emilia, since they left the Comets last year, everyone else is here making a huge ruckus, including my dad and his fiancé, Ernesto, Loretta and David, and I've never felt more loved or supported in my life.

It's fantastic, this little family we've seemed to build here. I have people I can count on and friends I know I'll have for life.

Greer signed another contract a few months ago, which means we're staying. I'm thankful, too. Macie is making some incredible strides with her hockey team, and I know she doesn't want to leave them behind. And selfishly, I didn't want to leave the beautiful home we built, which I still can't believe we live in.

We've come so far since Greer first asked me to be his date, and I'm terrified that one day I'll wake up, and it'll be just a really, really good dream.

I don't want that. I want this forever.

I want Greer forever.

I make my way back to my seat, taking in the last of the ceremony with an impatience I've never known before. I want so badly to just run to the people who matter most in my life and skip all these speeches that I have heard a thousand times before.

When it's finally over, we do the typical graduation thing and toss our caps into the air, then we're free.

I don't waste a single second and run to find Macie and Greer at our designated meeting spot.

I slow down when I see them, taking in the view in front of me: Macie and Greer, standing together and laughing at something, each of them holding a giant bouquet of flowers.

They look so much at ease together, a stark difference from the first few interactions together. Macie no longer calls him *The Jackass*. Instead, she calls him Jacob.

I didn't tell Greer this, but just last week, she asked me if he's going to be her dad, and if he does become her dad, can she call him that.

I cried for a half hour afterward.

Her question was so sweet and innocent, mostly because she has no idea how Greer feels about marriage. Do I want to get married again? If it's Greer asking, then yes. In a heartbeat. But I know the idea of marriage isn't something he's too crazy about, and I respect that.

"Mom!" Macie races down the hall, her arms outstretched as she runs toward me.

I crouch just in time to scoop her into my arms, hugging her tightly. She's getting so big, and soon, I know she's not going to let me hug her like this in public, so I'm going to soak it all up while I can.

"I'm so proud of you!" she says, and the tears leap to my eyes in an instant. "You did it!"

"I did. I did it."

She pulls away. "Greer said you could. He said that even when you thought you couldn't, he believed enough for both of you that you could do it."

I look up at the man who has meandered down the hall our way. He's grinning brightly down at me.

I rise to my feet and barely stand before he throws his arms around me, dragging me into his warmth. I sigh when his familiar scent washes over me and sag into him.

"You're incredible, Stevie."

"Only because I know I have you there to help me when I fall."

"Please," he says, pulling back to cup my face in his hands. "You were incredible long before I met you."

When he says it, it makes me believe it's true.

I give him a small smile, which is covered when his lips touch mine.

It's a soft kiss. A chaste one too. But it doesn't stop Macie from complaining.

"Are you guys going to kiss all day, or are we getting ice cream?"

I laugh, pulling away from Greer. "Ice cream."

"Yes!" She pumps her fists in the air. "I'll even let you ride shotgun in the fun car."

"Then where are you going to ride?"

"We can take her," my sister says as she approaches. She spreads her arms wide. "Steve…"

I fall into her embrace, hugging her tightly.

"Congratulations, big sis."

"Thanks." I squeeze her tightly before letting go. "You're the best little sister, you know that, right?"

"I know." She shrugs, then winks at me.

I'm passed around to everyone, giving them all hugs.

By the time we're finished, I'm a blubbering mess, feeling like a fool.

"This is your fault, you know," I tell Greer.

"How so?"

"You gave me this big family, and they've made me cry, so it's your fault."

"Well, don't dry your eyes just yet. I have something else that might make you cry."

I tip my head, brows crushed together. "Okay…"

"Do you want to get married?"

His words have me staggering back. "Excuse me?"

"I was wondering if you wanted to get married."

I look around at the group surrounding us. All eyes are on us right now, and I'm not sure what the hell is going on. Why is he asking me this here? Now?

"To…you? Or just in general?"

"Well, I'd prefer if it was to me, but I guess in general is fine too."

"Are you…" I can't even get the words out. They're stuck in my throat like I've swallowed a rock.

"I am."

"Greer…"

"Steve…"

He chuckles lightly, though it's not his usual laugh. It's a bit stilted and quiet. I realize for the first time that Greer's nervous. He's *never* nervous.

That means…

"I'm asking you to marry me, Stevie."

"She probably can't tell because you're just standing there like an idiot," Miller says, causing everyone to laugh.

Greer sighs, then drops down to one knee. "Stevie Thomas, I love you more than anything in this world."

Macie gasps. "More than hockey?"

"More than hockey," Greer confirms.

"More than me?"

"Shit."

He clears his throat, then peers back up at me.

"Stevie Thomas, I love you and Macie more than anything in this world." I grin at his correction. "I know I've been against marriage in the past, but that's because I didn't realize what I was missing. You. Macie, too," he says, looking over at the kid in question. She shoots him a thumbs-up. "But now that I know what I could have, I want more. I want *you*. Both of you. Forever. I want to be your husband, and I want to be Macie's dad."

Someone gasps, and someone else sniffles, but I have no clue who makes either sound. My sole focus is on Greer.

I can't believe this is happening. I can't believe this is happening *now*, with all of my friends and family surrounding me.

I can't believe that this man…this incredible, amazing man…wants to marry *me*.

"You can still be my dad, even if she says no," Macie whispers in a voice that's not so quiet, and her words melt my heart.

"No."

"No?" Greer says.

"No?" Macie echoes.

"I mean, *no*, that's not necessary."

"So, you're saying…" Greer trails off.

"Yes!" I yell, not caring that we're in the middle of a crowded hallway. "Yes, yes, yes!"

"Are you sure you mean it? I can't tell."

"Yes," I say more quietly this time.

"Really?"

"Please don't make me say it again."

Greer shoves to his feet, then wraps his arms around me, slamming his mouth against mine without hesitation.

This kiss is a lot different than the one before. It's not as soft or as chaste. Instead, it's full of love and the guarantee of forever.

When he finally pulls his lips from mine, he trails his kisses up my cheek to my ear.

"I plan to make you say *yes* every damn chance I get."

I shiver at the promise.

"Her ring, her ring!"

Greer steps aside, and I'm shocked as hell to see Macie holding her palm up to me, a beautiful gold ring sitting in the center.

"You knew?" I ask her.

She nods. "Yep. He asked for my permission last week."

"So that's why you were wondering if you could call him *Dad*?"

Macie nods, her eyes drifting from me to Greer, who is looking down at her with tears welling in his eyes.

"Is that what you want?" he asks her softly, and she nods again. "Yes. Yes, you can call me that."

Greer drops to his knees and pulls Macie into a hug. She holds him just as tightly, and my heart leaps into my throat as I watch them together. It's everything I ever wanted for her with the guy I never expected.

This might just be my favorite moment ever.

When they finally part, I don't miss Greer swiping at his eyes or the redness to Macie's.

They both sniffle and look anywhere than at each other.

Greer grabs my hand, then slides the ring over my finger.

"It's a perfect fit," I mutter.

"I'm just that good."

He winks at me, and I roll my eyes.

"You're annoying," I tell him.

"I know. But now I get to annoy you forever." He presses a soft kiss to my lips. "I love you, Stevie."

"I love you more, Greer."

"And I love you both. Now can we *puh-lease* get some ice cream?"

We all laugh at Macie's impatience.

As we head out of the school, the whole big group of us, all I can think is: *This is it. This is forever.*

I'll never take any of this for granted.

BONUS SCENE

"Whose pussy is this?"

"Yours."

"Say it again."

"It's yours."

"What's mine?"

"My pussy. My pussy is yours."

"You're fucking right it is, wife."

Wife.

I sigh when the last word leaves his lips, then again when he laces his fingers with mine, his thumb tracing over the ring on my finger.

I'm married for the second time but married for the first time to someone I truly love.

And I do love Greer. So damn much.

Not just because he's currently railing me so hard that I see stars but because of how incredible he is all around.

We've only been married two weeks, but he's an amazing husband and an even better father to Macie.

I can't imagine how life could get any better than this.

"Yeah?" he says, and I realize I've just spoken those last words out loud. "Just wait until I fuck your tight little ass with one of those toys we bought while I bury my cock inside of this cunt later tonight."

Oh god.

I shiver in anticipation of it.

Greer slips his hands between us, his fingers finding my clit. He rubs short circles on it while he fucks into me, and it doesn't take me long to combust around him.

"Fucking hell," he mutters as he follows me into oblivion.

He captures my mouth, kissing me hard and rough, promising me more is to come. I hate it when he slides out of me and rolls to the side, trying to catch his breath as I rest my head on his chest.

We're on the last day of our honeymoon, and while I don't want to leave Greece just yet, I do want to get back to North Carolina and see my daughter. We've never been apart for this long, and I miss her something fierce.

"I can't wait to get back home," he says quietly after several moments of us lying there.

"I was just thinking the same thing."

"I miss Macie."

"I miss her more."

He laughs. "Yeah, probably. She did call me *Jackass* at the wedding, so I have some beef with her."

"She said it affectionately." I run my fingers through

the soft fluff of hair on his chest. "She also called you dad."

I don't miss the stutter to his breath. "Yeah. She did do that."

I sit up a bit, wanting to look at him. "Does it freak you out?"

"Is it crazy if I say no?"

"Not at all."

"Then, no. It doesn't freak me out. I thought it might, but it doesn't. It feels…"

"Right?"

"Yes." He nods. "So right."

I sigh, then rest my head back against him. "I know what you mean."

"We're going to have a really good life together, Steve."

"But it won't be a long life together if you keep calling me Steve."

"What? You love that nickname."

"I really don't."

"Would you like to pick a new one? How about Fluffy Butt? Or Snuggle Bunny?" He snaps his fingers together. "I got it—Sweetcheeks McLovely Buns"

"You know what? I think Steve is fine."

"Nah. It's too boring now. I think Sweetcheeks McLovely Buns has a nice ring to it."

"I will push you off the balcony, Greer."

He laughs. "No you won't."

"I will too. I'll toss you right over."

"But if you throw me off the balcony..." He drags his hand down my back, not stopping until he's cupping my ass in a harsh grip. "Who is going to fuck this beautiful, beautiful ass of yours Sweetcheeks McLovely Buns?"

"I hate you."

"You don't," he says, rolling over until I'm on my back once again, and he fits himself between my legs. "You love me. You even promised to do so forever."

"I was drunk."

"Liar." He presses a soft kiss to my jaw. "You were sober."

"I was drugged."

Another kiss, this time closer to my lips. "As if I had to drug you. You were a willing participant."

"Well, then I—"

"Am completely full shit."

Then he kisses me, and it's that same desperate kiss he always gives me. That same passion and heat and so full of promises that I can't wait for him to keep.

He kisses me like I'm his, and that's just what I am.

"Say it," he commands like he can read my mind.

"I'm yours," I whisper against his lips.

"Yes, yes you are...Steve."

OTHER TITLES BY TEAGAN HUNTER

CAROLINA COMETS SERIES

Puck Shy

Blind Pass

One-Timer

Sin Bin

Scoring Chance

Glove Save

Neutral Zone

ROOMMATE ROMPS SERIES

Loathe Thy Neighbor

Love Thy Neighbor

Crave Thy Neighbor

Tempt Thy Neighbor

SLICE SERIES

A Pizza My Heart

I Knead You Tonight

Doughn't Let Me Go

A Slice of Love

Cheesy on the Eyes

TEXTING SERIES

Let's Get Textual

I Wanna Text You Up

Can't Text This

Text Me Baby One More Time

INTERCONNECTED STANDALONES

We Are the Stars

If You Say So

HERE'S TO SERIES

Here's to Tomorrow

Here's to Yesterday

Here's to Forever: A Novella

Here's to Now

Want to be part of a fun reader group, gain access to exclusive content and giveaways, and get to know me more?

Join Teagan's Tidbits on Facebook!

ACKNOWLEDGMENTS

This book wouldn't be possible without the support of these amazing people:

My Marine who is my rock. I love you Naley style: Always and Forever.

Laurie. I'm sorry for spelling your government name wrong. Forgive me?

My incredible editing team who is always there to make magic happen for me.

All the Bloggers, Bookstagrammers, and BookTokers who continue to show up and support me. It means everything. Thank you really isn't enough.

My Tidbits on Facebook. You're my happy place.

YOU. Thanks for taking a shot on this book. I really hope you loved it.

With love and unwavering gratitude,

Teagan

TEAGAN HUNTER writes steamy romantic comedies with lots of sarcasm and a side of heart. She loves pizza, hockey, and romance novels, though not in that order. When not writing, you can find her watching entirely too many hours of *Supernatural*, *One Tree Hill*, or *New Girl*. She's mildly obsessed with Halloween and prefers cooler weather. She married her high school sweetheart, and they currently live in the PNW.

www.teaganhunterwrites.com